ONCE *Burned*
DESIREE
HOLT

ELLORA'S CAVE
ROMANTICA PUBLISHING

An Ellora's Cave Romantica Publication

www.ellorascave.com

Once Burned

ONCE BURNED

80

Erotically Yours
Desiree Holt

Dedication

&

*As always, to my husband, my white knight and hero,
without whom none of this would be possible. To Helen,
editor extraordinaire, who makes my books sing and
knows more than anyone what that takes. And to Cindy,
whose friendship means more to me than she'll ever
know.*

Trademarks Acknowledgement

&

The author acknowledges the trademarked status and
trademark owners of the following wordmarks mentioned in
this work of fiction:

Dallas Morning News: A. H. Belo & Company

McDonald's: McDonald's Corporation

Star Trek: Paramount Pictures Corporation

U-Haul: U-Haul International, Inc.

Welcome Wagon: Welcome Wagon International, Inc.

Chapter One

The call came at seven-thirty in the morning, as Cassie Fitzgerald was getting ready for work. She was hardly prepared for either the sound of Harley Graham's voice or the news he was delivering. She hadn't spoken to him in years and now his announcement hit her like a blast of cold air.

"I'm sorry to be the bearer of sad news, Cassie, honey but your mother passed away early this morning."

She clenched the receiver to stop the shaking in her hand, processing his words. Her heart felt as if a fist was squeezing it and tears for a woman she'd wiped out of her life were like grains of sand behind her eyelids. Memories she'd kept barricaded in the closet of her mind sprang loose to assault her.

"Cassie? You still there?" Harley prodded, as the silence stretched.

She swallowed hard against the sudden tightness in her throat. "Yes, I'm here."

How did he expect her to react? She and her mother had never been close and the six years since she'd left home had stretched their relationship beyond the breaking point. Once a month she made the obligatory phone call, a tense conversation for both of them. Not even Diane's death had brought her back. *Especially* Diane's death. No, Diane's *murder. Say it, Cassie. Your sister was murdered.*

"I didn't know she was ill," Cassie finally managed, wetting her lips with her tongue. No, all her mother had done was complain about "that terrible Griffin Hunter" and moan about the loss of Diane. She could picture Harley on the other end of the call, holding the receiver with infinite patience. As a young doctor he had delivered both her and Diane, helped them through their father's suicide and now apparently tended the last of the Fitzgeralds who lived in Stoneham.

"She hadn't been doing too well lately," he said. "I wouldn't exactly say she was sick but she'd really been failing. I've been treating her for some heart problems but last night I guess she just gave up the ghost."

She could hear the reproach in his voice. His silent criticism hummed across the long-distance connection. Well too bad. He wasn't the one who'd had to flee to save herself. For six years she'd been able to shut Stoneham completely out of her mind — the only way she could save herself from emotional destruction. Now, damn it, she'd be back in the place she ran away from, pouring hot salt water into open wounds.

"I'll have to make arrangements to take some leave from the office," she told him. "But I can't take more than a couple of days." She would let them know right away that she wouldn't be gone for long. She had no desire to linger in Stoneham. The town held so many agonizing memories for her, had left so many emotional scars, that even a brief visit would strain all her emotional resources.

"I understand. I sent the body to the funeral home and Neil McLeod is handling all the paperwork for the estate. Your mother had him helping her with everything lately."

"Handling? Estate?" Cassie was puzzled. "What on earth could there be for Neil to take care of? My mother had nothing but the house and a small income."

"I guess she just wanted to make sure everything was tied up nice and neat. She knew her health was bad. She probably didn't want you to have any trouble with anything after she was gone." He cleared his throat. "He left the funeral arrangements until you got there. Thought you'd like to take care of that yourself. That okay, Cassie?"

"All right." There it was again, that slight accusatory tone. She pressed her fist to her forehead, trying to think. God, going back to Stoneham was like walking into the fires of Hell for her. But there was no way she could explain that to anyone without dragging all her secrets out of the closet where she kept them hidden. "I'll fly in to San Antonio and rent a car at the airport. Otherwise it would take me two days to drive to Stoneham from here. I still have a key to the house, Harley, so I'll go straight there."

"You call me when you get in, honey. Okay?" He gave her his office and pager numbers, extended his condolences again and she was left to her thoughts.

Her head was pounding as she tried to assess her situation. If there was one place she did not want to be it was Stoneham, Texas, a small town with big memories, none of them pleasant. Well, almost none of them. When she fled the town and her family, she left with the intention of never returning. She hadn't even returned for her sister Diane's funeral. Or her father's. She couldn't. There was too much pain. Now she had no choice. She was the only one left.

So here she was, thrust into it again. She would have to arrange for the funeral and burial, have Neil take care of probating whatever estate there was. Sell the house, definitely. Putting it in the hands of a realtor would be the smartest thing to do. Maybe Neil could help with that too. She certainly didn't want to hang around and deal with it. In fact, her preference would be to take care of everything she could from a distance.

She couldn't stay and that was that. Along with all the other memories she'd have to deal with, staying meant coming face-to-face with Griffin Hunter.

Just thinking his name made the heavy weight of memories slam into her. Yet beneath the anger and pain that were still fresh after all this time, she felt the familiar stirring in her loins, the heat igniting low in her belly and her nipples tightening. The mere thought of his name brought it all back.

No! She banged her hand on the counter. Griffin was out of her life and he'd stay that way. No erotic memories were going to change that. She would do everything possible to avoid him, slipping in and out of town before he even knew she was there.

Cassie swallowed two aspirins, trying to take the edge off the headache and called her editor. She already knew it wasn't a good time for her to take leave.

After a year of struggle, *The Sports Weekly* had finally turned a corner. Florida was filled with sports teams. The Tampa Bay area, squarely in the middle of the state and with its own major league and college teams, was an ideal place for a sports publication. It had been a real coup to be hired on as the only female reporter, a job she worked twice as hard as anyone else to keep.

They were approaching their next crunch in the schedule. Since they were two months into baseball season, with football looming quickly, everyone would be working nonstop. Well, unfortunately it couldn't be helped. Death didn't leave you many options.

Mike Rivard, her editor, listened silently while she told him what happened.

"I'm sorry," she said. "I know this is a busy time. I feel like I'm finking out."

"Cassie, it's always a busy time around here." His voice always sounded as if it came from the bottom of a barrel. "Sometimes other things have to take precedence. This is one of them. Go and do whatever you have to. Your job will still be here. Just call me when you get there and give me a read, okay?"

She promised to do so, feeling enormous relief. She and Mike had an excellent working relationship but she knew how tough on people he was. He surprised her with his understanding. She gave him her cell phone number in case anything came up and hung up.

It took most of the hour she predicted to get organized, putting a temporary stop on her newspaper and giving all her plants a good soaking. Finally she called her friend, Claire, who promised to keep an eye on her place, take in the mail and field any questions.

"Do you want me to come with you, Cassie?" she asked. "Dealing with this stuff can be very stressful."

Claire, her roommate in college for four years, was a paralegal for an attorney who did a great deal of estate work. When Cassie's life had come unraveled so long ago, it was Claire who saved her, who talked her into moving to Tampa after graduation and looking for a job there.

"No, thanks just the same. I plan to be there and gone before anyone realizes I was even in town."

"Well, at least let me drive you to the airport. Parking costs an arm and a leg there and just because you say you'll only be gone for a few days doesn't mean something won't come up where you'll need to be gone longer."

Cassie was actually grateful for the offer. By the time Claire arrived she was packed and ready.

"One suitcase?" Claire raised an eyebrow.

"I meant what I said, Claire. I don't plan on making this a long visit."

By lunchtime she was on a nonstop flight to San Antonio, Texas. She closed her eyes, fighting back the nausea at the thought of what faced her. *Stoneham.* The scene of so much pleasure, yet so much pain. And Griffin Hunter, who despite her most determined efforts, had lived in her dreams every night for the past six years.

Six Years Before

Summer in Central Texas. Hot sultry nights, beckoning with unspoken promise. The air redolent with the mingled scents of phlox and lantana and Texas bluebells.

As Cassie strolled slowly along the sidewalk she wondered why she'd decided to walk to the movies in this ungodly heat. Already her skin was sticky with the humidity and her clothes hung limply against her body. Leaving an air-conditioned house suddenly didn't seem the wisest thing to do.

But the house had closed around her, suffocating her. Diane, her older sister, was out living up to her wild reputation. Their parents, with Diane out of the house, were too engrossed in watching television to remember they had another daughter. No wonder she sometimes she felt as if she didn't exist in their eyes.

They were such a study in contrast, she and Diane. Two years apart, they might have been two worlds apart. Her sister blasted through life like a comet, her wild gypsy looks beckoning to every man who laid eyes on her.

Cassie was so rigidly proper, so bright and self-sufficient, her parents had long ago decided she required no supervision on their part. Cassie won the awards and gold stars while Diane accumulated detention slips for her deliberate violation of rules. Cassie went to college. Diane stayed home to work and live life in the raw.

Diane was like a flame that drew unwary moths, burning those who got too close. To her parents she was a bright star, vivacious, full of life, lighting up their universe. They were fascinated that they could have produced such a child, captivated by the colorful aura that surrounded her.

So while Cassie labored in bland anonymity, Diane did as she pleased and made her parents love her for it. Cassie had long ago stopped raging about the unfairness of it. She was focused on one thing—graduating and getting as far away from Stoneham, her parents and Diane as she could.

Even if she hadn't wanted company tonight and wasn't in the mood for socializing, she still had the fidgets. Sitting shut up in her room didn't appeal to her. A movie by herself seemed a good solution. Anything to get out of the house that felt more like a prison every passing day.

The lone movie theatre in Stoneham was only twenty minutes away. Walking to it had seemed like a good idea when she started out. Now as the moisture-laden air lay heavy on her skin and sucked at her breath, she wondered if she should just go back home and hole up in her room.

"Taking the night air, Cassie?"

The voice came out of nowhere, low, seductive, flowing over her like warm honey.

Cassie jerked her head around. Lost in her own thoughts, she hadn't realized she was in front of Griffin Hunter's house. "Griffin? Is that you?"

"It's me, sugar. Come on up and have a beer."

Griffin Hunter. Stoneham's resident bad boy. Ten years ago his mother had died and permanently altered life in the Hunter household.

"I don't know what you see in that boy," Mrs. Fitzgerald whined, every time Diane flew out the door with him and the rest of the "wild bunch".

"Griff Hunter's got it all, Mother," Diane would laugh. "And he sure knows what to do with it."

"His father fell into a bottle when his mother died and never came out," she said waspishly.

"If it hadn't been for Griffin, their landscaping business would have gone straight to Hell," Diane shot back. "That says something about him."

No one argued that he wasn't an excellent landscape gardener, a hard and dependable worker. But when he wasn't working, he was the acknowledged leader of the wildest crowd in the county, the ones who drank excessively and had wild parties. They were considered trouble. The police always had them on their radar.

And if there was trouble to be had, Griffin was square in the middle of it. Although very bright, he barely managed to graduate high school with his class. He didn't consider studying a high priority. He was in one scrape after another, always angry, always ready to brawl. His mother's death and his father's collapse into alcoholism gave him more license to thumb his nose at society.

Nowadays, only the business made him focus. He balanced his time between landscaping, hauling his father home from some bar and running at night with the crowd that made a hobby out of seeking trouble. A crowd Diane fitted in only too well.

He was the guilty pleasure of every female in Stoneham. Like a forbidden prize his wicked smile and sexy body charmed every one of them. Prepubescent teenagers, ripening adolescents, women both repressed and lusty—they all harbored secret dark fantasies about Griffin Hunter.

Say goodbye and keep walking, Cassie told herself, even as her feet ignored her silent direction and carried her along the path and up the steps to the wide front porch. Buried in her mind were her own secret fantasies about Griffin Hunter. The boys she dated, even in college, lacked any semblance of finesse, instead viewing sex as a competitive sport. How many nights had she lain in bed, wishing for Griffin's hands on her body instead of on Diane's, the pulse throbbing between her legs where heat pooled like liquid silver, her heart racing, her skin flushed.

"How come you're not out with Diane and the others tonight?" she asked.

"Didn't feel like it. How come you never come out with us? I'd show you a good time, sugar."

"I'm not Diane," she said primly.

"No kidding."

He was lounging in the glider, a beer can in his hand, one foot rocking the glider back and forth. Skintight jeans molded his muscular body, outlining a bulge at his crotch that Cassie averted her eyes away from. His half buttoned shirt exposed the crisp, curling hair on his chest. Sun-bleached hair, worn just a little long and casually disarrayed, brushed his collar. Cassie couldn't see his eyes in the dark but she knew they were a piercing electric blue.

Griffin looked like an Adonis come to life. Except Adonis never had such a roughly carved look to his face, or exuded such a sense of the dark side. She could certainly see what Diane saw in him.

Her heartbeat began to accelerate and faint heat gathered in her belly. *Danger!* a little voice shouted at her. *Go to the movies. Go home. Go anywhere. Leave.* But here she was, her feet firmly planted on the porch. She peered through the darkness at him, her breath quickening just at the sight of his dark angelic face.

"Is that a slam?" she asked, leaning against the porch railing.

"Come on over here and sit with me." He patted the section of the vinyl seat next to him. "Take a chance with the town bad boy. Come on, Cassie, I don't bite."

As if drawn by an invisible thread, she walked over and sat down at the other end of the glider. In the reflected light of the street lamp she could see Griffin's wicked grin.

"Keeping your distance?" He laughed, a rich, deep sound. "No, you're definitely not like your sister."

"I think this is a bad idea." She started to get up but suddenly his long fingers were clamped on one arm.

"Don't leave yet, sugar. We've hardly had time to get acquainted." He reached to the table beside him and handed her a cold metal can. "Have a beer, Cassie. Just one beer. Surely that won't ruin your reputation."

"Well…all right. Maybe one beer would be okay."

She sat stiffly, clutching the icy can in her hands, sipping from it automatically, wondering what she was doing there anyway. And trying to ignore the tension coiling within her.

"Home for the summer?" Griffin asked conversationally.

"Sort of."

She'd just finished her sophomore year at college. In two days she would be meeting her roommate, Claire, and four other friends for a week of white water rafting in Georgia. Then she would find a summer job that would keep her as far away as possible from Diane and her parents.

"How can you be sort of home?" he asked.

"Where's your father?" she asked, changing the subject.

"Where else would he be?" His voice flattened to a monotone. "The Winter Garden, waiting for closing time and someone to haul his ass home."

"So you're just whiling away the night here alone on your porch?"

"Maybe I was waiting for you, squirt," he said, his voice soft and seductive, whispering to her of forbidden pleasures.

"Why do you always call me that?"

"Squirt? I guess because you seemed so much younger than Diane."

"Because I'm not wild, like she is? Because I'm dull and boring?"

Griffin chuckled. "Anyone who calls you dull and boring hasn't bothered to take a really good look."

He was Diane's lover. One of her many lovers. All the times Cassie had seen him waiting for her sister to come flying down the stairs, smiling that wickedly sexy smile, exuding an unconsciously erotic air, she'd fantasized he was waiting for her.

Her shameful, dark desire for him, hidden in the deepest recesses of her mind, leaped to the surface. Cassie, the virgin, the ice queen, the nobody, hungered to have Griffin's arms around her, molding her to his body, touching her in all the mysterious places of her body. She ached to feel his penis inside her, his mouth on her breasts, his fingers tantalizing her clitoris that was swollen just from her fantasies.

Suddenly she realized she was no longer in her isolated corner. Somehow she'd moved across the glider — or Griffin had — and his arm was around her shoulders, his face dangerously close to hers.

"What do think, squirt?" he asked in his hot molasses voice. His mouth was inches from hers. "Want to take a walk on the wild side?"

"Don't tease me, Griffin." The nickname made her feel small and unattractive.

"Oh, sugar, I'm definitely not teasing. Maybe I should call you dewdrop."

She blinked. "Dewdrop?"

"Mm hmm. Fresh as the early morning dew on a blade of grass. I'd like to pluck you and lick you all up."

He bent his head and she knew he was going to kiss her. Common sense told her to push him away but she couldn't make herself move.

He waited the space of a heartbeat for her to move away or object, then his mouth came down on hers, hard, his tongue forcing her to open for him. She felt it sweeping into the dark recesses of her mouth, tasting her like a sweet dessert, flicking at nerves she didn't even know she had. Tentatively she let her tongue meet his, twist with his, duel with his — and she was lost.

Chapter Two
The present

❧

The plane landed in midafternoon. Cassie hadn't called ahead for a rental car, so by the time she retrieved her luggage and arranged for transportation, she was hitting the interstate at the beginning of rush hour. The Texas heat had enfolded her as soon as she walked outside, plastering her clothes to her body. Once inside the rental car she turned the air conditioner on full blast, praying for icy relief.

Her neck ached with tension, her head was throbbing and the clogged highway didn't improve her mood. Stoneham was still a good hour's drive away once she hit the outskirts of San Antonio and she didn't relish spending all this time in gridlock. She fiddled with the radio, trying to find a station with soothing music while traffic slowly inched along.

Finally, finally, she was beyond the city limits. Traffic was considerably thinner now and she could increase her speed. As she drove along I-10 she noticed changes since the last time she'd made this trip. Signs of progress were everywhere. New housing developments, strip centers, office buildings.

But not in Stoneham, I'm sure, she thought. Nothing ever changes there.

She was hot, tired and hungry by the time she pulled into the small town. It was just after six o'clock and daylight was fading. The exit road from the Interstate had dumped her off at the edge of downtown and now she skirted it, following familiar side streets.

As she drove, her eyes scanned automatically for any sign of Griffin, though she didn't really expect to see him just because he was in her thoughts. He was about the only thing her mother had talked about, bitching that she was sure he was responsible for Diane's death, yet he still walked around big as life. Cassie had a lot of unkind thoughts about Griffin Hunter, but accusing him of murder wasn't one of them.

He was out there, somewhere, doing whatever it was he did now, and sooner or later, they'd run into each other. Her stomach knotted at the thought. What could they even say to each other after all this time?

Before long she pulled up in front of the house she'd lived in most of her life. She noticed that giant oak trees still guarded the front yard and shaded the porch but they couldn't hide the slightly sad and neglected look the house now wore. The lawn and bushes obviously needed tending. The wooden trim around the limestone was faded and, in some spots, actually peeling. Shades pulled down at every window only added to the look of despair.

Cassie felt her stomach tighten as she took out her key, long unused, and opened the front door. A dank, musty odor hit her at once. Her mother may have been existing here but she certainly hadn't been living.

She snapped up the old-fashioned window shades, hoping a little light in the room would improve things but it only made them more dismal. A thin film of dust covered everything, accentuating the worn look of the furniture that had served them well for so many years. She walked slowly through the rooms, mentally taking stock. It was obvious that after her father's death, her mother had spent her life in as few rooms as possible.

Guilt reached out to touch Cassie but she chased it away. It was not her fault. None of it. For twenty years she had labored for her parents' love and approval. She was the forgotten child hidden in the shadow of Diane's brighter light. They probably hadn't even missed her when she left. And now she was the only one remaining.

Sighing heavily, she trudged up the stairs, lugging her suitcase. The bedrooms looked like relics from an old movie.

The heavy furniture in the room her parents shared looked austere, the coldness of it broken only by the rumpled look of the bed. Probably no one had thought to straighten it after they took her mother away. Well and exactly who would do that, missy? she thought bitterly.

Her parents had turned Diane's room into some kind of shrine, with pictures of her on every available surface. Everything else in the room as exactly as she'd left it six years ago, as if disturbing them would underscore the fact she was actually dead. A pink sundress still lay tossed across the bed, pink sandals tumbled onto each other on the floor as if the wearer had just slipped them off. Probably from the last time Diane had slept in this room. If she strained her ears, Cassie could almost hear Diane's laughter and a chill washed over her.

She had pushed the circumstances of Diane's death away for six years. Now, standing in this house, everything popped back into her brain bringing familiar memories and emotions. Diane might have been wild but what could there possibly have been about her to drive someone to commit murder? An unwelcome need to find answers was worming its way into her system.

With determination, she backed out of the room and went to her own, another site of little change but not for the same reason. Looking around she could have been the young Cassie again, dressing for high school classes or home from college between semesters. The same yellow and white wallpaper, the white ruffled bedspread with the daffodils sprayed across the surface, the little vanity with the yellow skirt where she'd applied her makeup. Now everything was old and faded. No nostalgia involved, just a sad memory.

Opening her suitcase, she hung up the few things she'd brought that needed wrinkles to fall out and pulled on a pair of shorts and a tee shirt. Thankfully someone had the sense to leave the air conditioning on, albeit at a high temperature and she bumped the indicator up as she passed the thermostat in the hall.

The kitchen yielded little in the way of food. No surprise there. She had no idea how or when her mother ate. The freezer held a half gallon of vanilla ice cream that she decided would do as her dinner.

Standing at the counter, spooning the creamy confection from the container, she called Claire to let her know she was okay. And finally she dialed Harley Graham's home number.

"I'm so glad you're here safely, Cassie." That warm voice had soothed her since she was a toddler. "I was beginning to worry about you. Have you eaten? Would you like to come by the house for a bite? Your mother ate so strangely lately I can't imagine you'll find much there."

"Thanks, Harley but I'm okay. I can get stuff tomorrow. I guess I just wanted to let you know I'm here and ask what happens next."

"The body's at Stoneham Mortuary. Still the only one in town. They're just waiting to hear from you about final arrangements."

"Will there need to be a big funeral?" She frowned, thinking of that unpleasant possibility of half the town showing up from morbid curiosity.

"I think a small service at the mortuary would be appropriate," he assured her.

Cassie realized there was a great deal left unsaid in that simple sentence. "I'll talk to them tomorrow," she told him.

"And Neil McLeod said to catch him in the morning. You know, he still handled all the legal work for your folks. He'll make time for you to go over your mother's papers."

"I'd like to wrap this up by Monday. Do you think that's possible? I really need to get back to work and there isn't much to hold me here anymore."

"I know this is hard for you, Cassie. Stoneham hasn't exactly been kind to your family." He sighed. "We'll make this as easy on you as possible but I think a lot depends on what you want to do. Talk to Neil first. Then if you want to chew anything over, give me a call."

"I can't tell you how much I appreciate this, Harley. You're a good friend as well as our doctor."

"You thinking of calling any of your old friends while you're here?" he asked cautiously. Like everyone else, he knew her leave-taking had been anything but pleasant and he had no idea who she'd kept in touch with. "Tonight's Thursday. In another hour they'll all be at Pete's Pizza."

"I think I'll pass. Thanks just the same." She was already battling too many old memories she felt was better left tucked away.

"Well, you know where to find them. Or me. Nothing ever changes in Stoneham, you know."

I know. Nothing except my life.

Six Years Before

They were in Griffin's bedroom, a room that reflected his masculinity in the stark oak furniture and the walls bare of adornment. The only relief was a framed photo of his mother on his dresser. The pale golden light from the street lamps poured in through the window, casting shadows on their bodies.

Cassie had no recollection of how they got there. One minute he was kissing her and wiping out all her brain cells. The next they were upstairs in his room, his eyes burning into hers, his hands hot on her face.

He undressed her with exquisite care, peeling away her blouse, sliding her skirt down to her ankles, then tossing it to the side. Deftly he unclasped her bra and slid it off with the ease born of long practice. As her breasts sprang free, he cupped them in his palms, his thumbs rasping against the nipples. When he bent and licked the hardened points—just a brief swipe of his tongue—she felt electricity jolt through her.

She barely felt him remove her panties, her last line of defense. Shivers chased themselves along her spine as his hands roamed her body and he murmured softly in her ear, seductively, reassuringly. He touched her everywhere—her shoulders, her back, her hips. One finger teased at her navel before his hand descended to the nest of curls between her thighs. With exquisite gentleness he combed his fingers through them, sliding down to the lips that guarded her virgin sheath.

Then she was lying on his bed, in his arms and he was whispering to her, naughty things, erotic words that made her skin burn. His mouth was locked to hers now, his tongue probing and tasting. Tentative at first, she met his challenge and as their tongues tangled together, fire shot through her. Fear and desire mingled in a potent combination, fueled by the unexpected intensity of her own response. This was unsafe, uncharted waters for her and she had no idea how to act. She only knew that whatever Griffin was doing, she never wanted him to stop.

Griffin lifted his head and looked at her, his breath catching as his eyes took in every detail of her naked trembling body. The street light shining through the window cast tantalizing shadows on her skin. Holding her in his arms, sensing her anxiety, he wanted to tell her everything would be all right, wanted to show her how he felt. Because Griffin Hunter had a secret of his own.

It was no coincidence that he'd been sitting on his porch when Cassie walked by. He'd spent many nights before heading out for his hell-raising, sitting and waiting as he'd done tonight, hoping Cassie Fitzgerald would walk by.

From the moment she'd invaded his dreams as a sixteen-year-old nymph, he'd been in love with her. Only she was Diane's virgin sister, off limits to the wildest boy in town. And had been all these years. Tonight when she came strolling by, his senses came alive. After all this time, he still wanted her, now more than ever.

What would she do if he told her the wildest boy in town wanted her for his own, not just for tonight but forever? Would she bolt from his arms, from his bed and run from his life? Or would she stay?

His hand began to explore her body in earnest, reveling in the velvety smoothness of her skin. Again he cupped one of her small, high breasts in his palm, feeling its heat, using his thumb to softly abrade the rosy nipple already hardened like a diamond. Gently he used his mouth on first one, then the other, biting softly, then soothing with his tongue, licking them until their wetness showed in the reflected light. His calloused fingertips caressed the sloping swell.

He took a long time teasing and tantalizing, paying careful attention to each breast in turn, kissing and licking the skin, sucking at the nipple swelling in response to his touch. Her breathing began to quicken and he could feel the skin tighten under his caresses.

"Griffin, I…" She worked to clear the fog from her brain.

"Ssh, sugar. Don't talk," he murmured. "Such sweet little breasts, just waiting for the right mouth to suck them."

He let his hand drift lower, lower, trailing across her navel down to her lower abdomen, the tips of his fingers just touching the beckoning triangle of curls. When he ran his fingers through them with a possessive touch, Cassie reached out a hand to touch him and encountered hot naked skin.

When had he shed his own clothes? Her hand jerked back but Griffin captured it with one of his and placed it on his chest, trapping it between them.

"Relax, Cassie," he crooned. "Let me make you feel good. Let me love you."

Carefully he cupped the palm of his hand against her feminine mound and touched the inside of her thighs, clamped so tightly together.

"Open your legs for me," he whispered. "Come on, sugar. It will all be worth it."

She was powerless to do anything but obey. She felt hot all over, inside and out. A slow throbbing at the entrance to her vagina was growing stronger, like a primitive drum beat. She resisted only slightly as he separated her legs. Then she felt that same feathery touch as he toyed with the curls covering her mound, just skimming the tops of his fingers over them. No one had ever touched her there before but letting Griffin do it seemed the most natural thing in the world.

"Okay, sugar?" he whispered, his voice hypnotizing her. "Don't be scared, all right?"

Her mouth wouldn't work. She just nodded.

"Good. You're gonna love this even more, I promise."

One finger parted the folds at her entrance and slid between them. She jerked but the arm cradling her held her in place. Griffin was gratified to find her already wet and slick, her labia slightly swollen, the skin hot. One finger slid easily into her, its passage moistened by her own lubrication. He waited until she'd adjusted, then carefully eased a second finger inside, testing her tightness, stretching her to ready her for his throbbing cock.

He moved his thumb lazily to the nub of her sex, lightly rubbing the tip of her clitoris back and forth.

Sparks shot through her body. "Oh, God, Griff. Oh, my God."

Sensations swept over her, rousing her body. She was frightened, terrified of the unfamiliar feelings consuming her. She wanted to pull back but her body wouldn't let her. Without any conscious thought she parted her legs for him even more.

"That's it, Cassie. Open wide for me."

He kept up the soft murmurs, coaxing her, soothing her. With his thumb and forefinger he peeled back the tiny hood shrouding her clitoris, exposing it even more to his touch, pinching it gently. She nearly exploded out of his arms, her body arching off the bed.

Suddenly the movement of his hand stilled. Cassie forced her eyes open.

"Griff? What's wrong?"

"Were you waiting for me, Cassie?" he whispered.

"What?" What was he talking about?

"I don't know whether to feel guilt or beat my chest, Cassie." He pressed soft kisses on the corner of her mouth. "You didn't tell me you're a virgin, sweet thing. Did you want me to be your first lover? Tell me. Was that it, darlin'?"

Her lips barely formed the word. "Yes." She didn't dare tell him how many nights she had lain in her virginal bed dreaming of just this moment. She was eager and ashamed at the same time but more than anything she was so aroused she couldn't think.

"I won't disappoint you," he breathed in her ear. "You'll be good and hot and ready for me. A little bit of pain but the pleasure, oh, sugar, the pleasure. I'll make you feel so good. Just close your eyes and feel, sugar."

She felt suspended in space. Her heart was beating so loudly she thought surely he could hear it. He stroked her inner sheath, his fingertips rasping the sensitive skin, reaching far inside to stimulate every muscle and nerve. All the while his thumb kept up its unbearable torment, back and forth, back and forth, on that hot, swollen nub. She clutched at the sheet beneath her, moving her body, wondering if she would go mad with the pleasure. Every sense was vibrantly alive.

Griffin could feel the first flutterings inside her, feel her fighting it. "Open your eyes and look at me," he demanded. "Let go, Cassie. Just let go. Come for me, sugar. Let it happen."

A mountain in her path couldn't have stopped her. Her body was beyond her control, betraying her with every response.

Suddenly she felt spasms racing through her. The intensity was too much, so much that it frightened her. She had to stop it. And then she convulsed, her head coming off the pillow, her thighs clamping around his hand. She was over the edge as her orgasm racked her body, wave after wave of pleasure beating at her, consuming her, liquid pouring from her into his hand.

Griffin pressed his mouth to hers, forcing it open, swallowing her moans as he pressed his fingers into her hard.

Then it was over and she lay panting on the bed. He could feel her, hot and wet and pliant, little aftershocks still making her vagina contract around his fingers. He withdrew his hand, cupping her mound gently.

"Felt good, didn't it, sugar?"

"Yes." She could barely speak the word.

"That's just the beginning, darlin'. Trust me, Cassie. I'll take you to the top of the world."

Slowly he slid down until his head rested between her thighs. He blew softly on the entrance to her still quivering passage, his breath like a hot breeze against her heated flesh, then began stroking her with his tongue. With just the tip he traced the line of her folds and the pink skin guarding her vaginal vault. Lightly, like a feather, he teased and tasted, lapping up the slick moisture from her orgasm.

She might have thought she was finished, undone but at the first lick of his tongue Cassie nearly came off the bed. Strangled moans came from her throat as his strong hands held her thrashing body in place. He showed her no mercy, gave her no room to draw back as he used his tongue relentlessly. Back and forth, around and around, until she was crying, begging, pleading for more.

Just as she thought she couldn't bear the exquisite pain for another moment, he thrust his tongue into her and she came once more, pushing at him, pulling at him, her hands holding his head. He held her thighs tightly as she rode out the storm and the quivering in her muscles began to subside.

She was still waiting for her pulse to slow when he moved back up and took her hand.

"Touch me, Cassie. I want you to know what you'll feel inside your body."

His shaft was enormous and nearly shocked her out of her fog of sensation. She felt the silky skin, the hard thickness and it was like nothing she'd ever touched before. The tip was wet and she used one finger to slide the moisture back and forth over the petal-soft skin. Griffin jerked, so ready from stimulating her that he had to grit his teeth.

"All right, sugar. You are wide and wet for me." He put his mouth close to her ear. "I'm glad you saved it for me, Cassie. Did you know you were always the one I wanted? The one I dreamed of at night?"

He shifted slightly to reach into the nightstand drawer. Cassie heard the tearing of foil and opened her eyes to see Griff sheathing himself in a condom. Then he moved over her, positioning himself, the head of his shaft at the entrance to her sheath. He was stopped almost immediately by the thin barrier of protection, the membrane that would yield to him at any minute.

"Look at me, Cassie," he commanded. "Open your eyes and look at me."

She opened them and saw his own eyes glittering with deep desire, boring into her. "A tiny pinch, darlin', That's all. There."

He pushed hard, once, and felt her recoil slightly at the pain but he held her in place. Inch by slow inch his cock invaded her. Beads of sweat popped out on his brow as he fought for control. And then he was in all the way.

"All right, sugar, here we go."

He put his hands under her hips and lifted her to meet him. Slowly, steadily, he began thrusting into her, watching her for signs that she was ready again.

He held her with his eyes, seeing new sensations grip her and wipe away the pain. Her tissues stretched around his penis, thick and hard and enormously aroused and reaching for him, clutching at him, drawing him deeper yet. When he saw her eyes widen with renewed desire he increased the tempo, harder now and faster, holding her tight against him so he could reach her deepest recesses, rocking her with the motion. His hands slid around her hips, his fingers slipping into the cleft of her buttocks, separating the smooth globes. He pressed his fingertips against the tight opening and that was all it took.

They came, falling over the edge together. Cassie felt as if she were shattering into a thousand pieces. She was flying, she was floating. Her body shook with the force of her orgasm and colors swirled behind her eyelids. She could feel Griffin's hot liquid jetting into her even through the thin shield of the condom, his iron maleness throbbing as his release came with tremendous force. She never wanted it to end.

Finally he collapsed on her chest, his heartbeat thudding against her, panting for breath. They lay in each other's arms for a long time, neither of them speaking. Griffin would have given anything to know what was going on in her head. He didn't ask because he was almost afraid of the answer.

He'd certainly had more than his share of sex but this was beyond physical. This was a claiming, a bonding, a giving of heart and soul. This was forever. As he poured himself into her, he never wanted it to stop, this feeling that was so all-consuming. For the first time in his life, Griffin Hunter knew what love was. It both scared him and embraced him.

Cassie twined her fingers in his long, wheat-colored hair, trying to get her brain working again. She had just given her carefully guarded virginity to the town hooligan, her sister's lover and she didn't even regret it. She didn't know what that made her do it but at the moment she didn't care.

Finally she roused herself. "Griffin?"

"Yeah, sugar?"

"I have to go. It's very late."

He sat up, taking her with him, smoothing her hair away from her face and searching her eyes. "Are you all right, dewdrop?"

She smiled in the darkness. The nickname tickled at her heart. "Yes, Griffin. I'm fine. Better than fine."

"I didn't hurt you?" He smoothed the hair back from her face. "God, you were so tight."

"And you're so…large." She smiled again. "No, I'm okay. Really."

"I want to see you again, Cassie."

"I-I'm going away the day after tomorrow, Griffin. I'll be gone for a week. Then I'll be heading back to the university."

"Come back tomorrow night? Please? If that's all the time we have, give us one more night. I'll make it even better for you. I promise."

She wanted to tell him if he made it any better she'd probably die. But her sister intruded in the moment they shared. "What about Diane?"

"What about her? She's got more fish to fry than she has a pan to put them in. It's you I want, darlin'." He put his lips close to her ear. "It's always been you I've wanted. In my story the bad boy gets the good girl."

He stroked her ear with the tip of his tongue and she shivered. She nodded wordlessly, knowing she'd regret it.

She almost stayed away, calling herself all kinds of a fool, ashamed of her wantonness. But the next night there she was, lured by the siren call of the most erotic experience of her life.

And Griffin was right. The second night was even better. He taught her things she'd never even dreamed of, helped her to scale new heights of sexuality with him. She was in a constant state of arousal, never getting quite enough of him.

And so for two nights, cocooned in the secrecy of his room, away from unsuspecting eyes, Cassie learned about love and sensuality from Griffin Hunter. She reveled in it, gloried in it, celebrated life and loving in the big king-sized bed with the street light pouring in on them.

When Cassie was dressing to leave the second night, Griffin pulled open the drawer of the nightstand and handed her a little box. He seemed hesitant, almost embarrassed.

"For me?" she asked.

"It's not much, Cassie but it's all I have to give you."

"You don't have to give me anything," she told him.

"Yes. I want you to have something that will always make you think of me."

She opened it and drew in her breath. Nestled inside was a tiny silver heart on a chain.

"I don't give my heart easily, sugar. But it belongs to you. Always. Take good care of it."

She was so full of unexpected emotion her heart nearly stopped. She clasped the gift to her, treasuring it, moved nearly to tears by his words. He helped her fasten the chain around her neck and kissed her softly on the lips.

"I'll see you when you get back," he said. "Let's not waste a minute before you have to go back to school."

She nodded, already counting the days, visions of wedding dresses floating in her head.

But when she saw him a week later, he was already married. To Diane.

Chapter Three
The present

ℰℭ

Cassie slept restlessly, waking frequently from the troubled dreams that plagued her. Being back in this house did nothing for her peace of mind.

Finally giving up and trudging downstairs, she found some instant coffee in a cupboard, boiled some water and made a cup for herself. Sitting on the barstool at the end of the counter, the telephone book in front of her, she began making the calls she'd been dreading.

The people at the Stoneham Mortuary would be happy to meet with her any time she could make it during the day. Donald Brandon, obviously under his father's tutelage, tried to engage her in conversation but his unctuous tones made her skin crawl. She planned to be in and out of that place as quickly as she could.

Neil McLeod, who with his father handled most of the town's legal work, took her call right away. "I've been waiting to hear from you, Cassie. I'm sorry we have to see each other under these circumstances but it will be a real pleasure to see you. I'm happy to take care of things for you."

"I have no idea what there is to do, Neil but Harley says you've handled everything for my mother."

"There's a small estate and of course, the house to deal with. Why don't you come by around noon and I'll take you to lunch?"

No social engagements, she told herself. Get it done and get out. "I'm really only here for a short time. If we could meet this morning that would help me a lot."

"How about ten?" he asked, his voice barely concealing his disappointment. "Maybe I can talk you into dinner."

"Ten is fine," she said, ignoring his other comment. "See you then."

She hadn't brought much of a wardrobe with her but she had packed her brand new summer pantsuit that would take her just about anywhere. The soft rose color set off her light blonde hair and warm brown eyes and accented the faint hint of tan she'd acquired. She found towels and showered, applied her makeup carefully and pulled her hair back into a gold clip to keep it neatly away from her face. Gold hoops at her ears completed the outfit.

She examined herself carefully in the mirror. At least she'd face the town in style.

Before she left the house she added a list of cleaning supplies to the list of groceries she needed. If she planned to sell the house, it couldn't be shown as it was and her mother didn't seem to have much in the way of household items. She might as well buy enough groceries to get her through the weekend. Public places like restaurants, where she might run into Griffin were to be avoided at all costs.

Her watch said ten sharp when she walked into Neil McLeod's law office. Six years ago when she was a junior in college, he'd been graduating from law school. He was tall and handsome then, athletic, with dark hair and deep black eyes. Maturity agreed with him, improving on those good looks.

What did he know about Diane's death, Cassie wondered. Had he kept up with her wild activities?

Her eyes, gazing around the room, spotted two framed photos on the credenza behind him. Cassie knew Neil had married Leslie Walters, daughter of his father's partner, right after graduation. One photo showed the two of them laughing on the deck of a sailboat. The other included two small children, boys, carbon copies of their father.

"Good to see you, Cassie." Neil stood to shake her hand and indicated a chair across the desk from him.

"You're looking well, Neil." She nodded at the photos. "Life must be good for you."

"Yes, it is. Dad and I share the practice," he told her, "and there's plenty to keep us busy. Leslie's father retired about three years ago. Heart attack. He keeps his hand in with a few cases but the doctors don't want him working full-time."

"I hope he's feeling well," she said formally. "You know, I was always surprised you stayed in Stoneham."

"Never had any desire to leave here, believe it or not. Leslie and I have made a wonderful life for ourselves here and it's a terrific place for kids to grow up. None of the city problems." He grinned at her. "How about you? Anything on the horizon? Maybe coming back here to settle down? Or is there a marriage coming up to keep you in Tampa?"

"Not if I can help it," she said emphatically. "Besides, I love my job and it keeps me busy enough. Listen, I'd love to exchange pleasantries but I'm trying to keep my time here as short as possible. Can you tell me what papers I have to sign, or what I have to do?"

He opened a file on his desk. "I'm sure you know the estate is not extensive. However, your father had been a real saver and invested wisely. Your mother had a good income and never touched the principal, so there's about two hundred thousand in annuities."

Cassie stared at him, astonished. "You're kidding!"

"Nope. Dead serious. Your mama made some arrangements, with my counseling, a few months ago." He look across the desk at her. "She had me do the paperwork to add your name to everything as a joint owner. Even the deed to the house. You're a joint tenant with right of survivorship." He pulled a sheet of paper from the folder. "This is a form for you to sign just for the firm stating that I have turned over all the assets to you. I'll give you a letter detailing everything.

You can cash out the annuity if you want. Just tell the company where you bank and they'll do a direct deposit."

"What about probate? That usually takes forever."

"There's no will, Cassie, because anything with joint tenancy automatically passes to the other owner. That's you. So no probate."

"But-But…" Cassie dug around in her mind for words. "My mother hated me, Neil. Why would she set things up this way?"

He shrugged. "I think your mama had a hard time with a lot of things. I'm sure she knew she'd been unfair to you. Maybe this was her way of making it up."

Cassie shook her head, struggling to understand it all.

"Anyway, this way you can wrap everything up quickly, which I thought would be what you wanted. I guess you'll be selling the house?"

She nodded. "Still only one real estate agency here?" she asked.

"Just the one," he agreed. "Jesse Markham and now his daughters. Jesse does the commercial and they do the residential. Want me to have one of them call you?"

"Actually, if you could have someone come by this afternoon, that would be great. I'll be home doing some work in the house. What else?"

"There's a small life insurance policy, about twenty-five thousand. It will cover funeral and other expenses. I've called the insurance company and asked for the paperwork to be faxed but this is Friday, so I'm not too optimistic about getting it until next week. I have copies of the death certificate for you, along with my letter, so there shouldn't be any holdup on anything."

"The bank?"

"Sure. Well, really, only the checking account, which is now yours. Howard Cook will take care of you when you get there. I already talked to him. 'Course, he's gone for the weekend too."

"Neil, I don't mean to sound pushy or ungrateful but you're right. I don't plan to hang around. In fact, I was hoping to leave here on Monday. Do you think that's possible?"

He leaned back in his chair, looking at her. "We'll do this as fast as we can, honey, but you can just write the weekend off."

She ground her teeth in frustration. "All right. If I have to, I'll call my boss and tell him I need a day or two more."

"Why don't you give me a holler this afternoon and I'll see how far I can get. Been to the funeral home yet?"

"No, that's my next stop."

"Well, shouldn't be too much of a hassle there. Your mother actually made all the plans and left them instructions."

Cassie stared at him. "She did?"

"Yes, ma'am. Said she didn't want anything big or anything fancy. You can tell Don Brandon he'll get paid as soon as the paperwork's done on the insurance policy. If he has any questions, have him give me a ring."

Cassie breathed a small sigh of relief, grateful to have all those decisions taken out of her hands. The words popped put of her mouth before she even realized she'd said them, startling both her and Neil. "What do you know about Diane's death?"

Why had she said that? She hadn't faced the issue in six years, hadn't even thought about it, so why had she suddenly brought it up now? When had Diane's death become a subject for her curiosity? Why did she even care? Being back in that house was doing weird things to her mind.

Neil looked at her sadly. "Aw, Cassie, what do you want to bring all that up for?"

"To tell you the truth, I don't really know." She shook her head. "I couldn't get home for her funeral, so I guess I'm just a little curious. All I ever knew was there was some kind of violence..." She stopped. "I don't know why I even asked. Forget it, okay?"

Neil seemed to weigh his next words carefully. "You know they thought for sure Griffin had killed her, don't you? But it seems he had an airtight alibi."

"Griffin? He was a suspect, right? That's what the newspapers said."

"Well, there was a lot of speculation going on there." Neil shifted in his chair as if he found it uncomfortable. "I hate to speak ill of the dead but your sister certainly pushed the envelope, as they say."

"They never found out who did it?"

"No, they haven't. And Griffin Hunter just walks around town, big as you please, still running his business. Although I guess if we had another landscaper around here folks wouldn't be putting up with him. Anyway, if I were you, I'd just leave things alone. No sense raking up past history."

Cassie stood up in a hurry, gathering her purse and keys. She had no intention of discussing Griffin with anyone. She'd worked very hard to keep him tucked away in a secret corner of her mind.

"I really have to go, Neil. Please see what you can do about the paperwork on everything and I'll call you later."

"I'll do my best but you know this town. Even tomorrow is too soon for everyone." He came around the desk and placed a kiss on her cheek. "Sure I can't talk you into lunch? Or how about dinner? I'd love to have you come out to the house and meet the family."

"I'm really not here socializing." No, that sounded too rude. "I mean, I'm just here to take care of business. To make sure things get done the way my mother wanted them. I appreciate the offer of dinner and everything else you're doing for me. I'll expect to hear from you."

She fled the office, her brain rattling. How could she get through this? With all the rage and pain bottled up inside her, socializing in Stoneham was impossible. She just wanted to escape without too much damage to her own emotional state.

* * * * *

Cassie hated the fact that Diane's death, which she'd kept pigeonholed in the back of her mind for six years, was suddenly swimming to the forefront of her consciousness. She had refused to discuss it with her parents, instead finding out what she could from articles on the internet. But whatever details she managed to find were sketchy.

Three months after Diane's marriage to Griffin Hunter, her battered body was found in a ravine at Stoneham Municipal Park. Suspicion had first fallen on the husband, always a prime suspect in cases like this. The only problem was, he had an airtight alibi and three witnesses to back it up. Besides, she could imagine Griffin doing a lot of things but committing murder wasn't one of them.

After that, the case just languished until it finally fell off the radar. Cassie had simply put it out of her mind. At the time she had been so angry with Diane she could have killed her herself. Being in Stoneham after all this time had brought it unpleasantly to mind.

Donald Brandon was oily obsequiousness itself when he greeted her at the mortuary. His impeccable black suit blended perfectly into the dark wood paneling on the walls. His hair looked as if he glued it in place every morning, every strand perfectly arranged. Cassie almost expected to hear organ and harp music drift in from the walls.

Donald held onto her hand so long she had to yank her hand away from him. As distasteful as he had been in school, he had gotten worse as he aged.

"I understand my mother left instructions for her funeral," she told him. "If you could just tell me what they are, I'll sign off on everything and we can get this done."

"I hoped we might have a moment to chat," he said, somewhat petulantly. "It's been a long time since you've been home, Cassie. We have a lot to catch up on."

"Actually, Donald," she said firmly, taking a step back, "I'm trying to get this done and get out of here by Monday, so if we can just get to it?"

A little frown creased his forehead. "I'm sorry but I don't think that will be possible." He sounded slightly disapproving.

"Neil told me my mother had made all the arrangements ahead of time. All I had to do was go over the details with you. I don't understand what the holdup could be? What could possibly take so long?"

The disapproving frown was still in place. "Today is Friday. I have to confirm the arrangements with the cemetery, place the notices in the paper, arrange for a service and prepare the body for burial."

"Well, exactly how long will this take?" she asked, impatient with the whole situation. This was getting worse by the minute.

"Your mother only wanted a small service, which we can do in the chapel here. But I'd say, with everything, Tuesday would probably be the earliest we can finish up."

"Tuesday! Donald, we're not burying the president here."

Donald gave her a stern look. "Cassie, I must say, I'm a little disappointed in you. This is your mother we're talking about. I know the two of you had issues these past few years but we here in Stoneham still believe in showing the proper respect for the dead."

Cassie gave up. "All right. Just do whatever you have to and call me when everything's finalized. I'm staying at the house." She paused. "By the way, what can you tell me about Diane's death?"

"Diane's death?" He kept his face carefully blank.

"Yes. I wasn't here at the time and it just seems strange no one was ever arrested for it."

"I'm sure I wouldn't know anything about it. Have you checked with Chief Dangler?"

"No but thanks for the suggestion."

Someone else to stonewall her, she was sure. Why wouldn't anyone talk about her sister's death?

Getting back in her car, she wanted to bang her head on the steering wheel. Her quick trip in and out of town was looking longer and longer. She needed to shake off the dust of Stoneham permanently, and the town kept reaching out its tentacles to trap her in its own special hell.

Pulling out her cell phone, she called Mike and gave him an update.

"Don't worry, Cassie, take whatever time you need. I'm sure this is a tough time for you and I don't want to add to your stress. Take all of next week. And don't worry about your paycheck."

This was more sympathy than she ever would have expected from this man. If only she could tell him that the toughest time was having to be here at all.

She passed the police station on the way to the grocery store and her car seemed to turn in on its own and park without her doing a thing. In the next minute she was shaking hands with Barry Dangler, the Chief of Police and telling him she was fine and yes, it was too bad about her mother. She thanked him for his condolences.

"I wonder if I could see the file on Diane's death," she said, social niceties out of the way.

"Now Cassie," he admonished, "why bring all that up now? It's been six years since it happened."

"I guess because I ignored it at the time and now I'm feeling some latent guilt." She uncrossed her legs and recrossed them. "And maybe a little bit the reporter in me."

"That's right," he nodded. "I heard you were working for a newspaper in Florida. But honey, there's just nothing to tell. Honest. I felt it in my bones that Griffin Hunter did it but he was covered up with witnesses."

He looked uncomfortable with his next words. "No disrespect, Cassie but your sister walked a lot on the wild side. Speculation was that marriage didn't change her social habits and Griffin was fed up with her and the situation. If he didn't do it, then maybe it was some guy she met that night, someone she provoked into a rage. She was pretty good at pushing people's buttons, you know."

Yes, Cassie thought, *especially mine*. "So are you saying I can't see the police report? Why?"

Dangler sighed and was silent for a moment. "The law says you can go to court to get this if you want, so I guess I'll just save us all that trouble. I think this is a big mistake and it won't make you happy but I'll do it."

"Thank you, Chief. When can you have it ready for me?"

"I'll have to get it from the dead files. All the old cases are in the archives. Give me until the first of the week."

Cassie tamped down her frustration. Everything was "next week". She was ready to just blow the whole thing off but her reporter's nose was twitching. Both people she had brought this up to wanted her to forget it, which only made her more determined to pursue it. She was stuck in town anyway, so she might as well get what information she could.

And just maybe she could finally shut the door on Griffin Hunter.

"Call me Monday afternoon if you haven't heard from me by then," Dangler told her. They shook hands and he ushered her out.

41

She stopped at the grocery store next. Cleaning supplies. More food than she first planned on since it appeared she was going to be stuck here for a few days. She rushed along the aisles, pushing herself to be home by early afternoon. She needed to call Neil and check on his progress and also see what he had been able to do about arranging a real estate agent to come out to see the house. She'd been in Stoneham less than a day and already she could feel it suffocating her.

She wheeled her cart out the door to the parking lot and stopped, frozen in place. Griff Hunter was leaning casually against her car, watching her.

Chapter Four

❧

Her breath was frozen in her chest. Swallowing hard, she made her feet move, one in front of the other, doing her best to ignore him, her eyes still drawn to him. This was a different Griff from the daredevil who lived in her darkest dreams. He was not only older but harder, less yielding. His hair was still sun bleached and too long, his body fuller but still tanned and muscular. Aviator sunglasses hid the remembered blue of his eyes but his mouth, which had pressed such passionate kisses on every part of her body, was set in an expression of bitterness. There was something almost lethal about him now. If she hadn't known him so well, she might have been afraid of him.

And something else defined his posture. Anger? Sadness? She didn't want to know. She especially didn't want to feel the quickening of her heartbeat, the tightening of her breasts, the instant hardening of her nipples and the primal beat that began throbbing between her legs. The heat had burned her once—scorched her—and she wasn't about to play with fire again.

But her brain apparently had taken a vacation, along with her ability to make a sensible decision and stick to it. All these years, all that pain and it took only seconds for her body to leap to life in the once familiar response.

She detoured to the trunk of the rental car, her keys in her hand, which trembled despite her best efforts.

Griff reached out one arm and pressed down against the lid of the trunk so she couldn't open it. "I heard you were in town. I came to see for myself."

"Please let me open my trunk." She tried to make her voice as flat as his.

"We have things to talk about, Cassie."

"You're wrong. We have nothing to say to each other."

"Oh but we do." He moved until he was standing right next to her, crowding her space. "We have a lot to say. We have unfinished business between us."

She looked up at him, anger flashing in her eyes. She hated him for what he'd done to her and even more for the memories he'd left her with. Every one of her failed relationships could be traced back to her inability to get Griffin Hunter out of her system. No one's kisses sparked such passion, no one saw into her soul the way he did. She wanted to kill him for destroying her life.

"Our business was finished a long time ago," she spat out. "We're done."

He lifted his hand and she opened the trunk, methodically stowing the groceries inside.

"I was sorry to hear about your mother."

"Thank you."

She slammed the trunk lid shut but when she moved to get into the car, he blocked her path. She forced herself to stare up at him, hoping her face gave away nothing of the turmoil inside her. "Please let me by. I have things to do."

"This is far from over, dewdrop."

"Dewdrop?" She wanted to smack him. "Don't you ever, ever call me that again."

"Fine, *Cassie.*" His voice had a hard edge to it. "Whatever you want me to call you, this time you won't be able to run away from me."

"Run away?" She looked up at him furiously. "I wasn't the one who ran off and married someone else. I wasn't the one who made false promises that I didn't keep."

His face was totally expressionless, everything hidden behind the dark glasses. "There's a lot you don't know."

Her eyes blazed at him. "Did you have a good laugh, Griff? Seducing the baby sister of your lover, taking a naïve virgin to your bed, then dumping her? Did you all have a good chuckle over that?"

She stopped, drawing a deep breath and fighting for control. She hadn't meant to let him provoke her that way and her anger was directed as much at herself as at him.

Griffin yanked off his sunglasses and gripped her arms with his strong hands. His blue eyes flashed in the sunlight. "You have no idea what you're talking about," he said in a tight voice. "And you're wrong. We aren't done. Not by a long shot."

As suddenly as he had grabbed her, he released her and stepped back. "We will be seeing each other, Cassie. Make no mistake."

Then, like smoke in the wind, he was gone.

* * * * *

Cassie sat in the driver's seat, shaking uncontrollably, unable even to fit the key into the ignition. The feeling was still there, that flash of intense sexual tension between them and he could still crack her shell with just a few words. She had to get out of town, had to get away from Griffin Hunter. She didn't need to go through the pain of losing him again. She'd spent six years blocking it out. She wasn't sure she had the emotional resources to do it twice.

Closing her eyes, she reached into the neck of her blouse and pulled out the long silver chain that she always wore, fingering the oversized locket at the end. Only Claire knew that inside the locket was the tiny silver heart Griffin had given her on their last night together. In all the time since then, despite her unbearable pain, despite the bitter memories, she had never, ever been without it.

She wanted to put her head down on the steering wheel and weep.

* * * * *

The afternoon was as unproductive as the morning. When she called Neil, he told her regretfully the insurance company wouldn't be faxing him anything until Monday.

"Sorry. The weekend, you know. But I'll call you Monday when they came in." The sound of papers rustled over the phone. "I did call Jesse Markham and he said one of his daughters would drop by and see you. Do you need some help going through the house? I'd be happy to offer my services."

"Thanks anyway, Neil but I can manage. As a matter of fact, I think it's something I need to do by myself."

"Well, I know you want to get back to Tampa as soon as you can, Cassie and that's probably a good idea. I'll do whatever I can to expedite things."

She had started the massive job of cleaning when Carol Markham dropped by briefly, interrupting her progress and leaving her card.

"Nice to see you, Cassie. I'm sorry about your mother. My condolences."

Carol was the younger of Jesse's daughters and four years older than Cassie. Some said she'd been on the fringes of Diane's crowd but she certainly looked prim and proper now. "We're all on our way to the lake for the weekend," she said with a breezy air. "How about if I come by late Monday morning? We can do a walk through and fill out the listing agreement. Sound okay?"

And if it isn't, Cassie thought? Stoneham apparently closed up for the weekend, just like it always had.

Carol's next words made her tense. "Oh and do something about the yard. Your mother really let it go. Call Griffin Hunter, or I can do it for you. He'll fix it up in a jiffy. Bye."

Over my dead body, Cassie thought. There had to be someone else she could call. She was still more shaken by their encounter than she could admit to herself.

She was interrupted again when Donald Brandon called to tell her he'd confirmed the memorial service for Tuesday, if that was all right with her.

Why did everyone ask her that, when she had no real choice?

"Fine, Donald. Thanks." She rubbed her forehead, where a headache was beginning to build.

"I spoke to the minister and he's agreed to perform the service. He also notified the cemetery and they'll prepare the grave site, right next to your father."

"Thank you," she repeated. "I appreciate you handling all of this."

"I hope everything meets with your approval." His slippery voice fairly slid over the wires.

"That's fine, Donald," she told him again. Did he want her to express undying gratitude? "Whatever you arrange is all right with me."

"I've run off some funeral notices and we'll get them around this weekend."

Stoneham's newspaper published once a week, on Wednesdays. The usual method of notification of events between times was flyers in all the local stores. No high-tech age in this town.

"Fine, fine. I'll touch base with you on Monday morning."

"I know this must be a trying time for you," he went on. "Perhaps you'd like to have dinner with me tomorrow night? A little companionship is always nice."

Another dinner invitation. What was it with all these men and meals? She'd never had so much as a hamburger with them when she'd lived here before.

"I don't think so, Donald. I really have a lot of work to get done in the house."

"Well, all right. But if you change your mind, just give me a call."

Her original plan was to finish most of the downstairs by the end of the afternoon but all the interruptions had given her a headache that was setting up shop behind her right eye.

Tomorrow, she thought. *As long as I'm stuck here for a few days, I might as well not kill myself.*

She pulled her pad of paper across the counter toward her and began listing things to check—utilities, mail, the newspapers. Whatever she couldn't sell she'd have to arrange for shipping to Tampa. Or give it away. Which might, she thought, be the best solution. There wasn't anything she wanted, truth be told.

And then there was the yard work. Carol Markham was right—the grounds were a mess. The signs of neglect were everywhere. A buyer would be put off by that and the fading trim. She'd ask Neil to recommend someone. Landscaper as well as painter. There simply had to be someone she could hire besides Griffin. Having him around would just open the can of worms she was trying to close.

Monday she'd get copies of the will, the death certificate and probate papers from Neil and take them to the bank so she could transact her business there. She had the few bills that needed paying and she'd take care of that right away. She sighed heavily. Why had she ever been so foolish as to think she could easily accomplish this over the weekend? Everything, it seemed, was conspiring to keep her here long past the limit of her endurance.

Still, once again she thanked God that in small Texas towns the legal procedures, where no one was contesting anything, didn't drag on forever. Otherwise she'd be stuck here until God knows when.

The ringing of the phone again startled her.

Now what?

"Just checking to make sure you're doing okay."

Harley's voice was steady and soothing and Cassie almost cried at its warm familiarity. "Not great but okay," she told him.

"I spoke to Neil and he said he'll do what he can to help you wrap things up here quickly. Time to bury the past, right, Cassie?"

She sighed. "I thought I'd already done that but it seems fate dug it up again. But thanks for checking up on things. The sooner done the better."

"I agree. Let me know if there's anything I can do."

Life had indeed conspired to tear open the scars of the old wounds and she wondered now if they'd ever heal.

Impulsively she picked up the phone and dialed Claire.

"Oh, Cassie, I'm so glad you called. I just this minute got home and was checking for messages. How's it going, gal?"

"Apparently life has connived to keep me chained to this stupid town," she complained. "Nothing's changed here, that's for sure."

"Is there a lot you have to do? Do you want me to come out there and give you a hand?"

"Claire, you don't know how wonderful it would be to have you here but no, thanks just the same. You have obligations and the stuff isn't that complicated, just tedious. Everything gets done on Stoneham time."

"How's Mister Silver Heart?"

Claire was the only one Cassie had ever confided in about Griffin. She'd fled to her that terrible summer and cried for days, overwhelmed by the awful sense of betrayal. After that, unable to return to Stoneham and see Griff and Diane in the bloom of wedded bliss, unable to cope with her parents' blindness where Diane was concerned, she'd spent every school break and summer at Claire's. The warmth her family surrounded Cassie with almost — *almost* — killed the pain that still lived in a tiny corner of her heart.

"I'm sure he's just fine," she answered now. "I'm avoiding him at all costs." Telling Claire she'd already run into him would open a dialogue she wasn't ready to have.

"You know, it's probably none of my business but this might be a good time to take care of your unfinished business with him too."

"Griffin and I are more than finished," Cassie said, her voice sounding heavy. "It's over and done. Period. You know that."

"Sure, sure. That's why you wear that locket with the tiny heart inside, right?"

"Claire…"

"All right, all right. But call me if you need to gab. I'll be in and out all weekend but I'll keep my cell phone on. Take care, sweetie."

Cassie realized she'd had nothing since coffee that morning, which might account for part of the headache. She was too tired from dealing with the day for anything elaborate and she felt the grime of the house covering her. Okay, a shower, cool clothes and a sandwich and milk. Just what she needed.

Passing Diane's room on the way to her own, she again stopped in the doorway. She could almost smell the scent of Diane's rich perfume, hear her throaty voice as she hummed to herself. Had someone flown too close to her flame, burned themselves and retaliated? She turned to escape the sense of choking when something nudged at her consciousness.

She stopped, forcing herself to wipe everything out of her mind and put on her reporter's brain. What was she noticing? What was wrong or out of place? Her eyes lit first on the dresser. That was it. Every drawer was open just a fraction, as if it had been closed hastily. Her mother would never do that. She was known for her prim neatness.

Cassie opened each drawer slowly, looking through the contents. Again, everything was almost neat but if you knew the history, you could see that things had been marginally displaced.

Next she turned to the closet. The folding doors were fractionally open, again as if someone had been in a hurry. The inside of the closet was messier than the drawers. Someone obviously had been looking for something and might have been running out of time, not able to be so careful.

The fine hairs on the back of her neck stood up and a shiver ran down her spine. Tomorrow she would go through this room more thoroughly. It was obvious, though, that someone had been in here searching. When? And what for? Most important of all, who had a key and could come here whenever they pleased?

That thought was more than unsettling. Tomorrow, first thing, she would call a locksmith and have all the locks changed. She knew it was the weekend but she'd pay double time for this. She'd never sleep comfortably knowing there was a stranger out there who could enter the house at will.

She stood under the shower a long time, letting the water wash away the day and its troubles. Dressed in shorts and a tee shirt, she headed back downstairs. She stood at the counter eating the sandwich she made, with ice-cold milk to wash it down.

The laptop she'd brought with her stared back at her from the kitchen table and she thought about plugging it in but just the effort of booting it up seemed more than she could handle. She could go through her mother's room but she needed a good night's sleep to tackle that. Finally, with nothing else to do and not in the mood for television, she decided to sit out on the back patio for a while. As dark as it was, she didn't notice the figure in the big lounge chair until she was almost next to it.

"I figured you'd be out here sooner or later." Griff's voice was like warm velvet in the darkness. "Sit down, Cassie. You can't run away from me in your own house. We have things to talk about and by God, we're going to do it now."

Chapter Five

❧

Cassie felt her throat tighten and her stomach recoil. Too many emotions battled inside her—anger, apprehension, desire and the one she'd buried so deeply she didn't think it would ever surface again. Love. She couldn't make words come out of her mouth. She turned to run back to the house but he was out of the chair like lightning, gripping her arms with incredible force.

"Oh, no you don't," Griff said, his voice harsh. "Not this time. You're going to sit in that chair and listen to me if I have to tie you down."

He forced her onto the lounger he'd just vacated and sat down on the edge beside her. One arm stretched across her body pinning her effectively in place, with no wiggle room.

"I'd appreciate it if you'd let me get up this instant." Her voice was cold with fury. "And get away from my house."

"Not until you hear what I have to say. You can scream if you want but think of the explaining you'd have to do when someone shows up to rescue you."

He was so close she could smell the mixed scents of soap and aftershave on his skin. His face still had that wickedly sexy look and his eyes, no longer hidden behind sunglasses, burned into her. But the laughter that always danced in them was gone. Now they looked like two dead pools of navy, reflecting no light at all. Still his gaze could make hot and cold flashes chase themselves over her body.

Her heart squeezed at the painful thought of all they'd lost.

"If I let you have your say, will you let go of me? And will you go away?"

"Yes. But you have to listen to everything."

"I cannot possibly imagine what you think I want to hear."

She was holding herself rigidly still, trying not to touch any part of him. She knew if she did, all the stored desire, the remembered passion, would come flooding back and she'd be powerless to refuse him anything.

"I have plenty to say, whether you want to hear it or not. Are we clear on this?"

She nodded mutely.

Griffin looked at her for a long time, taking in every bit of her figure that she knew was riper, more mature than his "dewdrop" had been. His long-ago words suddenly echoed in her head. How he'd wanted her, from the time she was just a teenager. Did he think she actually believed lust turned to love? Based on what—those memorable two nights hidden away in his bedroom, tasting all those illicit pleasures? Then why had he married Diane?

Looking in his eyes, seeking answers, she was shocked by the incredible pain she saw.

"How can I make you understand it all," he asked her, "when I still have trouble with it myself? I only knew that I loved you and that's never changed. Not even with the train wreck Diane had made of my life. Somehow I have to convince you of that, because I don't think I can give you up again."

"What can there possibly be to understand?" she asked.

"God, I don't even know where to begin here." He looked away for a moment, his eyes distant. "If I tell you that no matter what you saw or heard, you were the one I wanted since high school, I know you won't believe me. Why should you? But it's the truth. That night on the porch when I told you I was waiting for you? You thought it was a line but that's exactly what I was doing. Just as I'd done a lot of other nights. Waiting for you to walk by."

"Bull," she said. "Diane was always the one you wanted. Not me. I wasn't loose enough for you and your friends."

And Diane was the one he'd married.

"You're right about that. Even in high school you were the ice queen. You could destroy guys just with that cold, frosty look of yours. Did you know that? Everyone was afraid to approach you." His voice dropped slightly. "Me more than anyone. It took a lot of guts to do what I did that night."

"I don't believe you." But her voice was a little uncertain. Was that why she had so few dates in high school? She'd deliberately kept everyone at bay, unwilling to be painted with the same brush as her sister. Still, there hadn't been anyone who really interested her enough to drop her guard.

"Shut up and let me finish," he told her. "I meant every word I said to you those two nights. Everything. I was more than ready to stop running with that crowd. I thought when you came back from your trip maybe we'd see what kind of relationship we could build."

Cassie could still remember the shock when her mother broke the news of Griffin and Diane's marriage. Afraid she'd fall apart on the spot, she'd smiled stiffly, then locked herself in her room. Unwilling to face anyone and listen to the painful details, she'd endured hammer blows to her heart and shut out the world.

"You must have run out of patience, because when I came back, there you and Diane were, the happy couple. No doubt having a good laugh at my expense."

Griffin grabbed her so hard his fingers bit painfully into her soft flesh. He shook her until her head snapped back and forth. "Did you think I wanted you to just walk out of my life?" His voice was rough. "Do you think I wanted to marry Diane? Do you really think that's what I had in mind? We might have had our fling, although Diane had a fling with just about everyone. But you didn't marry girls like her. You only took them to bed."

"I didn't know what to think," she whispered, shaken by his fury. "I-I thought you'd just amused yourself with me, for some reason." *And burned me in the process.*

His eyes were blazing into her, like twin lasers. His fingers pressed her flesh even harder. "She was pregnant." He spat the words out as if they tasted bad. "Diane was pregnant."

Cassie felt as if someone had punched her in the stomach. "What? She was what?"

"You heard me. She was pregnant. She swore it was mine." He raked his hand through his hair. "I'm a lot of things, Cassie. I know what my reputation is and I've certainly done everything to deserve it. But this was my responsibility and I wasn't going to opt out of it."

"You didn't have to marry her." But she knew those were empty words. Griffin was right. He'd accepted responsibility for his father and he would have done no less for the the woman who'd told him she was carrying his child.

"Is that how little you think of me? I know you always looked at me as just another piece of trash, like everyone else in this town did. But believe it or not, I have some sense of accountability for what I do. Especially when it involves another person. A child." He was still gripping her arms, holding her in place. "Besides, I didn't think a child should have to suffer for an irresponsible act."

"My folks must have had a fit."

"They didn't know. No one did but me. I thought they'd have a hemorrhage over the runaway marriage but Diane was twenty-four, there wasn't much they could do about it and somehow no matter what she did, they were always accepting of it. I never could figure that out."

"Diane drew people like moths to a flame," Cassie said bitterly. "She had our folks wrapped around her little finger. And everyone else too, it seems."

"I tried to see you when you got back but you were here one day and gone the next. I didn't know how to find you and I couldn't very well ask your parents."

"I got out of town as fast as I could." She tried to shift in the lounger to a more comfortable position. "I spent the summer with my roommate. Did you think I wanted to stay around and watch you and Diane play house?"

"I was desperate to explain it all to you." He looked away from her now. "I didn't know what the hell to do. My dad was drinking himself to death and I had a wife who only wanted a name for her child and someone to pay the freight."

"I'd have thought she would get an abortion," Cassie said, hating the bitchy tone of her voice. "A baby would cut into her playtime."

"I actually asked her about it. God knows I wanted her to. Having a child with Diane was never in my plans. She said she was afraid of them. That something might go wrong. So there we were, pregnant Diane, drunken Dad and me, all in the house down the street. Can you think of a more fun scenario?"

"And what did you think I would do, play the doting aunt? Or didn't that cross your mind?"

"I didn't think at all and that's God's honest truth, Cassie. I was just trying to take it one day at a time."

"And then Diane was killed."

"Yes." He exhaled heavily. "Then Diane was killed. But I can tell you, the ink wasn't even dry on the marriage license before she was out running around again. I wanted her to settle down because of the baby, stop drinking, take care of herself but you know Diane."

"Better than I ever wanted to."

"I knew she was still sleeping around." Every word was edged in bitterness. "Hell, Diane could never be faithful to anyone. It wasn't as if I cared one hell of a lot, except I didn't want her to hurt the baby." He drew in a shuddering breath. "I'd already planned to divorce her as soon as the baby was born and file for sole custody. The Barbours' dog down the street was a more fit parent than she was."

"I understand you were the one and only suspect," Cassie said quietly.

"You got it. I know I haven't always been a nice person, Cassie but murder is a little out of my league. No matter what the circumstances."

"They never found out who did it." Her voice was so low she didn't know if he could hear her.

"No. No, they didn't. I think half the town still thinks it was me."

"But you have a business," she protested. "And apparently everyone hires you."

"As long as I stay in the yard and don't come in the front door, they're very happy to pay me for my work." His lips twisted ironically. "I guess it's okay to hire a murderer if he hasn't killed someone close to you."

There was such pain in his voice, her heart began to ache for him. Don't do this, Cassie, she berated herself. Stay out of the fire. Let him talk and then tell him to go.

"Okay," she forced herself to say, "I've heard what you have to say. Now you can go."

"Do *you* think I killed her? How about it, Cassie? Do you see me as a killer?" His voice was flat, his eyes hooded as he waited for her answer.

"No." She barely whispered the word. "No, I don't."

He suddenly leaned closer to her, his face so near she could feel his breath on her skin. He knew if he said it now there'd be no taking it back but he couldn't stop himself. If it was truly dead, this feeling they'd shared, he had to find out.

"Griffin…." She tried to push her head back into the chair.

"I never got to tell you that night that I love you, dewdrop," he said quietly. "And that is who you are, Cassie.

My dewdrop. I gave you my heart, but I figured we'd have plenty of time for that later. I wanted you to get to know me as a person, not just by my reputation."

Cassie's heart nearly stopped. Whatever else she might have said caught in her throat. Of all the things he could have told her, this was the last thing she'd expected. And the name. His nickname for her. The sound of it made her heart crack open.

Damn him!

"Say something," he prodded. "Tell me to leave right now or I'm going to kiss you."

Cassie couldn't move, couldn't speak. She couldn't do this, couldn't let him touch her. Part of the reason for her return to Stoneham was to get him out of her system once and for all. She wanted to make him pay for the hell he'd put her through. If she let him touch her now, she'd be his again.

She willed herself to jerk away, to get up but her muscles wouldn't obey her command. Then his mouth was on hers, parting her lips, probing gently with his tongue.

The kiss started out easy, tentative but then Griffin's hand tangled through her hair, pulling her head to him, holding her in place. The kiss deepened and she couldn't fight it, her arms automatically reaching around him, holding him to her. The kiss went on and on, his tongue sweeping erotically through her mouth, tasting its velvet cavern, teasing at all the wet corners and she didn't have the strength to break the contact.

Finally Griffin lifted his lips and looked at her hard. "It's still there, isn't it, Cassie. This thing between us. You can lie to yourself but you can't lie to me."

"Griff, I…"

But then he was kissing her again, feeding from her mouth, ravaging it with his tongue. He held her to him so tightly she could barely breathe.

"This won't go away, you know. I still love you." His voice was thick with emotion. "God, how I love you. And admit it or not, you feel the same way." He sat back, releasing her and gently brushed one cheek with his fingertips. "You haven't married, have you? Or found anyone to get serious with? I thought not."

"I had my reasons," she whispered.

"You don't have to tell me what they are. The kiss says it all. You gave me a precious gift, Cassie. I didn't take it lightly, whatever you think. I didn't have a real choice in what happened before. I won't let you run away from me this time. You can take that to the bank." He touched the locket around her neck. "What's in there, dewdrop? A picture of me?"

"No. No, it's not."

"You still own my heart, dewdrop. Nothing ever changed that."

And just like that, like fingers brushing away a magic curtain, six years disappeared as if they'd happened yesterday. The memory of that sleek, muscled body, the golden curls on his chest, the feel of his fingers on her, in her, was like a drug in her system.

He stood up, towering over her.

"This yard hasn't been touched in forever. I think your mother just kind of gave up on everything. I don't have anything scheduled for tomorrow. I'll be back in the morning and get to work on it."

She couldn't believe the switch in conversation. She might as easily just have imagined him saying those three words that were turning her upside down. Her body was aching for his hands, his tongue, his hardened erection and he was talking about landscaping? "I don't think…"

"That's right. Don't think. Just let this take us wherever it goes." He bent and kissed her lightly. "Good night, darlin'. See you tomorrow."

Then he was gone. Cassie sat on the patio for a long time, playing with the locket and feeling her lips where his had touched hers. She called herself all kinds of a fool, knowing she was staring danger in the face. She had to find a way to protect herself from this fire that threatened to consume her. Once burned was more than enough for her.

Griffin Hunter could whisper all the sweet words in her ear he wanted to. She knew the truth. In the vernacular, he wanted to fuck her and just like before, he'd do whatever it took to accomplish it. She just wished she didn't feel this awful, aching need.

Chapter Six

ဆာ

Sleep eluded Cassie. She tossed restlessly, dozing briefly, only to be awakened by the memory of Griff's mouth on hers, his maleness so close to her. Images of the past kept floating in her head. No matter how she tried, she couldn't chase them away.

Finally, at six o'clock, with the sun trying to slip in around the edges of the window shade, she decided to get up and get to work on the house. Pulling on the shorts and tee shirt she'd thrown over a chair, she pulled her hair back in a ponytail and made herself a pot of coffee. Today she reminded herself to eat, popping bread in the toaster while she filled a coffee mug.

She was munching on the last bite when she heard a truck pull into the driveway. A glance at the clock told her it was only six-thirty. Nobody started life that early in Stoneham. Peeking through the curtains, she saw Griffin lifting equipment out of a pickup labeled *Hunter Landscape Services*. Ignoring the flutter in her stomach, she opened the door and stepped out on the porch.

"I think this is a very bad idea." She tried to make her voice as firm as possible. If she let him into one corner of her life he'd take the rest. She couldn't do it again. He'd said he loved her but could she believe him? Trust him, after everything?

He looked up. "Planning on doing the yard work yourself?"

"No but..."

"Okay, then. I'll try to get as much done as I can before the worst heat of the day. I thought I'd get all the hand work done before starting the mower. Don't want your neighbors throwing rocks at me."

She started to tell him again to go away but her mouth had its own idea of what to say. "Would you like a cup of coffee?"

He stopped arranging his tools and looked at her for a moment, then nodded. When he spoke, his voice was as reserved as hers. "Yes. That would be nice. Black, no sugar."

"Easy enough."

Cassie girl, you are playing with fire again, she told herself. *How many times will you hold yourself in the flame?* She ignored the alarms going off in her head and poured coffee into a mug for Griffin, refilled her own and took them out to the porch. She sat down on the top step and motioned for him to join her.

"I appreciate the hospitality, Cassie. Not what I expected after last night."

Last night. She was still trying to decide if she had imagined it or not. Had he really said he loved her? Was the unbelievable story he told really true?

Under lowered lids she stole an all-encompassing look at him. His jeans and tee shirt hugged his body like a second skin. As he sat down, muscles flexed beneath the fabric, working smoothly and effortlessly. When she got to the bulge in his crotch her eyes slithered away.

Don't go there.

The aviator shades were in place again, making his eyes unreadable. Cassie wished hers were too. When he turned her face toward him, she was afraid of what he would see there.

"We still have a long way to go, sugar," he said, in his deep, liquid voice, "and I'm not rushing things. But I'm taking advantage of every minute you're here. Be warned."

She didn't know what to say to that. She was torn between wanting to run and wanting to throw her arms around him and bury herself against him.

"So," he said, changing the subject. "How's it been going? Anyone giving you a hard time?"

"No." she shook her head. "Not unless you count the fact that you can't get anything done until next year around here. I forgot this place operates on Stoneham time."

He threw back his head and laughed. "Oh, yes. Nobody hurries for anything around here. What's on your plate that you're so anxious to get rid of?"

She ticked off her items for him. "Cleaning out the house, listing the house, probating the will, having the funeral service, all that stuff. Neil McLeod's handling everything but he doesn't seem in any bigger hurry to get stuff done than anyone else."

"Get used to it, Cassie. You've been away too long. Nothing's changed."

Except my life, she thought. "By the way. Who would I call as a locksmith to bribe for some Saturday work?"

"You have to be kidding. What's so urgent it can't wait until Monday?"

She told him about Diane's room. "It's probably just my imagination but it makes me nervous thinking someone I don't know about has a key to this house." A thought struck her. "You didn't happen to come over and go through that room, did you?"

"I haven't set foot in this house since Diane died," he said, somewhat angrily. "And if I did, I wouldn't be sneaky about it." He drained his coffee. "I don't like the sound of this, though. Especially with you staying here all alone. Let me make a couple of calls."

He pulled his cell phone off the belt clip and scrolled through to find the number he wanted. Cassie listened while he cajoled someone into coming over, his voice finally almost threatening. "Just do it," he said. "You owe me enough favors it won't kill you to pay one back."

"I don't want you to impose on anyone for me." Cassie folded her hands in a prim gesture on her knees.

Griffin snapped the phone shut. "Phil Morgan does most of the locksmith work in town. He hates to work on Saturday but I rattled his cage a little. And I'm not imposing. He wouldn't mind calling me if he needed some work in a hurry."

"Thank you." She didn't know what else to day. "I appreciate it."

"Is the room still the way you found it?"

She nodded. "I checked everything then put it back the way it was. I thought of calling the police but I changed my mind."

"When I take a break, I want you to show it to me." He handed her back the mug. "Thanks for the coffee. I need to get to work."

Cassie dragged out the cleaning supplies she'd bought, found her mother's broom and vacuum cleaner and began methodically divesting the house of its accumulation of dust and neglect. She didn't know how long it had been since someone had really cleaned the rooms, or what her mother'd been able to do.

She made a mental note to call Harley in the afternoon and ask him more about her mother's condition. She felt badly about not getting back to him yesterday but her mind had been on other things.

A lot of other things. And instead of the answers she'd been looking for, she seemed to have come up with more questions than ever.

* * * * *

Cassie had just finished cleaning in the living room when the doorbell rang. When she opened the door, Griffin stood there with Phil Morgan.

"How you doin', Cassie?" Phil had been a big player in Diane's group but now he seemed intimidated by her little sister's presence.

Cassie smothered a laugh. "Fine, Phil. Just fine."

"Sorry about your mother. She was a nice lady."

"Thank you very much."

Griffin stepped into the house and took charge. "Cassie, why don't you let Phil know what all he needs to do. Then you can show me that thing you were talking about before."

"Oh! Of course. And thanks for coming out on a Saturday. I know I cut into your time off and I'm more than willing to pay for it."

Phil just nodded, then followed her as she showed him all the doors, even the one from the garage into the house. He made notes on a little pad of paper as they walked, nodding to himself.

"Okay. Let me get my stuff and I'll have it done in no time. I've got a portable key machine so you'll have a whole new set before I leave."

She was more grateful to him than she could have said.

"I want to see Diane's room." Griffin's voice was quiet. "Let's do it while Phil does his thing."

She felt strange standing with him in this room, painfully picturing Griffin and Diane together on this bed. Could she ever ask him all the questions that tumbled in her mind? Deliberately she tamped down her thoughts to focus on what they were doing and explained why something so slight bothered her.

"You're right," Griffin said finally. "Your mother invented neatness. Her housekeeping may have suffered the last few months but she never would have left stuff this way. And of course, it's been six years since Diane set foot in here."

He gnawed on his thumb, looking around, standing still for a long time as if memorizing details. He walked around the room once more, this time slowly, looking at the disarray in the closet, searching for some kind of indication of why someone had been there.

"What I can't figure," he said, "is what they'd be looking for. Diane didn't have anything of real value. Not even our wedding ring. I got what I could afford. And why now?"

"I asked myself the same thing. I can tell you my parents didn't change a thing in this room after Diane died. Did she spend much time over here?"

"As much time as she did anywhere, I guess, including our home." He tried to keep the venom out of his voice. "But she didn't have anything worth taking. Something else is going on here and it bothers me that I can't figure it out."

Phil was just finishing up when they walked out onto the porch. He closed the workbox on his truck and brought a set of keys over to her.

"The same key will open all the doors," he told Cassie. "I didn't know how many you'd need, so I made four. I guessed you were looking for extra security, so I also put deadbolts on the three outer doors."

"Thank you very much," Cassie told him. "This has been a big help. Let me get my checkbook and I'll pay you. Oh." She stopped. "It's an out of state check, is that okay? I promise you it's good."

"No problem." He smiled uneasily. "Uh, just pay me for the materials and we'll call it square."

"But that's ridiculous." She raised an eyebrow. "What's going on? You came out here on a Saturday, which is at least double time. I insist."

"Uh... Griffin?" He shifted nervously from one foot to another.

"Pay him what he says, Cassie. He owes me too many favors to charge for his time."

She saw it was useless to argue with them, so she wrote out a check for the locks and Phil fairly ran to his truck.

"I think that man's afraid of you," she said, a smile twitching at the corners of her mouth. "Do you beat him regularly?"

"At least once a week," he said in a solemn voice, then winked at her.

Her heart stuttered and she had to turn away. This was absurd and ridiculous and she had to stop it.

He went back to the yard work and Cassie tackled another room in the house. When her stomach began to grumble, she knew it was time for lunch. She debated about offering Griffin something, knowing she was wading into deeper and deeper waters but finally went to the door and hollered to him.

"If you like tuna fish, lunch will be ready in ten minutes."

He looked up from the side yard, startled. He wiped at the sweat on his forehead with his arm and looked at her, as if assessing her. "Okay," he said finally. "But I need to find a place to wash up."

"You can use the bathroom downstairs. Come on in."

She went back to the kitchen to fix their lunch.

What are you doing, Cassie?

In a minute she heard the front door open and close and his footsteps move down the hall. She was just putting their plates on the table when he came into the kitchen. His presence filled the room. His hair was still damp from running wet hands though it and he had obviously put on a clean tee shirt. Muscles rippled under the tanned skin and he smelled of maleness and the outdoors.

Despite the past, despite the pain she still carried with her daily, she wanted nothing more than to throw herself against his body and hold on for dear life. And that, she told herself, was a sure recipe for disaster.

Chapter Seven

80

"I think you'll need to soak the towel I used for about a week," he told her. "Sorry abut that."

"No problem." She fussed at the table settings. "I hope this is okay."

She had fixed tuna sandwiches with chips and pickles and large glasses of iced tea.

"This is fine, Cassie. You didn't have to fix anything for me. I usually just take a break and run down to the sandwich shop."

"I didn't mind. I was fixing something for myself anyway." Could she just stop being so fidgety? She felt like a fly that couldn't find a place to light.

It's just lunch. What's the big deal?

"Thank you for getting Phil out here and helping with the locks."

"No big deal. He really does owe me. And it was important to get it done. I'm not saying someone has a key to this place but no sense taking chances."

"I can't imagine why anyone would want to go through Diane's room." She brushed a stray hair off her face. "It just seems so strange."

"Do you know what kind of visitors your mother had in the last few months?" he asked her.

Cassie shifted uncomfortably in her chair. "I know this sounds awful to say but I actually haven't spoken to my mother since about six months before she died."

Griffin looked at her strangely. "Did you two have a fight? I know you haven't been back here since...well, for several years but I guess I assumed you all were still talking."

Cassie put her sandwich down, wiped the corner of her mouth and tried to think how to answer the question without putting herself in a difficult position. "You have to understand. It all had to do with Diane. She and I were total opposites. She was bright, vivacious, a charmer from the day she was born. I was kind of the afterthought. Dull gray. Nobody asked or expected very much of me."

"You sell yourself short," Griffin interrupted.

Cassie took a swallow of her iced tea, then went on. "No matter what Diane did, my folks were totally absorbed with her. They chalked up her wildness, her reputation, to 'youthful high jinks', as my dad used to say. She was the bright light in their lives.

"When Diane died, I was still so...well, I was still dealing with what happened when you two got married and I couldn't make myself come home for the funeral. They never forgave me. And when Dad died, my mother practically told me to stay away. That was fine with me. We've only had limited contact since then."

"I really messed up your life, didn't I." It was a statement more than a question.

"Actually, I think I probably did that all by myself." Her voice was low, quiet. "I really don't want to talk about it right now, if that's all right. Would you like some more iced tea? Or another sandwich?"

Griffin reached out and caught her hands in his. "I don't want iced tea and I don't want anything else to eat. I want you to look at me."

She stared at her lap.

He tugged on her hand. "Cassie? Lift up your head and look at me."

Reluctantly she raised her eyes to meet his, thinking what a bad idea this had been. She should have just let him get his own lunch.

"We're either gonna keep picking at this thing until it starts to bleed," he said, "or we open it all at once and hope it will heal."

"I keep telling you," she said in a sad tone, "there just isn't anything to say. This was a mistake, Griffin. I'm sorry. I appreciate your help with the locks and the yard but when you're finished I think you should just go."

Before I make a fool of myself again.

"Not a chance." He shook his head. "For one thing, I discovered something last night and you should have too. Whatever was there between us six years ago is still there. It's always been there for me. Diane got in the way and there's just no polite way to say it differently."

So he did remember what he'd said. But did he mean it?

He paused, watching her, then went on. "I know she was your sister but she just wasn't the nice person your parents thought she was. Diane was selfish, self-centered and she used people. She always hovered at the edge of a precipice, daring everyone to fall over it with her. When we were all running around like idiots it was okay, because she could drink and fuck with the best of us."

Cassie jerked, her face paling.

"Does that word offend you? I'm sorry but there's just no other word for it. None of us in that crowd bothered much with morals at that time. We were wild, then. All of us. Some nights I even slept in the drunk tank with my father. That's just the way it was."

"And is that the way it was with us?" she demanded. "Just…an exercise?"

"No," he said, his tone emphatic. "But that's another topic for discussion. I'm just trying to make you see something here. Diane was just a good time, a hard ride, as they say. One more place I could run away from the disaster my family had become. But I never loved her. She knew it, I knew it. I guess I hoped when I married her for the baby we could start something new."

"And did you?"

"Not even for a minute." He shook his head, a shadow of sadness sweeping over his face. "Diane really didn't want to be married but your folks would have had a fit if she was single and pregnant. The money wasn't so great then, either, which bothered her a lot. I don't know what she expected but it sure wasn't what she got. And of course, there was my dad."

"I heard he passed away about year after Diane," Cassie interjected.

"I can only tell you it was a blessing for both of us."

"I'm sorry." She didn't know what else to say.

"Yeah, well, aren't we all. Thank you."

He was still holding her hands tightly in his, preventing her from leaving the table. "When she told me about the baby I took it as some kind of sign to clean up my act. But Diane wasn't about to let a baby cramp her style. She bragged that she didn't even look pregnant. Most nights all we did was fight and she'd slam out of the house. It was a freaking disaster."

"Is that what happened the night she died?" Cassie asked quietly.

"You mean the night she was murdered? The night the whole town thought I'd killed her?" His voice was venomous. "Let's call it what it is, Cassie. You can't dress it up with nice words."

"I just… I don't…"

"The night Diane was murdered we had a big fight. That's what you wanted to know. Right?"

She nodded, looking at her lap again. He sounded so angry.

"I guess I'm just damned lucky I went to Phil's house instead of staying home and getting smashed. Two other people dropped by and we drank beer and watched a game on television. Otherwise I'm sure I'd be on the inside looking out through bars right now."

Without raising her eyes she said, "I never believed you killed her, Griff. I didn't think you could do something like that."

"You're a majority of one, I'll tell you that. People still look at me cross-eyed."

"But you do everyone's landscaping and everything," she pointed out again and frowned. "They still hire you."

"Only because they don't have a choice." He dropped her hands, stood up and took his dishes to the sink.

"We still have a lot of unsettled issues between us, Cassie. And we're going to settle them before you leave here. Make no mistake about that. If I have my way, Tampa has seen the last of you." He headed toward the front door. "I'll let you know when I'm finished so you can take a look."

Cassie sat in her chair a long time after that, trying to straighten out her brain and her emotions. Griffin Hunter, Stoneham's worst bad boy, had grown up. As a man who'd walked through Hell he was even more dangerous. Before, he had been a forbidden pleasure that she hungered for, beckoning her.

Now he was older, his wildness under control but still there below the surface. Letting him into her life again was a big mistake but she seemed powerless to stop it. If she kept opening the door for him, he'd walk right in and consume her. And that scared her.

If she was completely honest with herself, this was the reason she hadn't wanted to come back to Stoneham. Here she'd have to face the fact that she'd been in love with him all these years. No matter how much she kept denying it to herself, there it was. That's why she still wore the locket.

Those kisses last night. Powerful kisses that she had willingly accepted, that stirred something inside her. The imminence of more was just hanging out there, tempting her, keeping her on edge.

And his words. "I love you."

Could she trust what he said? And what could she do with that? Could she admit that she'd loved him all her life?

Those two nights with him so long ago haunted her memory. She had indeed saved her virginity for him, hoping shamefully that one night she would be the one lying in the bad boy's arms. Even after the disaster of his marriage, the months and years of crying and anguish, nothing could erase that exhilaration. Seeing him now brought it all back.

Walk away, she told herself. But she knew she wouldn't. She had built a fantasy on secret dreams and two stolen nights. Could she let down the bars long enough to find out if that fantasy was real?

* * * * *

Cleaning the kitchen took the longest of all the rooms and by the time she finished, Cassie needed a break. She decided to take the opportunity to call Harley Graham.

"Good to hear your voice, Cassie." His booming voice sounded so comforting. "Everything going okay there?"

"Yes, Harley. Just fine. Thanks."

"Ran into Neil and he told me you and he had met, gotten things started."

"Yes, we did." She sighed. "I didn't think everything would take so long. I guess I was dreaming if I thought I could do it in three days."

"Not around here, girl." he chuckled. "By the way, I'm passing the word about the funeral service on Tuesday. Hope you don't mind."

"No, that's all right. I don't expect a big crowd and that's probably just as well."

"You may be surprised, honey. Your folks lived here a long time."

Cassie thought a moment about how to frame her question. "Harley, did my mother have a lot of visitors during her last few months?"

"I don't know what you mean, Cassie. She had two or three friends who looked in on her. Neil came by every so often to check on her and get her to sign some papers or other. Thad Williams, the senior partner in that firm, used to do all the legal work for your folks. When he retired Neil took over but Thad still came around to see her now and then. What's this all about? You looking for someone specific?"

"No, no," she said quickly. "I guess I was just trying to get a picture in my mind of what was going on here."

"Well, if there was anyone else, they'll for sure be at the funeral. You can check everyone out for yourself."

"Thanks, Harley. And thanks for setting everything up here for me."

"No problem." He paused. "I happened to drive by your house a while ago and saw Griffin Hunter working in the yard. You hire him to do some work?"

"Uh, yes, well, that is, Carol Markham suggested I get him out here to neaten things up. I'm listing the house with her."

"Be careful, Cassie. Griffin may be a lot older and run a good business but I still don't think I'd trust my daughter with him, if I had one."

Cassie felt a knot forming in her stomach. "Thanks for the advice, Harley but I can handle Griffin. I'm older too. Remember?"

"Just call me if you need me. You know I'm always here for you."

Well, that went well, Cassie thought, leaning back against the counter. *No one to suspect of breaking and entering except solid citizens and a blatant warning about Griff.* She tore off a paper towel, wet it with cold water and put it on the back of her neck. Her headache was beginning to come back too.

"Are you all right?"

She hadn't even heard the object of her thoughts come in. He was standing inches away from her, crowding her again, towering over her.

"I'm fine," she said. "A little overwhelmed by everything, I guess. I just got off the phone with Harley."

"You're not sick, are you?" His voice was suddenly concerned.

"No, thank goodness. That's all I'd need right now. I'd just told him I'd check in with him today. I also wanted to see if he knew who was visiting my mother these past few months. I'm trying to figure out who'd be searching for something here."

"Did you get anything from him?"

"A list of respectable citizens and a warning not to succumb to your charms."

Griffin actually smiled at that. "Looking out for his surrogate daughter, was he? It's nice to know my reputation is still intact. You'd do well to listen to him. I have plans."

She started to say something but he took her hand and pulled her toward the front door.

"Right now I want you to come outside and see what I've done. The place sure was a mess."

Cassie couldn't believe how he'd transformed it. The grass was neatly mown, the shrubs trimmed perfectly, all the beds weeded. Even the shriveled rose bushes had perked up. He walked her around the side yard and into the back. The flower beds had sparkled back to life and all the edges of the lawn, including around the patio, were neatly and precisely trimmed. He had put fresh mulch around the crepe myrtle and sycamore trees.

"Griff!" She couldn't hide her amazement. "I can't believe it's the same place. This is fantastic. You do incredible work." She couldn't stop staring, overwhelmed by what she saw. "Did you learn all this from your father?"

"Yeah, right," he snorted. "Some from working with him, some on my own by trial and error." He looked away. "Two years ago I started taking agriculture classes at the junior college in San Antonio. I learned a lot there."

She looked at him, her mouth gaping open. Griffin Hunter going to college? She felt like she'd stumbled into a different time dimension.

"Close your mouth, Cassie, you'll catch flies. Did I shock you? They say education is for everyone, you know."

"It's just that…"

"That you never expected it of me, right?" His moved closer to her, his presence crowding her. "What exactly did you expect of me? Did you just want to give up your cherry to the town bad boy so you could have your own naughty memories? Was that it?"

The day had been too long, the tension too much, the frustration too great. She sank down onto a lawn chair and burst into tears. She blotted her face with the wet towel, knowing she looked as undone as she felt.

"Cassie?"

In an instant he was kneeling beside her, brushing away the hair escaping from her ponytail, wiping away the tears running down her cheeks. "Honey, I'm so sorry. That was a rotten thing to say. And I didn't even mean it. Look at me, sugar. Come on."

Sugar. She could still hear his voice whispering it seductively in her ear while he did unbelievable things to her body. While his fingers probed inside her, slick with her liquid and his thumb did things to her clitoris that six years hadn't erased.

The tears she had saved up all this time came tumbling out. She rocked back and forth, crying in huge gulping sobs, not even caring what she looked like. She just needed to cleanse her body of the pent-up suffering.

She hadn't noticed Griffin leaving her until suddenly he was back. "Here." He handed her a glass of water and two aspirin. "Take these and drink all the water."

She obeyed his gentle instruction. Her body began to slow its paroxysms and return to normal. "Thank you," she said.

"I think you've done quite enough work for today. The house looks great but you look a mess and you're exhausted." He took the glass from her and pulled her out of the chair. For a space of a heartbeat he held her against him, their bodies touching, his rigid penis pressing against the softness of her belly, her hardened nipples pushing into his chest. Forcing self control, he released her and took her hand. "Come on. What you need is a hot bath and a nap."

"A bath?"

"Works wonders, they tell me." He led her into the house and helped her put away the cleaning supplies. "I'd take you out to dinner tonight but I'm not in the mood to drive fifty miles to a restaurant. If we parade around in Stoneham, your reputation will be shot by tomorrow. Take your bath, take a nap and I'll be back about seven-thirty. We'll order some pizza, okay?"

"Pizza?"

"Yeah. You know, the flat dough with all the stuff on it. And I'll hide behind the door when the delivery boy gets here." He grinned.

She gave him a shaky smile in return.

"That's better," he said. "So. Seven-thirty okay?"

"Do you think this is such a good idea?" She knew her voice was quavering.

"I think it's a fine idea. And you will too, once I get back here."

He pulled her against him again, cradling her against his chest, stroking her hair, soothing her. "I'll see you in a while, okay?"

She nodded. "Okay."

He started toward the front door, then stopped. "We're going to face this, Cassie. You may not want to but you've got so much bottled up inside you and I have so much to say. There's no running away this time. I'll see you later."

Chapter Eight

ɞ

Cassie had to agree that Griff was right. The bath was great medicine. She'd stuck some bubble bath in her suitcase for whatever reason and now she dumped most of it into the tub. Leaning her head back, she sank into the welcoming warmth and let the softly lapping water and heady aroma do its work.

What an ass she'd made of herself. She cringed just thinking of it. And what a fool he must think her but it was an emotional catharsis long overdue. Maybe now she could take care of business in Stoneham, shake the dust from her shoes and get on with her life.

But what was she going to do about Griff? She thought of him with a mixture of dread and anticipation, her dilemma still swirling around her. The imprint of his lips still lingered and the memory of his touch wouldn't go away. She'd come back to Stoneham still full of anger, determined to close that chapter of her life. Since then all she'd done was let herself be drawn tighter and tighter into his web. He had asked the right question of her, though—what did she want from him? Too bad she didn't have a pat answer. Did she want to push him out of her life forever, or was she willing to risk her heart one more time?

This was a different Griffin Hunter from the untamed careless boy who had taken her to his bed. That's what he had been then, a boy, even at twenty-four. This was an older Griffin, matured by the challenges life had thrown at him. A man and a greater threat than the boy had ever been.

Leaning back in the tub, she let her hands drift to the nest of curls between her legs, recalling how Griffin's hands had felt so long ago, teasing at those same curls, invading her body with a magic touch. This was a fantasy of long familiarity, played out whenever the memories of him became too hot to turn off. She spread her knees wide, letting the hot water lap against her skin and rubbing her fingers against her labia. She tingled just from thinking of those two nights with him and she rubbed her puffy skin between thumb and forefinger.

She regretted not bringing her vibrator with her, the poor substitute for Griffin that eased her frustration on many nights. Idly she let one finger slide over her clitoris between the labia, past the throbbing flesh that begged for stimulation. When she slipped a finger into her vagina and began sliding it back and forth, she closed her eyes and imagined it was Griffin's hands, Griffin's fingers. Her vaginal muscles clenched around the intrusion and she began moving her hand in and out, faster and faster.

When she placed her thumb on her clit, she imagined it was Griffin's thumb, circling and teasing. Her hips began jerking as the heat built inside her. Bracing her feet on the bottom of the tub, her head barely above water, she increased the tempo, bucking against her hand, until she could feel the tremors start. And then she was there, her whole body clenching as the spasms rippled through her.

But her fingers were not Griffin's, her hands were not his. And nothing she could provide on her own was a substitute for the thick hardness of his cock as it probed at her entrance and pushed up inside her.

She lay back in the tub, weak and only mildly satisfied. Why had she done this? Instead of bringing herself relief, she'd only stimulated herself to an edge that she might just fall over.

Better make up your mind, girl. The evening is approaching. Open that door and there's no going back.

She dried her hair and brushed it until it shone. Tonight she let it fall loose to her shoulders, not restrained by a clip or ponytail holder. She pulled on fresh jeans and a summer sweater in deep rose, clipped little gold hoops in her ears and swiped pink lipstick across her mouth. Putting on the war paint, she told herself. Did she even have a clue as to what she was doing?

Downstairs she closed all the drapes, sealing herself off from the world, and turned on only the kitchen light. There was no space for prying eyes to peer through.

At seven-thirty, waiting for the doorbell to ring, she was startled by a tap on the back door. She pulled aside the curtain on the little window. Griffin stood there, grinning at her.

"I didn't even hear you drive up," she said, opening the back door. "Why didn't you come to the front? Don't tell me you're worried about the neighbors."

"Yes and no."

He stepped into the utility room, pulled down the shade beneath the curtain on the door, and threw a small canvas bag on the counter.

"What's that?"

"My stuff. I'm spending the night."

Just like that. Suddenly she felt suffocated and her chest hurt.

"You can wipe that look off your face, Cassie. I have other reasons, which I'll tell you about over pizza." He grinned again. "Although I can't say I haven't entertained naughty thoughts about you."

"What reasons?" Her voice sounded strangled.

"Later. But that's why you didn't hear me. I walked and came in the back way. No one sees me arrive here or leave."

He propelled her into the kitchen. "Let's order the pizza. I'm starved."

Insisting she answer the door to the delivery boy, Griffin shoved money into her hand to pay for it. He skillfully avoided her probing questions while they ate and Cassie tried to sit as quietly as she could. But the sexual stimulation she'd given herself in her bath had left her whole body one big throbbing pulse.

If only I could attack him, then send him on his way.

After they'd finished the last crumbs and cleaned up, he took her hand and pulled her into the living room. Sitting down on the couch, he tugged her down beside him.

"First of all, I don't want you to freak out about what I'm going to tell you. I have to let you know, though, because it's why I made up my mind to spend the night."

She looked at him questioningly.

"The whole business with Diane's bedroom bothered me. What could someone possibly want that an airhead like Diane would have? Then when I was working in the yard, I saw where someone had been digging around some of the shrubbery, close to the house."

"What?"

"It wasn't landscaping work, I can tell you that. They were digging for something and then trying to cover it up. Then I remembered Diane had planted some of those bushes with me, when she was doing her 'let's do some yard work together' thing. It dawned on me someone might have thought she'd buried something there."

"I can't imagine what it would be." Cassie was astounded. Diane wasn't a complicated person. What would she have that would cause this stir of activity?

"Something's going on," he continued, "and I don't feel easy about it. With your mother gone now and you here by yourself, whoever it is might decide to get bolder. I don't like the idea of you being all alone here."

"But where will you sleep?" she asked.

"You could always invite me into your bed, sugar," he drawled but at the panicked look in her eyes he became serious. "I'm sorry, Cassie, That wasn't funny. And I owe you a big explanation about this afternoon."

He stood up, stuck his hands in his jeans pockets and stared at the wall.

"I don't even know where to begin here. I can't apologize for my life and I won't. I was what I was and I did what I did. Nobody held a gun to my head. Even before my mother died I lived for the excitement. I liked my bad boy reputation. After that it was easy to use her death as an excuse."

He stopped, gazing straight ahead.

"The disaster with Diane never should have happened. Oh, I liked her all right and she was great in bed. But nobody in that crowd ever expected anything lasting of anyone else. That's why we could be so free with each other. The pregnancy shocked me. Only once had I not used a condom but I guess that was enough.

"I told you she really didn't want to be married but she wanted money, something she mistakenly thought I had. She was certainly bored when I told her I thought we should clean up our act." He kept his back to her as if afraid to face her while he talked.

Cassie sat immobilized, barely breathing, just listening. "And what about us?"

She had to know the truth whatever it was.

"I wanted you the first time I saw you in your little cheerleading outfit." The words exploded in a whooshing breath, as if the confession had been hidden too long. "But I knew you'd never go out with me. You were just the stuff of my dreams. Then you went away to college and time went by. The first summer you went off somewhere to work but the next year, when you came back, I took a look at you and realized I was in love."

"In love." She echoed his words, tasting them, testing them.

He turned to face her now, a rueful look on his face. "Beats all, doesn't it? Shocked the shit out of me. And that was a problem, you see. Because how would I ever get you to think that way about me? I sat on my front porch for three nights running, hoping you would walk by and I could get you to come up and talk to me. I never expected what happened to happen."

"Didn't you?" She could hardly get the words past her throat.

"No. And please don't think I took it lightly, because I didn't. Those two nights we had together kept me going for the past six years. I gave you my heart, Cassie and then you ran away with it. I've never gotten it back." He stood in silence now. "When I tell you now that I love you, I'm not just saying what I think you want to hear. I've never said that to anyone else. Not even Diane. Or maybe especially not to her. Because you're the only one I've ever loved."

Cassie didn't move, didn't speak, not knowing what to do next.

"I don't expect you to say anything," he told her. "I just wanted you to know. I don't have any illusions about the future but it was important to tell you how I feel." He came to stand next to the couch. "I also wanted to apologize for this afternoon. That was a rotten thing to say. I've just been storing up so much anger all these years it jumped out without my thinking."

"Why didn't you ever call me?" she asked. "You could have found me easily enough."

He shrugged. "Too ashamed. Too proud. Besides, what did I have to offer? What could I say? 'Hi, Cassie. Your sister's dead. The town thinks I killed her. I didn't and now I want us to be together?' Do you know how that would have sounded?"

"You could have told me how you feel."

"Would you have listened then? Ask yourself that. Now," he said, visibly pulling himself together, "if you could direct me to some sheets and blankets, I'll fix myself up on the couch. I'd feel weird sleeping in your parents' room and I sure as hell won't sleep in Diane's room."

They stared at each other through the gloom of the room, the gathering dark underlining the silence. She knew she should run upstairs, lock herself in her bedroom and in the morning run back to Florida as fast as she could. Instead, she just kept looking at Griffin, searching for some kind of answer.

Finally she broke the spell. "You could sleep in mine." She said it so softly she wasn't sure he heard her.

He gave her a hard look, his eyes like cold steel. "Don't say that unless you mean it, sugar. I've only got so much control left in me. When I bury myself deep inside you, I won't let you walk away again."

Cassie could no more have stopped what she did next than halt a runaway train. She had lived with her memories for six years. She'd sworn she'd never come within ten feet of him again but now, here, she knew what a false promise that was. As badly as she'd been burned, the flame still beckoned temptingly. Not knowing what would happen afterwards, if he even meant half of what he said, she still obeyed the insistent call of her body. Standing up, she took his hand and led him to the stairs.

With her back to him, she said, "It's been a long time since I've done this so I'm probably a little out of practice. Of course, they say it's like riding a bicycle—the body never forgets."

Chapter Nine

✌

She faced him in her room, suddenly more nervous and afraid than she'd ever been in her life. Even more than the first time in his spartan bedroom. Griffin's memories of her, just like hers of him, were light years past. Would he still find her as desirable? Would the passion still be there? She lifted her hands, palms outward.

"Help me," she said.

He captured her hands in his, looking at her steadily. "Cassie, I have to tell you this. I had no right to ask you what you really wanted of me, because I have nothing to offer you. And you have to know if you hook up with me, this town will be pointing its collective fingers at you. It won't be pretty."

"Do you think I care one bit what this jerk town thinks?" She twisted her lips. "What has it ever done for me?"

His fingers rubbed sensuously against hers. "Last chance to back out, sugar. You're up here in your bedroom with the town bad boy. My reputation hasn't changed." His face was dead serious. "But neither have my feelings for you."

"Maybe this is what I always wanted, even before our first night together." She could hardly believe she was saying this. She gripped his fingers hard. "Maybe you were *my* secret fantasy and I've still been wanting you all these years. You didn't warn me the last time, or didn't it mean anything to you?"

"You can't imagine how much it meant." His voice was tight. "What about you? Did it mean as much to you? Have other men been able to set you on fire like I did?"

"No one," she whispered.

How could she even begin to tell him the way the touch of other men had turned her off, how no one else could awaken that hot flame of desire in her, make her body shiver and tremble in anticipation.

He cupped her face in his hands, leaned down and kissed her. If she thought his kisses the other night were exciting, tonight they made her blood race. Threading one hand through her hair, he pulled her lips tighter against his. She opened her mouth to him and he explored it slowly with his tongue, making her respond with hers. This kiss was like a feeding frenzy that went on and on. She leaned weakly against him, unable to stand on her own.

Gently lifting his mouth from hers, Griffin backed up to sit on the edge of the bed, guiding her toward him with gentle hands and very slowly undressed her. He took his time, not hurrying anything, each piece like wrapping paper exposing another piece of the gift. Pulling her sweater over her head, he traced the tips of his fingers over the swell of her breasts above her bra. He could feel their tautness and their heat. His palms itched to hold their fullness. Reaching around behind her, he unclasped her bra and let it fall. He drew in his breath as her breasts sprang into full view, high and erect.

For a moment he could only stare, drinking in his fill. The pert breasts of the young girl had become the mature breasts of a woman, the sight of them causing his mouth to go dry and his blood to heat. He grazed her nipples with his thumbs, touching the pebbled surface as if it were crystal, feeling them contract into hard points. Gently he kissed each of them in turn, sucking them until he felt them enlarge in his mouth, swirling his tongue around their tips, then closing his lips over larger portions of the creamy flesh. When she began to sway, he held her in place with his hands firm on her hips.

"God, you are so beautiful." His tone was reverent, almost awestruck. "Cassie, Cassie. You are still the light in my heart."

Her head was thrown back and the tempo of her breathing began to increase.

He unsnapped her jeans and slid the zipper down, leaning forward to press his lips against the soft skin of her stomach as he did so. Pushing the jeans down, he nudged her to step out of them, leaving only the tiny scrap of silk that passed for her panties. Then that was gone and she was naked before him.

His eyes raked over her as if memorizing every inch of her body, his eyes drawn automatically to that familiar triangle of curls covering her mound. He touched the tip of one finger where her thighs met, slid it up into the curls, then down, feeling their silkiness and the faint layer of moisture that told him she was already aroused.

Cassie gasped at his touch, nearly falling forward.

He tightened his grip on her, holding her in place. With his knees he nudged her thighs further apart and moved his finger lightly between them, seeking the warmth of her folds. He stroked one finger along the length of her labia, probing the outer edges, his touch eliciting a delicious shiver from her.

"Sweet, sweet Cassie," he said huskily. "How could I ever have been so stupid as to lose you?"

With his touch and the sound of his voice, everything came flooding back to her, every touch, every caress, all the secret yearnings in her dreams all these years. Cassie gasped in remembered pleasure, the pain she'd worn like a hair shirt gone, dissipated in this one moment. Just like that, the past six years disappeared and she was back in his bed with him, consumed by an uncontrolled passion. This was where she should be, no matter what.

"Remember that? Remember my fingers touching your sweet little cunt lips? Does it still feel good, sugar? You know it does. And I'm about to make you feel a whole lot better."

Somehow then he was out of his clothes and he had her lying on the bed next to him, cradling her with one arm. His free hand drifted to the apex of her thighs again and she opened her legs for him without prompting. He pressed his palm against her damp mound while he kissed her eyelids, the tender spot behind her ear, the hollow at the base of her throat where her pulse was beating its rapid rhythm.

He touched every outside inch of her femininity, teasing the curls, stroking the softness of the slick skin, taking his time with his exploration. When he found her already swelling clit and began to move his thumb over it, she jerked as if arrows of lightning had shot through her. She lifted her hips toward him and a soft moan escaped her lips.

"Easy, sugar. We've got all night and I'm in no hurry."

Touching the warm vaginal opening he felt how wet she already was and slid one long finger into her damp, moist needy channel. Her tightness made his own rock-hard cock throb and he gritted his teeth, chasing the automatic response.

"Open your legs wider for me, Cassie," he whispered.

She obligingly parted them, twisting her body up to him, little cries of passion rushing from her lips.

He moved his fingers easily in and out of her vaginal vault, stroking her nub with his thumb, watching her, knowing when to slow down, when to speed up. He knew just how to bring her to the edge, then back off, driving her to the point where every inch of her body was quivering with hot need.

He kissed her abdomen, his lips open and hot against her satiny skin. Reaching far inside her hot channel for her most sensitive spot, he curled his fingers to rasp against it, then drew back. "Do you remember this, Cassie?" His voice was low and deep. "Do you remember how it felt? Talk to me, sugar. Tell me what you like. How it feels. Tell me what you like me to do."

Cassie remembered it all too clearly, along with the overwhelming sensations it caused. But she couldn't open her mouth to save her soul. Still in the grip of conflicting emotions, she could follow the dance Griffin was leading her through but speaking of it was still beyond her.

Instead, she moved against him restively, hungry now, needy, wanting him closer. Her hands roamed over his chest, pulling at the crisp chest hair. She heard him groan with pleasure as she found his flat nipples and teased them with her fingernails. Heat was spiraling through her, pooling between her legs and an insistent throbbing pulsed through the wet muscles of her heated channel.

"It's all right, Cassie. I can wait to hear you say what you want. Right now your body's doing all the talking I need. God, how it's talking," he whispered. "I love you, Cassie. God help me, I love you more than my life."

Her eyes began to glaze and her movements quickened. His fingers danced over her, slid into her, teased at every sensitive spot.

"Griffin." Her voice cracked.

"Yes, darlin'? Tell me. Come on, tell me that you want this. And this. And this. Come on, Cassie."

She was pulling at him, sliding her hands over his hot skin. She couldn't stand it. Her mind was whirling.

"Tell me. Did anyone else make you feel like this?"

"No, no, no." She was thrashing now, tossing her head back and forth, rocking against him. "Nobody. Just you."

"You know it, sugar. Only me." He put his lips to her ear, stroking the inside with the tip of his tongue. "You're mine, Cassie. Only mine. Say it," he commanded her. "Say it now."

"Yes. All right. I'm yours. Please, please, please." She was begging now, nearly sobbing with need. Her body shook with frustration, reaching for that elusive peak of fulfillment, the moment when her womb would contract, her vaginal walls would clench and spasm after spasm would roll through her body.

He laughed, a low, throaty sound, his own desire evident in the huskiness of the tone. "All right then. Here we go." He thrust his fingers deeper into her, pressing his thumb hard against her sensitized clitoris, his hand drenched with her lubricating moisture. He felt the heat that had risen from inside her spread out, engulfing her. Her body was like a furnace against him.

"Come for me, Cassie. Just like before. Let me feel you come. Now." When he felt her pulling against him, her body arching toward him, he leaned close to her ear and whispered, "I love you, Cassie."

And that was all it took. Rockets went off in her head and she thought surely she would fly apart. The tremors deep within her went on and on and on, convulsing around his fingers, her body straining against his touch. Wave after wave of ecstasy washed over her. Small tremors like aftershocks fluttered inside her. He consumed her, as if it would never reach conclusion. Then, finally, he brought her down and the tremors began to slow.

She lay back against the pillows, panting, her heart racing so loudly she thought surely he would hear it. Pleasure still pulsed through her softly. She looked up at Griffin and his face held a satisfied look. But with his next words she could feel herself responding again.

"I want to be inside you," he whispered in her ear. "I want to feel you around me, feel your hot wetness on my cock. God, Cassie, I want to bury myself in your soul."

He wanted to taste her, the feel his tongue stroking those hot, wet walls, let her essence roll onto his tongue. The memory of how sweet she tasted had never left him. But it had been so long and his dreams of her so vivid, his own arousal now demanded satisfaction. His groin felt painfully tight, his penis twitching and his testicles hung full and heavy. More than anything, he wanted to make her his, to capture her body and her heart and never, ever be without her again. He wanted the dream to become reality.

Cassie tried to mold her body to his, her legs clasping around him as she urged him to enter her. Panting, vibrating from the intensity of her orgasm, still she was ready for him again. She wanted him at the very center of her body, penetrating her vagina, the tip of his penis touching her womb. She wanted to feel him convulse inside her like that night so long ago.

"Hold on a minute, darlin'. Don't move."

He slid back from her, reaching beside the bed for his jeans and the condom he had tucked in the pocket, just in case.

"I'm clean," he told her, tearing open the foil. "I give blood every three months so I get tested regularly." His face was deadly serious. "And Cassie? I haven't been with anyone else for a long, long time."

"I haven't either. I wish…" Her voice trailed away.

"What, darlin'?"

"That there could be nothing separating us, not even that thin latex. But I know…"

"I want that, too. But we have plenty of time for that. Later. And right now I'm dying here I want to be inside you so badly."

He managed to sheath himself, gritting his teeth as he felt his orgasm lurking in his body. He was through talking. His rock-hard shaft was swollen and hot, throbbing with need. No amount of control would stop him now. Groaning he pushed her hands aside and mounted her again, positioning himself between her legs.

Cassie reached down to take him in her hand, guide him into her and he lost it.

"Okay, Cassie," he told her, his voice unrecognizable.

Slowly he slid into her hot, wet sheath. Beads of sweat popped out on his forehead as he fought to hold off his climax, to make it last. Cassie gave him no respite. She lifted her hips to meet him, calling on her memories of their long-ago nights together, milking his hot erection. She rocked back and forth, urging him on.

"That's it, sugar. Yes. Oh, God, Cassie."

He began to thrust hard against her, grinding his pelvic bone against her sensitive nub, pulling her hips tight against him. Their sweat-slicked bodies moved together, faster and faster. He could feel her body gathering, feel her clutching at him. Just when he thought he couldn't wait any longer, he felt her clench around him and, panting hoarsely, he let go.

Cassie felt his hot, thick cock filling her completely, stretching her tight vaginal walls, damp flesh clutching steel-hard flesh.

Their climax was so intense it shook both of them. Every muscle in Griffin's body trembled with the effort, while beneath him, Cassie convulsed violently, arching wildly, thrusting her hips to meet him, pulling him deeply into her. Slick skin slapped against slicker skin, sliding against the cool, cotton sheets.

Finally they collapsed together, Griffin's head beside hers on the pillow, both of them gasping for breath, their rapid heartbeats thudding together. She had her fingers tangled in his hair and she whispered his name over and over.

"I love you," he said again, feathering light kisses on her cheeks, her forehead, her eyelids.

The words were so soft she almost thought she imagined them. "I love you, Griff." How good it felt to say it. All the years she had denied it to herself, now she could tell him without reservation.

Time seemed to expand as they lay there, twined together, his hand stroking her with infinite tenderness. When

Griffin tried to move, she held him in a tight embrace, her grasping muscles refusing to let him pull out of her body.

"Condom," he whispered and pulled out to dispose of it before trouble came calling.

Then he was back beside her. He stroked her face, thinking how many nights he'd wanted this again and never thought to have it. The sight of her at the grocery store the other day had slammed into him like a bulldozer. All he'd been able to think about was burying himself deep inside her and never letting go.

Now he was there and he intended to keep that promise to himself. Whatever it took.

Chapter Ten

ॐ

With the slowing of his breathing, rational thought returned to Griffin. The only thing he'd been able to think about was wanting Cassie again and having her. But six years wasn't as long as she thought and Stoneham was an unforgiving town. She had no idea the barriers that lay between them and he'd been foolish to put her in a position where she'd have to deal with them. Now they had things to discuss, things his brain had blocked out in his haste to bury himself in her again. He was right when he'd told her the nasty gossips would be sharpening their tongues. One of them needed to start being smart about this.

"Cassie." With great effort he lifted himself on his elbows and looked at her face. "Look at me, sugar."

"What?" She lay beside him in an attitude of complete satisfaction.

"We have to talk about this."

"About what?" She nestled against him, her skin against his, his penis lying at rest inside her as if it had belonged there forever. "Why are you always wanting to talk?"

"Because we have things to say." He shook his head. "Listen, sugar. This is important. I've waited a long time, hoping you'd come back. Hoping I could find a way for you to forgive me for what happened."

"I wasn't sure I could," she told him.

"I know, and that scared me to death. Because I wanted you—still want you—more than anything else in the world. But what happens next, Cassie? What's our next move? There are things you have to know before this goes any further."

"Like what?" There was a tiny hitch in her voice. "You know, I hated you for so long, even while I never got over loving you. When I had to come back here I dreaded seeing you, because I knew all those feelings were still there."

"Ah, Cassie…"

"No. Let me finish. One minute I want to kill you and the next you're professing undying love and we're going at it like two minks. So what is it you want to tell me? That this was just sweet talk to scratch a six-year-old itch?"

The words stabbed at him and his body tightened in anger. "Is that what you think? That I'm such an asshole I'd do anything to prove I could get you into bed one more time?"

He tried to slide his cock from her body and roll away from her but she refused to let him.

"Don't pull away," she demanded. "You pushed this thing, now you have to tell me where we're going with it. I guess-I guess just because you said you love me doesn't mean you're planning a long future with me."

The silence hung between them.

"Don't you know a future with you is the only thing I want?" he said at last, shaking his head sadly. "But I owe it to you to be realistic here. I told you. I'm a pariah in this town, a marked man. If we're together people will be talking about you all the time. I don't want to put you in that position."

"So I was right. This *was* just about getting me into bed for one night." Her body shook with anger. "That's your unfinished business?"

"No, sugar, it's way more than that." He slipped out of her with great care and leaned up on his elbow, his hand caressing her cheek. His voice was low when he spoke. "I never thought you'd come back. When I saw you, I… God, Cassie. You think letting you go again would be easy? I said I love you and that isn't a lie. But if I love you, I have to think about what's good for you, something I should have done to begin with. And what about your life in Florida? Your job?

Would you give it all up to live in a small town and be an outcast like me?"

She chose her words carefully. "A job is a job. I can get one anywhere. Since the night I left here, there hasn't been anyone else for me, Griffin. As angry and bitter as I was, when I looked at any other man, I saw only your face. I was sure I'd never see you again. Then my mother died and here I am. We just did things and said things to each other. Do you think it would be easy for me to walk away from that, regardless of what the town busybodies do or say?"

"I'm trying to do what's right for you, Cassie. I love you but life isn't even the same for us."

She pushed herself close against him, running her hand up and down his arm. "No, it isn't. But that doesn't mean it's bad. We could make it good together. You keep saying you love me. Do you mean it?"

He looked down at her cautiously, not sure what she meant.

"Do you really love me?" she prodded, holding her breath as she waited for his answer.

Time stretched endlessly until he spoke. "I have loved you for as long as I can remember," he told her slowly. "If I'd been someone other than who I was, I would have told you a long time ago. But what could I offer you then? What can I offer you now? Certainly not respectability."

Now she was the one who pushed away. Hard. "I guess I forgot to ask that question. Is that what I'm supposed to do? Ask what you can offer me?"

He had never seen her this angry, not even when he'd insulted her earlier in the day. She was raging, all the lovely indolence of sex instantly gone.

"Exactly what is it you think I want, Griffin Hunter?" Her eyes were fiery, determination etched on her face. "Answer me that."

"I told you." He formed his words in a flat monotone. The moonlight glancing in through the window outlined the sharp angles of his face, giving it a harsh look. "I'm an outcast in this town. People tolerate me but the men lock up their women and the women harbor secret thoughts of shameful sex with the town exile. Not to mention the fact that Diane's death will always hang over my head. I had no right to do this tonight. You have to want more than that out of life than what a relationship with me will do to you."

"Tell me that you love me again," she insisted.

"God, Cassie." He drew a ragged breath. "You just don't give up. All right, I love you."

"You know, I was the one holding back, afraid to give myself to you again and you came on here like gangbusters. Now you want to pull away and I'm ready to jump off a cliff with you. How stupid is that?"

Very slowly she opened the locket still hanging on the slender chain. When Griffin saw what was inside, he clenched his jaw. Emotion flashed deep and dark in his eyes.

"A long time ago you gave me your heart and told me to take care of it for you. I've been doing that ever since." She pulled him back down beside her and curled up close to him. "You keep saying we have a lot to talk about. Well, we've talked. And I'll bet we've got a lot more talking yet to do. Maybe I've got more to lose than you do, although I doubt it. But if I'm willing to chance it, why aren't you? Or were you lying to me just now?"

With a groan he pulled her into his arms and slanted his mouth hard against hers. This wasn't just a passionate kiss, it was a searching kiss, a probing kiss, claiming her, his tongue seeking answers that eluded his brain.

"All right, Cassie." He lifted his lips and stared straight into her eyes. "You want the truth? Fine. I want you more than my next breath. I feel as if I've loved you all my life." He raked his hand through his hair, desperation lining his face.

"Then…"

His voice was harsh. "You'd better be prepared for a hard ride but if you've got the guts to do it, who am I to argue."

In answer she shoved him back on the bed, leaned over him and took his shaft in her hand, gently stroking it, feeling the ridges that pebbled the velvety skin. "You're right, we have a lot to do, so we'd better get started."

Before he realized what was happening, she knelt beside him and leaned forward. When the heat of her mouth enclosed his hardening cock, he nearly came off the bed. Her tongue swirled and dipped and licked, covering his hardening erection with the warm moisture of her mouth.

"Jesus, Cassie." His hands gripped her head, his fingers weaving through her hair.

She lifted her mouth from its journey. "Am I doing it wrong?" Her question had a worried sound to it. This was something she'd read about in great detail but never had the desire to do with anyone else. "Help me, Griffin. Teach me how to pleasure you." She bent to her task again, loving the sweet-salty taste of him, the feeling of his penis growing and expanding in her mouth.

"Gently," he told her, his voice hoarse, his words sounding like rusty steel. "Touch my balls, Cassie. Tease them with your fingers. Yesss," he hissed, as she cupped the heavy sac and stroked it from back to front. "That's it. Oh, God, you're killing me."

She swirled her tongue at the tip of his cock, stroking the drop of liquid she found there over the rest of the head, then sucking the entire erection into her mouth. She moved her hand on his balls in cadence with the rhythm of her mouth, sucking and caressing and licking, until time lost all meaning for her.

She heard Griffin's harsh cries, felt his body thrusting against her, as she lost herself in the erotic joy of pleasuring him.

"Cassie, I'm gonna come," he groaned, trying to lift her head away.

She responded by clamping one hand tightly around his cock, pushing him harder into her mouth and stroking the shaft with her tongue. The hand at his testicles felt the pre-orgasmic tightening and then with a harsh cry he exploded into her mouth.

She felt the liquid jetting down her throat and she swallowed reflexively, still sucking and stroking until the last convulsion of his climax had left him. When she lifted her head, her mouth was wet with his semen and she licked every drop of it from her lips.

"Cassie," he moaned, pulling her toward him. "Oh, God, Cassie." He kissed her, tasting himself on her lips.

Against his mouth she said, "Now you belong to me too."

* * * * *

Whenever Cassie looked back on this night, she remembered it as a reawakening. The first frenzy of stored passion abated, followed by long, slow exploration. *Do you like this? How does that make you feel?* Griffin was experienced where she was not and he used his expertise to bring her to one shattering orgasm after another. For Cassie it was an unveiling, an awakening of her shuttered senses. For Griffin, it was the most completely erotic experience he had ever had, in a life full of them.

He insisted on turning on the light. They had only ever made love in the dark but now it was important that they see every inch of each other.

Griffin snapped on the lamp, then lay back against the pillows. Cassie looked at his naked body and began to tremble again. He was all sleek muscle, tanned hot skin and power. She touched the heavy mat of gold curls on his chest, running her hand lightly over them, touching his dark, flat nipples that peeked out.

In the brightness of the lamplight she took his shaft in her hand, staring at it in wonder, caressing it, exploring the tip with her finger, so gently that even as spent as he was, he almost came in her hand.

Swearing at his near loss of control, he covered her hand with his and moved it to the side, maneuvering her to lie flat on her back. With hungry eyes he examined every inch of her body, touching it in all the secret places, memorizing her. He ran his fingers over the hollows at her hip bones, teased at her navel, brushed his hands against her breasts now swollen and heavy with passion. With delicate strokes he laved the hard, rosy nipples, grazing them with his teeth, then soothing them with his tongue.

Gently he bit the tender spot between her shoulder and her neck, nipped at the pulse pounding at the base of her throat. Not even her arms were left untouched.

Kneeling before her he pulled her legs over his shoulders, leaving her entire vaginal area open to his assault. With gentle fingers he parted the lips and just stared his fill at the slick, pink flesh and soft, pouty lips exposed there. He separated them more, a fraction at a time, until her entire channel was exposed to his heated gaze. He brushed back the curls clinging there, damp with the fluids of her sexual release, so that no inch of pearly skin was hidden from his sight.

"Do you like this, darlin'? Can you tell me yet what you want? Can you say the words?"

Cassie lay there moaning, so wrapped in a sexual fog that even if she'd known the words to use her mind wouldn't command her mouth to form them.

"It's all right, sugar. I can read you even if you don't say the words. But one of these nights you will, Cassie. You'll feel free enough to talk to me like I talk to you."

Then, lifting her hips, he carried her to his mouth and in one swift stroke plundered her with his tongue. In a frenzy of feasting he lapped every internal inch of her, scraping his tongue against the sensitive flesh, flicking the tip against her clitoris now so sensitive just the merest touch made her jerk in response. Her skin was so tender, so delicious, he thought he would never get enough of her.

The more he stroked her with his tongue, the louder the mewling sounds emanated from her throat. Only his strength kept her anchored in place as he took her higher and higher, using his tongue and his teeth to touch every nerve in her hot, secret places. He was like a man possessed, so famished for every inch of her that he couldn't find enough ways to take her.

When he heard a low, moaning sound escaping her and felt her body begin the clutch of orgasm, he pressed her thighs apart with his forearms and opened her vaginal entrance with his fingers as wide as he could. While his penis twitched to slide into her, he was obsessed with watching her body convulse in passionate response to him.

His breath jerked as he watched her sweet pink flesh clench and unclench and heard her screaming his name as her climax rolled through her. His hungry gaze reveled in the sight of her hot fluid pouring from her opening and into the cleft of her buttocks.

His cock was so swollen, his body so aroused, he could barely contain himself. He wanted to plunge himself inside her and never pull out but he wanted more of her body first, more possession to slake his need. Griffin had been with a lot of women in his life but compared to Cassie everything else had been calisthenics. Cassie touched his heart, his soul, making him want to brand every inch of her as his.

Her fists were still grabbing the sheet and her body still shaking when he flipped her over and began kissing the length of her spine, wet, moist kisses, punctuated with swift stabs of his tongue. He was like an addict, unable to get enough of her. No matter how much he drank of her essence, he couldn't slake his thirst.

He nipped at her ankles and slid his mouth up the insides of her legs, little feathery touches that had her squirming with desire. Every spot was an erogenous zone—her calves, the backs of her knees, the juncture of her thighs at the crease of her buttocks. She moaned softly as he pressed each moist imprint on her tender skin.

When he reached the base of her spine, he kneed her legs further apart, separated the luscious globes of her buttocks, dipped his head low and began lapping the juice that only seconds before had seeped from her body. His hands cradled her as he pulled her up to him and his tongue sought the rosy inner flesh that had given up its secrets to him.

She bucked under his ministrations, calling his name over and over, begging, pleading, demanding his entry into her body. As his tongue licked away the last of the liquid, he stroked the cleft with his thumbs, pausing at the tight opening he had yet to penetrate only long enough to hear her cries intensify.

Barely remembering in time, he reached for another condom and rolled it on with shaking fingers. Then he pulled her to her knees, separated her folds and with one, swift stroke thrust himself into her from behind.

The moment his cock was fully buried in her he stopped, unwilling to have the feeling of ecstasy end too quickly. This was where he belonged, he'd always known it. He'd cherished the little spark of hope that this would happen for so long he could hardly believe this was real. Cassie. The woman who'd stolen his heart. The woman now willing to step into the mess that was his life without regrets.

Gritting his teeth to restrain himself, he began a slow, steady, thrusting movement, his hot hands holding her hips, as he described to her in erotic detail everything he was doing to her and everything he wanted to do.

Then the delicious feel of her snapped his control. One final stroke and he emptied his seed into the condom, his hands at her abdomen pulling her tight against him.

Exhausted at last, they slept, Cassie curled into Griffin's body. When they woke the room was still dark and Cassie urgently needed the bathroom. On her way back to the bed she peeked through the closing in the curtains to see the sun shining full force outside. Yanking the curtains back together, she slipped under the covers, savoring the feel of Griffin against her. She was totally relaxed, in the greatest sense of peace and security she'd had in a long time. Every muscle in her body was sore, every bone ached, but it was a satisfying feeling rather than an unpleasant one.

He'd been relentless, taking her every way possible, teaching her how to pleasure his body as he'd pleasured hers. Each time he'd carried her to new heights of passion, her brain told her she couldn't take any more. But he'd soothed her, petted her, taken her back down, then started all over again.

They'd done things together she'd only read about, yet none of it made her self-conscious or uncomfortable. With Griffin, exploring new boundaries was exciting to the senses. Because she loved him. There it was. The thing she'd been running away from since she'd left Stoneham. Without Griffin her life had just been a succession of colorless days. Now, here they were, together and she wasn't about to let it fall apart again, no matter what she had to do.

And no matter what anyone else said. Gossip could only hurt if you let it.

Lying in blissful lassitude, she was startled to feel the tip of Griffin's erection pressing against her and she automatically shifted her legs to open for him.

"A great way to start the day, sugar, don't you think?" he breathed into her ear, lifting one of her legs and draping it over his hip. His hand stole toward her clitoris, searching it out in the still damp curls and pinching it between two fingers. He felt her jerk in response to the stimulation.

"Will we ever get enough of each other?" Even as her body protested another assault, heat still stirred in her loins.

"I hope not." Adjusting her to accommodate him, he entered her from behind, then put his hand on her stomach to hold her tightly against him. He rocked slowly against her, his fingers reaching into her lips still swollen from the night before, testing her for readiness. When he felt her wet with desire, relaxing to take him, he thrust more fully. In the slowest, gentlest coupling yet, they climaxed just like that, lying there molded together.

"I love you, Cassie Fitzgerald," he said and today his voice was more certain. "You know you're mine now, with all that goes along with that."

She nodded. "I love you too, Griffin Hunter."

He leaned his head next to hers so he could speak directly into her ear. "Nobody ever knew about us, Cassie. Not a soul."

She stilled in his arms.

"I know you've had to wonder, all this time. Those two nights were private between you and me and too important for me to trash with loose talk."

"I was always unsure." She turned her face to look at him. "I didn't think you would but then the wedding and everything happened and I didn't know what to think. I only know the last six years have been hell for me."

"Me too, sugar. Me too." He stroked her arm, her cheek and kissed her temple, his heart thumping against her back. "For the first time in years, I can feel peace stealing through me. Soothing me. I don't know if I can find the words to tell you what you mean to my life but I'll spend forever doing what it takes to make you happy."

Finally, with great reluctance, they pushed themselves out of bed and showered together. Then Cassie went downstairs to make coffee while Griffin shaved. He came into the kitchen as she was pouring liquid into two mugs and she stood on tiptoe to give him a light kiss. His hair was still damp from the shower and he smelled tantalizingly of soap, aftershave and his own maleness.

"I need to go home and change," he told her. He was wearing the chinos and sport shirt he'd had on last night. "What are your plans for today?"

"I've got to finish cleaning the upstairs," she said. "It's driving me nuts. I don't know how my mother stood it. I also want to go through her room and see if she has any papers lying around I might need. Harley said Neil took care of everything but I want to find her checkbook, things like that."

"Want to take a little drive?" he asked.

"Where to?"

"Just some place I'd like to show you. Not far."

She raised an eyebrow, staring at him but his face gave nothing away. "Can you give me a couple of hours? Then I'll be ready."

"Sure. We'll stop somewhere for lunch." He sat silently for a few minutes, obviously running through some things in his head.

Cassie knew they had a lot of ground to cover and for the moment she was content to let him take the lead. But when he didn't say anything, she broke the silence. "I've made up my mind about something."

He looked at her warily, unsure of what was on her mind. "And that is?"

"Neither of us will have any peace in our lives until there's some solution to Diane's murder. I get the feeling the police didn't look any further than you and when that didn't pan out, they just stopped looking. Maybe they hoped you'd do something to kill your alibi."

Griffin had always felt the same way. Nothing was said but for months, everywhere he went Chief Dangler was there, watching him. If he asked about progress on the case, he was put off or just outright ignored. After the death of Cassie's father, people just stopped talking about it altogether.

"And how is that going to change?" he asked, his voice laced with bitterness.

"First of all, Dangler said he'd get me a copy of the police report and the autopsy. I've worked on newspapers long enough to read police documents. Then I want to go to *The Stoneham Recorder* and have them pull their back issues for me. I read what I could online but *The Recorder* didn't have a website then. I'm thinking maybe there might be something in one of the articles that will point us in a new direction."

"Cassie." He raked his fingers through his hair. "You aren't a trained investigator. You can't just go charging into something you know nothing about."

"I'm not charging," she told him. "Just investigating. If we could come up with a new lead or fresh piece of evidence and if Dangler won't follow it up, I'll hire a private detective."

Cassie stared into her coffee cup. "I discovered my mother had quite a little nest egg and she left it to me. Maybe I can use some of it to make up for all the tragedy."

Griffin just looked hard at her, then brought up what had been on his mind. "The money is immaterial. You can't stay here alone at night. The risk is too great, with someone running around out there trying to find something. I'd worry too much about you. We need to move you to the motel, with people around you."

"Stoneham Tourist Cottages? Puhleeze." She shook her head. "Anyway, I've already come up with a solution." Her eyes flashed with mischief. "You'll just have to move in with me."

"Cassie." He slammed his mug on the table, sloshing the coffee over the rim. "Damn it. That is the stupidest thing I've heard. Do you have any idea how tongues will wag? The vestal virgin and her sister's killer?"

Cassie burst out laughing. "If that weren't so funny, I'd be insulted. Give me a break, here. Anyway, it's my home and I can invite anyone in that I want. Besides, do you have a better solution?"

He opened his mouth to protest further but the phone rang.

"Hello? Oh, hi, Neil. How are you?" *Neil McLeod*, she mouthed. "Yes, thanks, I'm doing fine. You saved me a phone call, as a matter of fact. I was wondering what time I can come by the office tomorrow to sign whatever documents you have and start completing the process we need to wrap things up." She nodded her head. "Uh-huh. Uh-huh."

Griffin was busy wiping up the spilled coffee. He watched her face as she spoke.

"Yes, that was Griffin you saw here yesterday. Did everyone in Stoneham just happen to drive by my house? Uh-huh. Well, I appreciate your concern but I'll be just fine. Yes, he will be coming back. As a matter of fact, he's staying with me while I'm here."

Griffin nearly turned white but Cassie was grinning at him, her face convulsed with laughter.

"Yes, Neil, of course I understand. But I assure you, I'm perfectly safe with him. He hasn't killed anyone recently, has he? Well, there, you see? Thanks for calling. I'll see you tomorrow about one."

Griffin looked at her with anger and hysteria battling in his eyes. "You know I want to shake you, you idiot? That was a stupid thing you just did."

Suddenly a great laugh welled up and burst from him.

Cassie stopped holding herself in and in a moment they were both screaming with laughter, releasing the remaining emotion they'd both stored up for so long.

"You know Neil was on the phone to his wife as soon as you hung up," he told her, when he could finally catch his breath. "By noon the whole town will be in an uproar."

"So what? They need something new to talk about, anyway. I just hope it doesn't affect your business."

"I'll worry about that if I need to. Who knows, I might have plans nobody knows about." He sighed. "I guess I'm ready for it if you are. But darlin', I hope you really do understand what's going to come down on us."

She put her arms around him. "As long as we're together, Griff, that's all that matters."

He sighed against her sweet-smelling hair. "I don't know what I ever did to deserve you but I plan to do my damndest to make sure you don't get away."

"We'll make it. I'm tougher than you think." She grinned. "Tougher than this town thinks. Just watch my style."

Chapter Eleven

℘

Cassie blotted her forehead with her shirt tail and pushed some errant strands of hair out of the way. She was finally finished with the upstairs, everything but Diane's room, when Griffin returned. He'd changed into jeans and a tee shirt and scuffed boots of soft leather. She'd just put the spread back on her mother's bed when he walked into the room, startling her.

"Your front door was unlocked." His tone was accusing.

"I'm sorry. I can't believe I didn't pay more attention, especially after changing all the locks."

He frowned at her, worry creasing his forehead. "Well, you need to start doing that. Anyone with a mind to can just walk right in."

"I promise I'll remember from now on. What's that?" She pointed at the box he was carrying.

"Just what's left of Diane's things." He lifted it and looked at it as if it was a strange animal. "Your father came and collected all her clothes and stuff. These are just odds and ends I never had the stomach to go through."

Cassie placed her hand gently on his arm. "Why don't you put it in my room and we'll go through it tonight."

He didn't move, just stood watching her.

"What? Do I have a smudge on my face?" She wiped at it with the cloth in her hand and grinned up at him. "I promise I'll shower again."

He shook his head, watching her closely. "So, you've made up your mind about this? Just plant me on your front porch for everyone to see?"

"When you told me we were far from done, that we had unfinished business, did you think I was going to sneak you into the house like a thief in the night?"

He shrugged. "I didn't think that far. When I saw you all I could think of was wiping away the past six years and getting you in my arms."

"We have nothing to hide, Griff. And if we're going to have a relationship, I won't do it hiding behind bushes." Her eyes flashed fire. "You have a problem with that?"

"No, sugar, I don't but I'll ask you again. Are you sure you want to take on this town?"

She looked directly into his eyes. "You said you've never told anyone else you love them. Am I right?"

He put his hands on her shoulders and pulled her next to him, tilting her face up so she could see him while he spoke.

"No, Cassie, I've never said that to anyone before. If I had, it'd have been a lie. Because ever and always, there was only you."

"Are you healthy?" she asked, wondering why she hadn't thought to ask before.

The muscle twitched again. "Yes. I get tested regularly. I'd be a fool not to."

She didn't want to know what prompted his religious attention to that. She just hugged him, then stepped back. "Well, then. We're all set. And the town can just go to hell. What's in that other hand you've got behind your back?"

She tried to peer around each side of him but he sidestepped her. "Close your eyes."

"What?"

"Come one, Cassie. Close your eyes."

She squeezed her eyelids shut, wondering what was coming next.

"Okay. Now open them."

Her eyes not only opened but widened when she saw what he was holding.

"One perfect rose," he told her, holding it out to her. "I planned to get you a dozen but I saw this one in a bud vase by itself. It's absolutely perfect, the petals just about to open." He leaned down and placed a soft kiss on her lips. "That's what you are for me, dewdrop. A perfect rose about to flower in our love."

Cassie felt tears prick her eyelids. The last thing she'd expected from Griffin was romantic language and gestures. She took the box from him, setting it on the bed and threw her arms around him, nearly knocking the rose from his hand. "Oh, Griffin. I truly, truly love you."

"Go get cleaned up and I'll find something to put this in. I want to fix it so it blooms for a long time."

She was showered and dressed, Griffin locked the front door behind them and they were outside ready to leave, when a car pulled into the driveway. It parked behind Griffin's truck, blocking them in. Cyrus McLeod, Neil's father, got out and came over to her.

"Nice to see you, Cassie." He kissed her on the cheek.

"What can I do for you, Cyrus?" She was sure he was the advance guard and she wasn't in the mood for him. "I thought you'd be in church."

"I was hoping we could visit a minute, honey. Got a cup of coffee for an old family friend?"

"Actually, we were just leaving." She noticed that he'd ignored Griffin altogether.

Now he looked over at him. "Griffin, you think you could give us just a minute here?"

"Stay where you are, Griff." Cassie's tone was firm but polite. "Cyrus, if you have anything to say to me, you can say it in front of Griffin. And if it's anything negative about him, you can save your breath."

Griffin moved up to stand behind her, his hands resting possessively on her shoulders. Cassie leaned back into him, drinking in his strength.

"See, now, that's the thing," Cyrus told her. "There's a lot of things you just don't know, honey. You need to listen to me before you make a big mistake here."

"Neil called you, didn't he?" She spoke through gritted teeth. "He needs to mind his own business."

"Now Cassie. He's just concerned about you, like the rest of us. We all saw Griffin here yesterday and figured he was after you."

Cassie was so angry now she could barely speak. She clenched her fists at her side, trying for come control. "Listen to me, Cyrus. Apparently the whole town decided to drive by my house yesterday and spy on me. I'm sorry that's all you people have to waste your time on. I know everything I need to and if you're interested, Griffin wasn't after me, I was after him. Now, if you could move your car, we have someplace to go."

She brushed past Cyrus and climbed into the passenger seat of the truck.

"Nice to see you too, Cyrus." Griffin inclined his head, then went around to the driver's side, fighting a smile.

Cyrus McLeod stood at the edge of the driveway, face grim, watching the two of them. Finally, left alone, he got into his car and backed out into the street.

Griffin burst out laughing, a good warm sound that rumbled up through his chest. "I'd give a month's income to have a picture of the look on Cyrus's face when you blew up at him. But I'll tell you, he won't forget that for a long time. And the whole town will know about it before the day is out."

"Forget the town." Cassie pounded her fist on her knee. "I hate this town. Maybe I always have. My sister may have been the town tramp but when she was murdered and they couldn't pin it on you, they just blew it off. When my father died, nobody seemed to care and I'd guess my mother was just left to wither away in this house. Now everyone's on their high horse because you and I are playing house? Give me a break."

Griffin reached over and placed a warm hand on her thigh. Just the touch of his fingers on her skin sent shivers up her spine. "I don't think I ever realized what a little spitfire you are," he chuckled. "It'll give me a whole new perspective tonight when we're in bed."

"It will certainly make it interesting when we're married."

"Cassie, I'm asking you again, because this is important. It's about a lot more than sex. Are you very sure this is what you want?" His tone was deadly serious.

"And I'll ask you again." She played with his fingers in her lap. "Aren't you?"

"More than you can possibly know. This isn't something I take lightly. That farce with Diane not withstanding and my reputation aside, this is what I've always wanted. If you can believe that."

"I believe it," she said softly, Lifting his fingers to her lips she kissed each one in turn. She turned his hand over and licked his palm delicately. "So stop asking me the same question over and over, or I might change my mind."

Griffin shifted in his seat. "Cassie, if you keep doing that we'll have a wreck for sure."

She grinned at him, then dropped his hand back in her lap. "I'm saying this for the last time, Griffin Hunter. This was the last thing I expected when I came back here. I was prepared to hate you for the rest of my life. But I love you, and if I have to live in this cesspool of a town to be with you, well, that's fine. But it would be nice if we could both get out of here."

"Then maybe you'll be interested in what I have to show you. If you're determined to do this, our little trip becomes even more important."

"So mysterious," she teased, her eyes twinkling. "How about a hint?"

But try as she might, she couldn't pry any more information out of him.

"Just wait," he said. "I want you to see this without any preconceived notions."

Their closeness in the truck filled the air with snapping sexual tension, so electric they had to force themselves to use restraint. Even when they stopped for lunch at a roadside diner they took every opportunity to touch hands, or brush against each other. Just sitting across from each other, heat smoldered in their eyes and they shared unspoken promises of the night to come.

The dashboard clock read three-thirty when they pulled into a town about twice the size of Stoneham.

"Where are we?" Cassie peered through the side window, trying to catch a familiar sight.

"Marble Hill."

"But I mean, where *exactly* are we?"

"About an hour from Austin. Just keep your eyes open."

As Griffin drove through town at a leisurely pace, Cassie took in the limestone buildings lining the main street, an eclectic mix of shops and places like the feed and hardware stores. On the side streets Griffin pointed out where the schools were, the clinics, all the other things that make up a town.

As they headed out on the far side of Marble Hill, Cassie noticed a large nursery on the left, just out on the highway. "Do you buy any of your stuff there? It looks like a pretty big place."

"Sometimes." A tiny smile tipped up the corners of his mouth. "I'll show it to you on the way back."

They had driven another ten minutes when Griffin turned off on a narrow road. On both sides pasture land stretched to the horizon, dotted with oaks and sycamore and the mountain cedar so prevalent in the Hill Country. On one side of the road cattle grazed peacefully. On the other horses gamboled in the sunshine. The scene was a picture suitable for painting.

Griffin pulled up and stopped next to a For Sale sign set at one corner of the fence. "Come on." He took her hand and led her along the fence line. "So? What do you think?"

Cassie was bewildered. "I think it's beautiful. There's a big hill back there that would be perfect for a house and all this land for livestock. Why? Who owns it? Is someone building a house here?"

He turned her to face him, his eyes probing hers, trying to read her thoughts. "I hope that I am," he told her. "Dewdrop, I've been wanting this for a long time. Remember when you said it would be nice if we could move some place together? The old home town is nothing but a dead-end for me now and I'm ready to kiss it goodbye. Besides everything else, no matter what anyone ever finds out I'll always be linked to Diane's death."

"You'd really move?" She wished he'd take off the damn sunglasses hiding his eyes.

"In a heartbeat. That nursery you saw at the edge of town is also for sale. I've been talking to them, trying to see what kind of capital it would take to buy it. I've been wavering on this for months, waiting to see if either the land or the nursery sold. If they did, that could be my convenient excuse for failure."

She tilted her head, one eyebrow cocked. "Did you want to fail?"

He wiggled a hand back and forth. "Maybe before but not now."

"Why didn't you tell me about this earlier?"

He put his arms around her and pulled her close. "I had to make sure you meant what you said. You don't know how afraid I was that you were just getting me out of your system. Or maybe getting back at me."

"Oh, Griff." She swallowed the tears clogging her throat.

"If there's going to be any you and me, it isn't going to be in Stoneham. We'd be two outcasts and that's not what I want for you."

"How would you manage this? It's a big financial commitment."

"I could get a decent price for the house if I put it up for sale. The business too. And I've got enough saved for escrow to hold everything until I have the rest of the money." He tipped her face up to him. "I love this kind of area but what about you? Think you'd like living out here in the hills?"

"Are you kidding? It's beautiful. The town looks great. They've got the most interesting shops and I saw signs for several restaurants. And with the landscaping I spotted when we drove down some of the residential streets, you've got a ready-made customer base." She threw her arms around him and hugged him tight, then stepped back and looked up at him. "But do you know enough about running a nursery?"

He laughed out loud. "All the upright souls in Stoneham would be shocked to hear this but remember me saying I took a couple of courses at the junior college in San Antonio?" She nodded. "Well, actually, I got a degree in landscaping with a minor in business management. Pretty surprising for the town hellion, right?" He actually blushed telling her.

"Griffin! My God!"

Cassie was astounded. If someone had told her she would go back to her old home town, fall into bed with the man who broke her heart and promise to make a new life with him, she'd have sent them for therapy. Yet here she was, doing exactly that.

"I know. I can hardly believe it myself."

She was speechless.

"Well, say something?" he said nervously. "You love it? You hate it? What?"

For an answer, she pulled his face down to hers and kissed him, mouth open, tongue searching. She thought she'd never get enough of the taste of him. "I love it. And I've got some ideas too."

"Then let's do this right." He pulled off his sunglasses, a serious look on his face. "Will you marry me, Cassie? Will you risk the rest of your life with me?"

"Yes. Yes, yes, yes." She planted another kiss, this one quick. "Now let's go home and talk."

The euphoria of the afternoon lasted until they reached her house and walked up on the porch. Griffin had taken her key and was about to open the door when he stopped, hand frozen.

"What is it? What's wrong?"

"Cassie, it looks like our housebreaker has been at work again."

Chapter Twelve

ঙ

"What do you mean?" Cassie started to shake.

"There's scratches around the lock." Griff squinted at it. "Like someone tried a key that didn't work and played around with it. Stay here while I check the other doors."

Cassie waited on the porch in a fit of nervous impatience, twisting her hands in agitation. Why was this happening?

Griffin was back in five minutes. "Whoever it was tried every door. I guess we're lucky they didn't break a window or anything. Cassie, I think you should call the police."

"No." She was emphatic. "I can just see Dangler looking at us suspiciously and forming his own ideas. We'll take care of things ourselves."

"Darlin', whoever it is could be dangerous."

"Then you'll just have to protect me." She gave him a shaky smile. "Let's go on in."

Griffin unlocked the door, then went back to his truck, opened the lid on the bed and took out two suitcases.

"Griff?"

"Yeah?" He carried the luggage up to the porch.

"I'm really glad you'll be staying here with me."

"*Living* with you, sugar. And not a moment too soon, sugar. Someone wants into this place in a bad way and I'm not leaving you unprotected." He set his suitcases down and framed her face with his hands. "I can't let anything happen to you. Not now when we've finally gotten this thing right." He placed a soft kiss on her lips. "Okay, let's get a move on here."

She helped him put his things away in her room, got out her laptop and made him sit at the kitchen table with her. Booting up the computer and slipping easily into reporter mode, she questioned him as she would interview someone for a story.

"We have to figure this out, Griffin. Nobody else is going to do it, so I guess it's up to us."

"I'm just not sure we can find out anything, Cassie. God knows, no one would like it better than me but after six years the trail has to be ice cold."

She cocked an eyebrow at him and jutted out her chin. "I'm a reporter. I may write sports stories now but I cut my teeth on everything under the sun. It doesn't matter what you're looking for, the questions are still the same—who, what, where, when and why."

"All the same, Miz Reporter," he warned her, "you need to be careful. People don't like people digging into things around here."

"Apparently not," she told him, "since they didn't do much digging into Diane's murder."

"And someone already is after something in this house," he went on. "Something that might actually have to do with Diane's death."

"Okay, I'm not arguing with you about that. I was the one who thought something was out of sync to begin with, remember?" She nibbled at her lower lip. "Besides, what else here would interest them? So come on. Let's get started."

In full reporter mode, Cassie took him through every detail of the night Diane was killed, pulling things from his brain he didn't even know were there. Under her experienced prodding, a picture finally began to emerge for her.

In three months of marriage, Diane had done little to alter her pattern of living. She still worked during the day, a make-work job at their father's office he'd created for her. Anything for Diane, Cassie thought wryly. And each night when Griffin got home she was already there—dressed, primped, perfumed, eyes flashing, urging him out to enjoy the night life. She blew off his argument that all her running around wasn't good for the baby. If he wasn't willing to show her a good time, there were plenty of people who would.

"Money was tight then," he told Cassie, "and I was taking jobs more than an hour away just to bring in the extra cash. I tried to explain to her I was tired, that we didn't have extra money to blow now since she spent every penny she made so I was supporting both of us. Not to mention my good-for-nothing father."

"And what did she say?" But Cassie could imagine Diane's reaction.

"She'd just get that sneer on her face and head out of the house, slamming the door as she left without me." A bitter look twisted his features. "My father was a continuing problem too. The only good thing was he was seldom home when we were. He slept all day and drank all night."

"I'm sorry. I really am." She chewed on the end of her pen. "Was there anything different about Diane right around that time?"

He frowned. "Yeah, I guess. She was edgy in the weeks right before she…died." A muscle ticked in his cheek. "Something was on her mind but I thought maybe it was the pregnancy. She was dreading the arrival of the baby and I already figured out if anyone was going to care for that child it would be me."

"Exactly how were you going to do that working all day?" Cassie was losing a battle with the anger welling in her.

Griffin shrugged. "I hadn't figured it out yet. I couldn't even get her to stop drinking."

"Didn't she know about fetal alcohol syndrome?" The anger was turning into a cold rage. Cassie's entire life had been derailed for a child the mother didn't even want.

"Oh, yeah." He couldn't hide his bitterness. "But she was determined to enjoy the high life as long as she could."

"I'm surprised she didn't get an abortion. It would have solved a lot of problems."

"Before she told me, maybe. But for some reason the idea terrified her, although we'd all have been better off. Except by that time I was already emotionally invested in the baby and I'd never have let her do it."

Cassie got up and snagged two cold beers from the fridge, opened them and passed one to Griffin. She took her time drinking from her own bottle trying to cool down the fury that was burning inside her. Damn Diane anyway.

"Usually she made it a point to ask me to go with her but not that night. We'd started fighting as soon as I got home," Griffin told her. "Mostly about money and her drinking. One thing led to another and we started screaming some pretty ugly things at each other. Then she just stormed out and screeched off in her car."

"Did you get the idea she had some place specific to go?"

"Maybe. I don't know. I keep trying to remember. If I hadn't been so pissed off, I'd have called around to see where everyone was and find out who she was with. But I was getting to the point where I almost didn't care."

"What did she usually do when she went out by herself?"

Griffin shrugged. "Hang out with the same people I used to run with. Only by then I was looking at things differently and money was a big issue." He made a face. "Somehow, after finding out about the baby and getting married, it all didn't seem quite right anymore. Or as exciting."

"Impending fatherhood will do that to you," Cassie said with a tinge of resentment.

Griffin picked up one of her hands from the keyboard, separating the fingers and lacing his own through them. "The whole thing wasn't anywhere near what I had planned. There I was in a huge hole I'd dug for myself and missing you more every day. I was sure you hated me."

Cassie could feel her pulse accelerate at the touch of his hand. She'd tried to hate him all this time but that had lasted only until his kiss. Well, love and hate were two sides of the same coin, weren't they?

She stared at the computer screen. Scanning what she'd input. "She didn't give you any hint about what was bothering her?"

"None. I knew marriage and the baby were cramping her style, though. Diane was never one to be monogamous."

Cassie gripped her pen until her knuckles were white. She'd known exactly what Diane was like—needy and greedy, unconcerned about the lives she ruined.

She wet her lips. "Let's go back to that night again. Do you think she was meeting someone? Is that possible?"

"I guess anything is possible." Griffin leaned back in his chair, eyes closed. Suddenly he leaned forward and opened them.

"I nearly forgot. She had this little purse, more like something you keep your makeup in, I think. The last couple of weeks she carried it with her everywhere. When we went to bed at night, she took great care to stash it somewhere. At first it bugged the shit out of me and I tried looking for it when she was asleep. Then I just gave up, figuring, what the hell."

"Obviously she had something she didn't want anyone else to see. Too bad we don't know what."

With Cassie's prodding he filled in the details of the rest of the evening. He'd changed clothes, called Phil and invited himself over. Two other guys were there and they all watched a game on television, drinking beer and talking about nothing. He'd gotten home around one but Diane was still out. Angry and depressed, he'd gone to bed and was immediately asleep. At three o'clock in the morning Barry Dangler and one of his deputies banged on the door and woke him up.

"A patrol car, checking Stoneham Park for late night couples, spotted something in one of the bushes by the ravine." His hands gripped the beer bottle. "It was one of Diane's shoes. They discovered her body in the ravine. Her dress was torn and she'd been beaten to death."

"Was she raped?" Cassie asked the question as evenly as she could.

Griffin shook his head. "No. They found no evidence of it."

"And exactly how did they decide you were the prime suspect? You were in bed when they came to tell you."

"It wasn't rocket science. The whole town knew why we got married and what a disaster it was. I guess Dangler just figured I'd had enough and killing her was the best solution." He pushed back from the table. "Enough. Let's leave it until tomorrow. I'm sure whoever's trying to get into this house has something to do with everything but I'm done talking about it for today."

"You're right. Anyway, Dangler said he'd have the incident and autopsy reports for me tomorrow. Maybe I can find something in them. Then we'll decide where to go next."

He rubbed his forehead.

"Headache?" she asked.

"Just a little one. A couple of aspirin and I'll be fine."

Cassie hit the save key and shut down the laptop. She got up from her chair and went to stand behind him, rubbing her hands at his temples. "I give good head rubs."

He caught her hands and pulled her around to face him. "Let's go upstairs," he said hoarsely. "I've got something else that needs rubbing more."

* * * * *

This time it was different, the first frenzied hunger somewhat abated. They took their time with each other, exploring, experimenting, learning all the little signals that lovers in tune with each other use.

Griffin paid careful attention to every part of her body, touching her, tasting her, relearning everything he'd discovered the night before. He kissed her until she was almost mindless, his tongue stroking deep inside her mouth, stealing her breath.

"This is not sex, Cassie." His voice was hoarse and strained. "You can bet on that. I love you so damn much. Making love with you comes straight from my heart, sugar."

"I couldn't be like this with anyone else," she whispered.

She met him, just as eager as he was, her own tongue as heated an instrument as his. Their kisses were almost like the act of sex itself and heated their blood until they were filled with rivers of fire.

Cassie was bolder now, more sure of herself with him. Before he had taken the lead and she was the recipient. But her one act of daring the night before had given her a taste of something she wanted more of.

She took his swollen, throbbing penis in her hands, tracing the veins on the sides, sliding over the soft skin that hid the ridged flesh beneath it. Her fingertips slid over the head of his cock in wonderment while her tongue probed at the tiny slit at the top, licking the salty fluid that seeped from it with tiny, delicate laps. When she leaned forward and ran her tongue the length of him he groaned, burying his fingers in her hair, holding her head in place.

"More, dewdrop." His voice was thick with desire. "God, your mouth is like warm honey. Do it, darlin'. That's it. Yes, let me feel that tongue. Cassie, Cassie, Cassie. You take me to heaven, did you know that?"

When she took his balls in her hand and began to do the same thing with the heavy, weighted sac, he almost came off the bed. Cassie saw his muscles clench with the effort to maintain control but she was having none of it. The taste of him the night before had only whetted her appetite.

She took a page from his book, running her tongue over the seam at his hips, flitting over his abdomen, down the insides of his thighs. With her fingertips she sought and found his flat nipples, pulling and teasing at the tips as he did to hers, excitement rushing through her as she felt them swell and harden.

She was wild with wanting him, with welding him to her. When he tried to pull her up to lay on top of him, she shook her head. Taking him deep into her mouth again, she tickled and squeezed his balls, feeling them tighten in response. With her hands and her tongue, in the rhythm she'd learned so easily and quickly, she relentlessly coaxed his orgasm from him. When the hot liquid splashed on her tongue, she swallowed triumphantly, sucking deep and hard to get the last salty drop.

"Damn, sugar." He could barely get the words out. "You're sure a quick learner. I'm a wreck. But I think you did yourself in, darlin'. As tired as I am, as active as we were last night, you didn't leave anything for yourself."

She moved up to lay her head on his shoulder, inhaling the musky scent of him. "That's all right," she assured him, a tiny grin on her face. "We've got plenty of nights ahead of us. I love you, Griffin. With all my heart."

She reached up to kiss him and discovered he wasn't kidding about being tired. He was already asleep. Smiling, she nestled her body close to his. Even the aching, unfulfilled need was worth it, when she knew she had the ability to give him so much pleasure.

It amazed her that she could be so uninhibited with him, so unselfconscious. But she was learning that when the love between two people was as real as this, every physical act was merely an expression of that love.

And she was right in what she told him. They had a lot of time to make up for it.

As early as she was up the next morning, Griffin was already gone for the day. A note was propped up against the full pot of coffee.

"A full day's schedule. See you at six. I love you." He had drawn the outline of a rose on the paper, with one drop of moisture clinging to a petal…a drop of dew.

Cassie knew what it meant for him to have written that and she clutched the note to her heart. She was sure that in his whole life she was the only one he'd ever been that open with, that trusting. This was his way of telling her that she could trust him too. She smiled, pressing the note to her heart.

She called Neil and told him to expect her at one and to please have the single document ready for her to sign. Then she called Donald to check on the funeral arrangements and the cemetery. Finally she called the police station to remind Barry Dangler she'd be by in the early afternoon for the reports on Diane's death. The bank she'd worry about after she had the letter from Neil in hand.

The rental agency was fine about extending the contract for the car. They'd add on another week. If she needed more, she should just call them.

The two calls she dreaded making she put off until last.

When she reached Mike Rivard and gave him the news she was resigning and wouldn't be coming back, he was so silent that for a minute she thought he'd hung up. "Mike? Are you there?"

"Yes." He sighed heavily. "I guess you know what you're doing, Cassie. But you're leaving me in a real bind here."

"I know and I'm truly sorry. It's just that things here are, well, different from what I thought. I have more loose ends to take care of than I expected."

"What's his name?" he asked, his voice brusque.

"What? What do you mean?" She was startled.

"Any time a reporter as good as you are walks out on what could turn into a plum job, it's always a girl. Or in your case, a guy." More silence. "I hope he's worth it, sweetheart. I guess I should wish you good luck."

"Thanks, Mike. I really appreciate the way you're taking this."

"Who knows? Maybe one day you'll decide you like the Florida life again and we'll find a spot for you."

She thanked him a second time. "I'll have to make a trip back to get my car and close things up. I'll stop by and see you when I pick up my check."

"You'd better," he growled.

She felt a little sad after she hung up. Mike had been good to her, hiring her when other editors wouldn't have. But she had no regrets. She'd given him value for every dollar he'd paid her.

Her call to Claire was both harder and easier. Harder because they'd been so close for so many years and now, for the first time, would really be going their own ways. Easier because Claire made it so.

"The bad boy must be really good," she joked. "Six years and the past disappears just like that."

"I know, I know."

"Just remember, girlfriend. I was the one who listened to you cry all those months and patched up the cracks in your heart."

Claire had been her lifesaver. Not just for giving her a place to call home until graduation. She'd introduced her to the right people in Tampa, which made getting her first job a lot easier.

"When this is all over, I'll tell you the whole story and you'll understand."

"What about your car and your apartment? You can't just dump them."

"I have a new lease on my desk that I'd need to sign if I were staying. Otherwise I'm up the end of next month. I think I'll take next weekend, fly back and take care of stuff and bring my car back. And the rest of my clothes."

"Bring that hunk with you." Claire laughed. "I'm dying to get a gander at him."

Cassie spent the rest of the morning tearing Diane's room apart, looking for something, anything, that someone might be searching for. She emptied drawers and looked under and behind them, pulled everything out of the closet, looked under furniture. She even crawled under the bed to see if anything was hidden under the box springs. Nothing.

As she walked out of the room, the telephone rang and she ran to her room to get it.

"Glad I caught you, Cassie." Harley Graham's voice has that paternal tone to it. "I think we need to discuss something, honey."

Cassie's stomach clenched. "Are you all ganging up on me?" she demanded.

He was silent for a moment. "I'm not trying to lecture you but you've been away from this town for a long time. There are things you don't know about, things best left alone. Griffin Hunter isn't someone you should be letting into your house and your life."

"Is that right?" she gripped the phone so hard her hand hurt. "Well, thanks for your concern, Harley but Griffin and I are doing just fine."

"Let me give you a piece of advice, then. If you're so dead set on hooking up with him, I suggest you leave your sister's death alone. Stir things up too much and Hunter could end up in jail."

Cassie was seething. Hanging onto her temper with a frayed rope, she said, "I'm going to pretend we didn't have this conversation, Harley. I have to go now. 'Bye."

She barely restrained herself from slamming the phone back into the cradle. Checking the time, she showered, ate a quick sandwich and left for her appointment with Neil, girding herself for yet another attack. Today she dressed in cool navy cotton slacks and a sleeveless navy and pink top, pulling her hair up in a ponytail and tying pink and blue ribbons around it. Silver hoops at her ears completed her outfit. Not bad, she thought, checking herself in the mirror. Casual without being too informal. Just the right note. Texas was beginning to turn up its thermostat and she needed comfort, not style.

Neil and Cyrus were both in Neil's office when she got there. Her stomach knotted at the sight of them. This would not be fun. She was not in the mood for a lecture and she saw only disaster in this meeting.

"You're looking lovely as always." Cyrus rose to take her hand.

Okay, we're going for charm today, she said to herself.

"I'm fine, Cyrus. Thank you. I didn't expect to see you here today. I didn't think things were so complicated it would take both of you to handle it."

"Just making sure we cross all the I's and dot all the T's," Neil told her. "Sit down, Cassie. Would you like some coffee? Iced tea?"

"Iced tea would be nice, thank you."

Neil buzzed his secretary with the request, then leaned back in his chair.

Cassie looked at both men for a long minute. "All right, let's have it. Is this more of what you came to visit me about yesterday, Cyrus?"

"I want you to understand that we only have your best interest at heart," he began.

Cassie cut him off. "I'm sure you huddled together after your stop at my house, so why don't we just cut to the chase. If you want to talk to me abut Griffin Hunter, forget it. End of discussion."

"Cassie." Neil's voice was firm. "You've been away from Stoneham for years. College, then work. You probably don't even remember the reputation he had when you lived here. And let's not forget Diane's death. As far as the town is concerned, he's still the top suspect. He's not someone you want to spend time with."

Cassie mentally counted to ten. "I know a lot more about Griffin than you think." Her voice was much calmer than she felt. "And probably more than you or anyone else in this town does. Besides, he was cleared in Diane's death, remember? I appreciate your concern but please stay out of my personal business."

"You know, your mother's estate could be considered sizable by some," Cyrus persisted.

Cassie gaped at him. "You think Griffin's after my money? How absurd. And even if he were, that's also my business. So. Did you file the papers this morning? The courthouse can't have so much business that you didn't get it done. And the insurance forms."

The two McLeods looked at each other.

"What? You think you'll hold me hostage with paperwork?" She leaned forward and stared each of them in the eye in turn. "Guess again. I thought we could do this in a friendly manner but I'd be perfectly happy to get a lawyer from San Antonio to straighten this out."

Cyrus stood up and looked at Neil. "I'm done here. Maybe you can talk some sense into her but I doubt it." He walked stiffly from the office.

"You're making a big mistake," Neil told her.

"Then it's my mistake. I appreciate your concern but everything's fine. Show me what I have to sign."

Neil used every opportunity while he took care of her paperwork to interject comments but Cassie ignored him. She sat while he faxed the claim forms back to the insurance company, making sure she got a name and phone number so she could follow up on the processing herself. He handed her the letter to sign listing all the financial arrangements that had been made, attaching a list of assets that she now owned. She put all the copies of the paperwork in her purse and stood to leave.

Neil walked her to the office door. "Are you planning to stay in the house or sell it? Just curious, you know."

"I'm listing it with Carol Markham. She came by and dropped off her card the other day. Thank you for arranging that."

He put his hand on her arm, a gesture that made her skin crawl.

"You'll need some help going through everything," he said. "I'd be more than happy to do that. Your mother had great confidence in me these past years."

Cassie shook her head. "Thanks anyway but I think Griffin and I can manage."

"Cassie, you should be aware that you're hooking up with a viper. You don't know what you're letting yourself in for."

"On the contrary. I know exactly who I'm taking into my house."

"Then at least rethink this nonsense about reopening Diane's case. Let her rest in peace."

Cassie's jaw dropped. "In peace? With her killer still running around loose? You see, I'll never believe Griff did it, so the real killer is still out there somewhere."

"Honey, do yourself a favor. Clean everything up and go back to Tampa. You have a nice life there."

"Thanks for everything, Neil. I think I can tackle it from here." She left him standing with a polite smile pasted on his face.

She didn't fare much better with the chief.

"It's all over town," he told her.

"Oh? And exactly what are you talking about? The funeral? Does that mean I should expect a big crowd?"

"Cassie, you know exactly what I mean. There isn't a person in Stoneham who doesn't know you're playing house with Griffin Hunter." He fixed her with a grim stare.

"Well, Chief, I'm so sorry that everyone hasn't anything better to do here than discuss my private life."

"I think you're deliberately missing the point, Cassie. Forgetting about your sister for a minute, you come from a fine family. I knew your folks real well. Griffin Hunter is pure trash. He'll be nothing but trouble for you."

She had to grit her teeth to keep her temper in check. "I'll keep that in mind. Do you have those reports for me?"

He picked up a large envelope on his desk, tapped it against his fingers, then reluctantly handed it over. "I don't know what you expect to find here. There isn't much. If you don't know how to read them, you might misunderstand a lot of stuff."

She didn't want to tell him that for a solid year in Tampa all she did was read police dailies looking for any kind of story to follow up. She was afraid he'd change his mind about giving the envelope to her.

"You might also want to remember that there's still a chance to discredit Griffin's alibi," he added.

"After six years?" She shook her head, incredulous.

"Fine, Cassie. Whatever. I'll see you at the funeral tomorrow." As she stood to leave, he rose too. "You let me know if you need anything, okay?"

She wanted to tell him it would be a cold day in Hell before she asked anyone in this town for anything but she kept her mouth shut. This week she still needed people to talk to her. She didn't want to burn her bridges just yet.

Her final stop was at the bank. Howard Cook had been their family banker for as long as she could remember. She knew from her sparse contact with her mother that he'd been a big help selling her father's accounting practice when he died and investing the money for her.

He came out of his office to get her as soon as she walked into the lobby. "Neil called and said you'd be down," he said. "Nice to see you, Cassie. Come on into my office and we'll take care of stuff."

"Thank you." She swallowed a sigh, wondering what *this* encounter would be like.

He fussed with getting her in a comfortable chair, asked his secretary to bring them coffee, then opened a folder he had on top of his desk and looked at the top sheet. "Neil told me you had all the right papers, honey. This should be simple enough. All we need to do is take your mama's signature off the account and we'll be set. We'll just need a copy of Neil's letter and the death certificate. Or you can open a new account if you want to and we'll transfer the balance over."

"I want to draw it all out."

Howard's eyes snapped wide open and he stared at her. "Cassie, there's a tidy sum of money here. And all the direct deposits from the annuity go in here. That'd be a mess for you to change."

She almost laughed out loud at his expression. "I'd like a cashier's check, please and I'm taking care of the arrangements for the annuities."

Howard sat back in his chair, hands folded in front of him, his gaze firm on her. "Forgive me for intruding where I'm not wanted but I understand you've been, uh, seeing Griffin Hunter since you got to town."

"Yes." She nodded.

Here we go again.

She kept her face carefully blank. "In fact, I'm thinking of taking out an ad in the paper, just in case there's someone who might have missed the news bulletin."

Howard leaned forward in his chair. "Now, honey, this is just a small town where everyone takes care of everyone else. That's all."

"Like you took care of my sister?" she snapped.

His face turned an ugly shade of red. "Your sister brought her troubles on herself. You've always been the nice girl in the family. I guess folks just want to keep it that way. You'd do well to remember that, despite that alibi, Griffin was the only one with a real motive."

"Well you can tell *folks*," she said, underscoring the word, "that I appreciate their concern but I'm doing just fine. I don't believe Griffin killed my sister, not for a minute. He's not after my money but if he were, it's my money to give. Now may I have a cashier's check? I'll sign the form to close the account."

Howard finally gave in with poor grace and in fifteen minutes she was done. "I hear you're selling the house."

"My, my, the town has been busy. Yes. I'm listing it with Carol Markham."

"Well, if you need any help going through all that stuff, sorting through things, you just let me know."

Cassie escaped with her temper still intact.

Before heading home, she drove to the other side of town to the tiny Bank of America branch. They'd opened up just before she left, serving everyone who didn't want Howard Cook sticking his nose in their business. She already had the account with them she'd established in Florida so it took just a few minutes to make the deposit. She felt somewhat better getting her financial affairs out of the gossip sheet.

Tired and sweaty, she finally headed home. But rattling around in her mind was the question of why people were so eager to help her sort through the things in her mother's house. What was it these men thought she'd find? And were hoping she wouldn't find.

She began to get that itch on the back of her neck that plagued her whenever she was on the trail of a dicey story. Someone was definitely up to no good.

Chapter Thirteen

𝕤𝕠

She was lying on the living room couch when Griffin got home, a cold rag draped across her forehead and a glass of wine at her fingertips.

He leaned over and kissed the tip of her nose. "Hard day, sugar?"

"You don't know the half of it." She pulled off the washcloth and sat up, fire in her eyes. "I swear to God, Griffin, I don't know how you live in this place."

He chuckled. "Get the third degree today, did you? And warnings about bad boy Griffin Hunter?"

"You don't know the half of it. Everyone wants to mind my business for me. I don't think they'll be quite as friendly after everything I said, though."

"Did you give 'em hell, sugar?" He grinned.

"You bet." She went over to him and started to put her arms around him but he held her away.

"I need a shower before you touch me. I have every kind of dirt and fertilizer stuck to me."

"I'll come shower with you." Her boldness with him was continuing to grow.

The blue in Griffin's eyes turned a shade darker. "Come on, then," he told her, in his low husky voice.

Under the hot, steady stream, they took great care soaping each other's bodies. Not an inch of skin on either one was left untouched but when Cassie began stroking Griffin's hardened cock he pushed her hand away.

"Uh-uh, dewdrop. I'm not wasting it tonight. I have plans for later." He nuzzled her ear, licking the rim of it with the tip of his tongue. "Oh, sugar, I want to do things with you that haven't even been invented yet. I wish I could suck you into my body and keep you there forever." Then, in direct contradiction, he leaned her against the shower wall, spread her legs with his feet and used his fingers to bring her to orgasm.

"No fair," she gasped.

He laughed, a warm sound rumbling up from his chest. "You recover faster than I do."

Cassie was in no mood to cook, so Griffin went out to pick up Chinese takeout. She refilled her wineglass and sat down to read what she'd gotten from Barry Dangler.

The incident report didn't offer much. The patrol officers first on the scene had given their story of finding the body. The crime scene people hadn't been able to do much with the site. None of the ground around the area had yielded any good prints to analyze, and scour as they might, they could find nothing to indicate who might have been with her.

She turned to the autopsy report, which was fairly straightforward. Diane had been choked—although that wasn't the cause of death—struck several times on the head with something hard, and her body tossed down the ravine. Any of the blows to the head could have killed her. And just for good measure, the fall also broke her neck.

Cassie was halfway through the rest of the details when something stopped her cold. She read it three times to make sure she was not mistaken. She was shocked, enraged, furious, every kind of angry she could think of. If Diane had been standing in front of her, Cassie would have killed her herself. She pounded her fist on the table until it ached, then threw the folder across the room. She needed to tell Griffin about this.

Taking deep, gulping breaths she paced the room, somehow pulling herself together. She'd wait until after dinner to tell him. Let him eat first. Give him some time to settle down after a work day. She hoped she could manage it.

By the time Griffin returned, however, she'd picked up the papers from where they'd fallen and arranged her face into a pleasant mask.

Somehow she pushed everything to the back of her mind while they ate, although the food tasted like sawdust. She talked about her meetings that day, even laughing about all the warnings people had given her. *What an actress I am,* she thought.

When she told him about closing the account with Howard Cook and moving it to Bank of America, he laughed out loud.

"I'd give a week's pay to have seen the look on his face when you asked for the check. Serves the old bastard right. I always thought he blabbed too much about the business of the people who banked with him."

"Moving the money just made sense, anyway, since I already have an account with B of A. It just gave me a lot of satisfaction to do it."

While they cleared away the debris, she mentioned the other thing that stood out in all her conversations. "Everyone wants to help me clean out the house. Including the chief. And Carol Markham, who stopped by with the listing agreement."

"It sure makes you think there's something here someone wants."

"Yes but what?" Cassie was as puzzled as she'd been before.

"We can talk about it later. It's still light and it's cooled off. Let's go sit on the patio."

"Good. There's some stuff I need to go over with you."

They settled into the lounge chairs, Cassie clutching the folder she'd gotten from Dangler. The line from the report slammed back into her consciousness, if indeed it had ever left. One sentence, so damning, so destructive to so many lives. She swallowed against the nausea, determined to calm herself.

She glanced sideways at Griffin. "I quit my job today."

He turned his head to look at her. "How'd your boss take it?"

She shrugged. "After the whining and bitching he was great. He wished us well."

"You told him about me?"

"Didn't have to. He guessed and I didn't deny it." She cleared her throat, choosing her next words with care. "I thought I'd go back this weekend. I still have my return ticket. I need to close up my apartment, make plans to get rid of everything. Pick up my car."

"Can you do it all in two days?"

"Probably not but Claire can handle the cleanup details for me." She waited to see what he'd say next.

"You'd better give me the flight details, so I can make my reservation," he said at last.

"I was hoping you'd say that." She reached out and took his hand. "Besides, I want to show you off to Claire." She also wanted a chance for him to see the person she was while she'd been doing what she now saw as marking time. "I'll get my ticket. It's in my purse on the counter. I changed the reservations to Thursday."

"I'll do it. You sit there. Tomorrow I'll take a minute to reschedule my Friday jobs. No problem." He went into the house to make his arrangements.

Cassie tried to settle the butterflies tap dancing in her stomach. She'd procrastinated long enough. When Griff came back out, she'd have to tell him what she'd discovered. Rage surged through her again and she forced it back.

The screen door slammed. "All set," he told her.

She waited until he'd dropped into the lounge chair again. "I pried the information about Diane's murder loose from Chief Dangler today. The description of the crime scene was pretty graphic. Lots of blood."

Griffin grimaced. "I wouldn't know. They gave me very little information. They were interested in seeing what I could tell them."

"I know they did a DNA swab to see if any of the blood on her body was yours."

He nodded. "Yes, they did."

"Griffin, there's no easy way to say this so I'll just say it straight out." Her hands curled into fists. "The baby wasn't yours."

Chapter Fourteen

಄

Griffin didn't say a word. The silence grew between them until it was almost palpable. Cassie sat very still, trying to relax the knot in her stomach and keep her hands from shaking. Reading it hadn't been half as bad as saying it out loud.

When he spoke, his voice sounded hollow, as if he were at the bottom of a well. "Are you sure?"

Cassie bit her lip. "Yes. It's all right here in the lab reports and the autopsy. There was no DNA match whatsoever."

"God damn it," he exploded and launched himself out of the chair. He paced the patio, running his hands through his hair, jaw clenched, tension radiating from his body.

Cassie waited in nervous silence. Obviously no one had told Griffin the results of the tests at the time. Were they waiting for him to slip up, admit to something? How many people had Dangler shared this information with?

"I should have demanded a test from the beginning." He bit the words off savagely. "Your sister was a tramp, Cassie. I'm sorry to say it but it was the truth. She slept with anyone who appealed to her." He dry-washed his face. "Of course, I wasn't any better."

"Griffin…"

"Let me finish." He was so angry he could barely get the words out. "They knew. All this time, they knew. No one told me. I grieved more for the baby than I ever did for Diane. Shit."

Cassie willed herself to sit still, let him work out the battle within himself.

"Diane certainly knew, I promise you." His words were rough, vicious. "And I was the poor sucker she reeled in to take on her responsibility. I have not one doubt that when that baby came, she'd be gone and I'd be left to handle things. Diane was definitely not the maternal type."

He paced some more, cursing steadily, fists clenched. Finally, he drew a deep breath, seemed to gather himself and sat down again. "That certainly opens up a whole new can of worms, doesn't it?"

"Yes," Cassie agreed. "It does. I hate to ask but do you have any idea who the father could be?"

"Not a clue. But I think she carefully chose who she went to with her news, picking the one of us that would be the easiest mark. Also, I was the only one running any kind of business. Everyone else was sort of drifting through life and holding down a succession of odd jobs. If she was going to dump the baby afterwards, she at least had enough conscience to want it to have some kind of security."

Cassie felt a tightness in her chest. "Griff, I wish I knew what to say."

He pounded his fist on his thigh. "I think she wanted to make sure she cut you out too, Cassie. Diane was always jealous of you and somehow she knew how I felt about you."

"Jealous of me?" Cassie was astounded. She tried to read his face but darkness had descended like a black drape and there was no light coming from the house. "In God's name, why?"

"You were the smart one, the bright one, the one with all the awards. Diane played your parents for all they were worth, because her charm was all she had going for her."

Cassie couldn't assimilate the information. She'd had no idea how Griffin Hunter felt about her until those fateful two nights. It certainly hadn't been obvious. How had Diane known? Had her sister really done this deliberately?

"You always overlooked Diane's shortcomings," Griffin went on. "Two such completely different sisters—Diane, the wild child, grabbing at life with both hands and you, the object of every respectable man's dream. You had no idea how all those proper young men felt about you, did you? You didn't even know how great sex could be until that night, did you, sugar?"

She shook her head wordlessly.

"Damn," he cursed. "All this time, just wasted."

Suddenly he was on her, pulling at her, lifting her from the chair in both arms. Then they were on the grass, his body pinning hers beneath him. He slammed his mouth against hers, tearing at her clothes with his free hand until she was completely naked. His tongue stabbed into her, bruising the inside of her mouth, reaching deep into the dark hollow.

She heard the clink of his belt buckle, the rasp of his zipper, felt his movement as he jerked his pants down. Heard the rip of foil and the distinct snap of latex as he sheathed himself, and she marveled that he even had the presence of mind to do so.

"This is what I always wanted," he breathed into her ear. "This. Not Diane. Not anyone else. Just you, and me inside you."

"Yes," she breathed. "I want this, too. I want to feel you in my body."

In one swift movement he thrust her legs wide apart, bracing his arms under them so she was totally open and exposed to him. He didn't care if she was wet or ready. This wasn't about her. With a thrust that was pure possession he was inside her, buried in her, feeling her tight around him.

"Mine, Cassie. All this time, you should have been mine." His voice was hoarse, guttural. "Well, you're mine now." He plunged into her, going deeper each time. "Take me, Cassie." He was practically sobbing as he drove into her. "It should have been you. Always, always, always."

"Always yours, Griff." Her words caught on a breath. "Forever."

She didn't flinch at the pain of the intrusion, didn't try to push him away, even as she felt his engorged penis stretching her unbearably, scraping her vaginal walls. She could feel his rage, his pain, his despair at the destruction of his life all pouring into her and she wanted to absorb it all. To ease it. To make him whole again. *This* was what she could give to him. *This* was the proof of her love.

In just seconds he came with shuddering force, hips jerking, harsh, guttural sounds emanating from his throat. She clung to him with her legs around his hips and rode out the storm with him.

Then it was over, as suddenly as it had started. He lay panting on her chest for a moment, then heaved himself off and stood. He grabbed his handkerchief from his pants pocket to dispose of the condom, yanked up his pants and zipped them. He whispered a quiet thank-you that the houses on either side were only one story. No prying eyes to look down on them.

"Well, that showed a lot of class," he said, not looking at her. "Now you know what kind of bastard I really am. You should pay attention to all those warnings you heard today."

Cassie forced herself to her feet. She didn't even bother with her clothes, just stood naked on the lawn, the evidence of her own climax drying on her thighs. Deliberately she went to him and slid her arms around him, pressing her face against his back.

He was taut as a drum, every muscle in his body rigid.

"I guess they'll have a lot more to say tomorrow," she said, as gently as she could.

"I should tell you to run, Cassie, just as far and as fast as you can. Go back to Tampa. Get your job back. Get the hell away from me, if you want to save yourself." He wouldn't turn around.

She stepped in front of him. "You don't mean that. That's just rage, Griffin. And pain. You have a right to be angry and hurt and all of those things. You've had your life nearly destroyed. But if you really want me to leave, you have to tell me you don't love me. Can you say that?"

"I practically raped you, for God's sake. The woman who means more to me than my own life." He shook his head in disgust. "That would be enough to chase away anyone with brains."

"That wasn't rape. That was hunger, and agony, and the need to feel whole again." She reached out a hand and placed it gently on his arm. "There's no way you could do anything like that to me. Besides, I didn't hear myself screaming for you to stop. Did you? I love you, Griff. If I can absorb your pain then I want to do it."

"Cassie—"

"Tell me that you don't love me," she insisted, "and I'll throw you out of the house right now." She was shivering in the night air. She wrapped her arms around herself to ward off the chill. "Well? Can you say it?"

Griffin looked at her as if seeing her for the first time. "My God, you're freezing. Here." He picked up his shirt and made her put it on, pulling it together in front. He looked at her for a long time. "If I wanted to do the best thing for you, I'd say whatever it took to get you to run me off. But I can't. Because I do love you, Cassie. God save us both."

"Well, then. Let's go inside and figure out what to do. I think we've given the neighbors enough of a show for tonight."

She picked up her clothes and her papers and walked into the house, displaying more dignity than she actually felt. It was important for Griffin to know that she understood what had just happened and that she was a willing participant. That it changed nothing between them.

In a moment, she heard him follow her inside.

* * * * *

They faced each other in the kitchen. Griffin's face was still lined with so much pain Cassie wasn't sure she could stand it. She wanted to reach out and touch his cheek but she needed first to make him understand she was okay with everything, that she understood his wrath and it hadn't changed her feelings for him.

"I don't even begin to know how to apologize to you." His voice was filled with desperation. "I can't explain what I did. Even at my very worst I never treated a woman like that. I just needed to be inside you, to feel us connected, to bind us together. I needed something clean, something real. And I needed to get rid of all that anger."

She took one of his hands in both of hers and leaned forward, rubbing her face against his chest, hearing his heart thudding beneath her ear. "It's all right. I know. I understand. You can't chase me away. What kind of love would we have if I couldn't understand what drove you to this, what was behind it? It will take a lot more than that to get me to walk out of your life."

"God, you're amazing." He pulled her tightly against him.

Cassie looked up at him, trying to send him messages with her eyes. "Diane did a lot of damage to both of us. I don't even know yet how to deal with my own feelings, so I can hardly imagine yours. But we have to get past all of this."

She could tell he was searching for the right words to say.

"I think…I think just now I wanted to erase every trace of her from my body, to make sure there was only you. I wanted to take back all the wasted years. I just…"

"It's okay. I understand. Truly. We have to go forward, Griffin. And we have to do it together."

"I don't deserve you." He kissed the top of her head. "But God knows, I love you more than anything. If you'd run, I don't know what I would have done."

"Okay, then." She looked up at him. "I think we need another shower and some coffee. Then we can take a better look at this situation." She grinned at him. "We can shower together and save water."

The shower did more than wash off the grass and dirt from their bodies. It washed away the fury, the feeling of helplessness, the desperation that bubbled up after six years of hell. Griffin stood in the shower stall under the spray, just holding Cassie against him, letting her strength flow into him, until they both began to feel waterlogged. When they stepped out, he kissed her for a long time, a very gentle kiss but one that said more than any words. And when they were dried and dressed again, it was better between them.

Cassie made coffee, then filled a mug for each of them. They sat down at the kitchen table, where so much of their life seemed to be playing out.

"Now we have to figure out why nobody ever told you about the DNA and who the real father of that baby was."

"Easy," he said, his voice bitter. "In a town this size it wouldn't be difficult to match DNA. Someone's gone to a lot of trouble to cover this up and make sure the focus was only on me."

"I hate to do this to you," she told him, "but you've got to try to come up with some names. He could easily have been the person who killed her."

"I know, I know." He pinched the bridge of his nose. "I've just blocked so much of it out of my mind that it's hard to bring it all back. Besides, Diane used that charm on everything in pants. It didn't matter if it was me, the dentist or the bag boy at the grocery store."

When they had completely filled one page of paper with likely candidates, Cassie threw down the pen and shook her head. "This isn't getting us anywhere. We'll end up listing every man in town. There has to be a better way of doing this."

"No kidding."

They sat in silence for a moment, then Cassie snapped her fingers. "Did they give you back Diane's things after the…afterwards?"

Griffin frowned. "What things?"

"You know, her clothes, any personal items."

"No. I didn't even ask. Why?"

Cassie was doodling on the pad in front of her, lower lip caught between her teeth. "Didn't you say Diane always had that little purse thing with her?"

"What about it?"

"I'll call Dangler in the morning and ask about it. My best guess is it's still held as evidence, even though the case is cold. But if it's not there, it could be what our mysterious stranger is looking for."

"He'll be angry again because you're digging this up, you know. He still thinks I did it."

"Too bad for him."

Griffin narrowed his eyes. "There's one other thing we haven't considered."

"What's that?"

"Dangler could be covering up for someone. The people who hold power in Stoneham take care of each other. If Dangler knew — or even suspected — who Diane's lover was, he might just be doing a favor for an old friend."

Cassie felt sick. The possibility was very real and if that was so, their job would be a lot harder and a lot more dangerous.

They were both so emotionally drained even the coffee couldn't keep them awake. Climbing into bed, physically and emotionally exhausted, they fell asleep holding each other like lost children.

* * * * *

When Griffin got up at his usual early hour the next morning, Cassie rose with him. The day would be a busy one for her and no doubt unpleasant and she wanted time to prepare herself. "Come to the funeral," she urged him.

"Better for you if I don't," he argued.

"Do you think I care what any person in this town thinks? This is my choice, not theirs."

He pulled her to him and held her close, his lips brushing her hair. "Listen to me this once, Cassie. This will be a difficult day for you as it is. Don't make it worse for yourself. And it will be if I show up at the church."

He was right. She hated to admit it but he made sense. Whoever chose to attend would make their disapproval evident. Worse yet, they would make Griffin feel uncomfortable and she didn't want that. "All right. But be here when I get back, okay?"

"You bet." He hugged her, kissed her lightly, then was gone.

Carol Markham had left the listing agreement and Cassie signed it, tucking her copy in the folder with the other papers she was accumulating. Then she called the agency.

"You can come by before noon to pick it up," she told Carol when the woman came to the phone.

"Oh, honey, I don't want to make you do business on the day of your mama's funeral," Carol protested.

"My mother won't be any less dead," she said, her tone pragmatic.

Next she called the insurance company and asked for the claims processor whose name she had pried loose from Neil. He came on the phone in seconds.

"Yes, Miss Fitzgerald, we have all the paperwork and everything's in order." He paused. "On the life insurance we'll simply send you a check but on the annuities…" His voice trailed off.

"Yes?" she prompted.

"I'm not sure cashing them out would be a wise move. We could just transfer your name as the beneficiary and you'll receive monthly checks."

"I understood I could opt for the lump sum cash-out." She'd asked Neil very specifically about that. The amount, two hundred thousand dollars, still stunned her.

"If that's what you want, then of course we can do that," the man said.

"You're right. That's a significant sum but my mind's made up. Let me give you my bank account number and you can do a wire transfer."

Her next call was to the management agency for her apartment in Tampa to tell them she wouldn't be signing the new lease agreement. She would, she assured them, drop off a check at their office on Friday for one more month's rent, to give her time to do whatever was needed. No problem, they assured her.

Her final call was to Barry Dangler, which resulted in no information at all.

"Yes, we still have all your sister's things." He sounded abrupt. "But since it's an unsolved case they can't be released."

"Okay. Can I just come by and look through them?"

"What is it you're looking for, Cassie?" Anger was creeping into his voice. "Is there something you think we missed?"

"No. I just wanted to see the stuff. Is that all right? Is there some problem I'm not aware of?"

"No problem, except her killer is still loose. Bury your mother today, Cassie and call me tomorrow. But I'm telling you, get off whatever crusade you're on and close the door on this."

Her head was beginning to ache again. She dug aspirin out of her purse and swallowed two with the rest of her coffee.

She was dreading the afternoon more than she wanted to admit to herself. If she was lucky, only a few people would show up and the service would be short.

Shortly before noon, Carol came by to pick up the listing papers. "I just want to say again how sorry we are about your mother." She was wearing her sympathetic face. Cassie wondered if she practiced in front of a mirror. "It was too bad you weren't able to come home for your sister's funeral, or your father's."

Cassie refused to rise to the subtle dig. "Thank you for taking care of this." She handed the contract to Carol with exaggerated politeness. *Just sell the house and get out of my life,* she wanted to tell her.

"What are you planning to do with the furniture and things?" Carol asked.

"If whoever buys the house wants it, they can have it. I won't be needing it."

"I imagine you'll be going back to Tampa?"

"My plans are actually somewhat up in the air at the moment."

Get out of here!

"I hear those plans might include Griffin Hunter." Carol's eyes had an avaricious glitter to them.

Cassie sighed. "If you don't mind, I need to get dressed for this afternoon. Whenever you want to show the house, just let me know. I put my cell phone number on the contract so you can get hold of me wherever I am."

She managed to push the woman out the door and close it firmly behind her. Her headache was blasting back with the intensity of a rocket-propelled grenade. The sooner she and Griffin got out of this town the better.

At last she put on the one dark dress she'd brought with her and her low matching heels. A deep breath and she was ready.

Chapter Fifteen

∽

All Cassie could think of was the opening line from *A Tale of Two Cities.* "It was the best of times, it was the worst of times." More people came to the service than she expected, filling the small chapel at the mortuary. People she didn't even recognize crowded every corner of the room. Curiosity-seekers, she decided.

The room was hot and stuffy, the air cloying with the scent of the flowers banked tastefully around the platform the casket rested on. She couldn't begin to imagine who sent them, unless people were salving their consciences. The babble of voices, hushed though it was, didn't do her headache any good.

Donald Brandon greeted her with his practiced unctuous attitude, patting her hand and mouthing condolences. "I've made all the arrangements for the cemetery following this. They'll be expecting us."

"Thank you."

She recaptured her hand and turned to the coffin. She and her mother had never been close, even on the best of days. But her death marked the closing of a chapter in Cassie's life and she felt a strange sadness. Here was a woman who never knew how to enjoy life, except through a daughter who brought violence and evil into it.

Donald positioned himself next to her, acting as the official greeter. His voice grated on her nerves, its oily syllables sliding smoothly from one sentence to the next. She longed for a Star Trek transporter.

Beam me up, Scotty.

Neil was there with his wife. At best a nodding acquaintance of Cassie's, Leslie McLeod mouthed platitudes of comfort then moved away.

"I'm happy to see you haven't dragged Hunter along with you today," Neil said with approval.

"More for his sake than mine." Cassie curled her lips in a nasty expression. "I didn't want to subject him to the brand of etiquette this town practices."

"You know, you really need to take time to think about what you're doing," he admonished her. "I hate to sound like a broken record but..."

"Then don't," she interrupted. "I've had about all the advice I can take. By the way, I took care of everything with the insurance company this morning so that's one more chore you can cross off your list."

Neil shrugged and moved off to join his wife.

Next in line was Cyrus, with his obvious disapproval in contrast to his sympathetic words. "Your mother was a lovely woman."

"Yes. She was." What else could she say?

"I don't think she'd be happy at the path you're taking."

"Cyrus." Cassie was beyond exasperation. "Could I please just bury my mother without another lecture?"

He looked as if she'd slapped him. "Of course, Cassie. I'm sorry to intrude on your grief."

Last came Thad Lewis, Cyrus' former partner and Leslie's father. At the look on her face he bit back whatever he'd been planning to say. "I understand you're listing the house," he said instead. "Carol will get an appraiser out but I've been doing a bit of that since I'm not practicing much anymore. I'm sure you'd want someone to evaluate the things inside the house so you get fair market value."

"Are you offering to go through the house with me, Thad?"

He missed the dangerous edge to her tone. "Why, yes, as a matter of fact. At your convenience, of course."

"Thanks anyway but I've got it covered. You know, it seems like a lot of people are anxious to go through what's in the house. You wouldn't have any idea why, would you, Thad?"

He backed away. "I'm sorry if I offended you in any way. I was just trying to be helpful."

The pastor, Andrew Howell, provided the only soothing note in the room. He drew her to one side, away from the sideways glances and spoke with her about her mother and what he planned to say.

"I know this sounds terrible," she told him, "but my mother and I hadn't been close in years. If ever. I'm sure whatever you've prepared will be just fine."

"You're fortunate to have so many friends to help you through this." He glanced around the room.

"Forgive me, Pastor but these are not my friends. They're gossips sniffing around my private life. My sister was murdered, my father drank himself to death over it and my mother died totally out of touch with reality. And of course, in case you haven't heard, the icing on the cake for them is the fact that I'm living with the town pariah. So if you really want to do something for me, get this over with so I can get away from everyone here as soon as possible."

If he was shocked by her words Andrew Howell was too well trained a professional to show it. "Of course. Absolutely." He led her to a chair in the front row.

Cassie was sure the service was nice but it washed over her like a passing cloud. Only the fact that the pastor's lips stopped moving and Donald touched her arm signaled her that it was over. Then she got trapped in an argument about transportation to the cemetery.

"I think I should drive you," Donald told her, trying to guide her to the door.

"No, thank you." She jerked her arm away. "That's very nice of you but I'd prefer to drive myself."

"Leslie and I will be happy to take you." Neil was suddenly beside her. Leslie nodded, her face carefully blank.

"Please." Cassie moved to the side. "Thank you but I really need this time to myself." She all but ran to her car, leaving everyone staring after her, their unasked questions hanging in the air.

The graveside ceremony was blessedly brief. Cassie dropped the traditional white rose on the casket, turned and walked away. It saddened her that she felt nothing, not even regret.

"Cassie."

She turned to see Barry Dangler hurrying to catch her. He huffed slightly as he jogged to where she was standing.

"Here." He handed her an envelope. "The list of items we catalogued the night Diane was killed. If you want to come by and see them for yourself, just call me." He stopped to catch his breath. "Here's the last piece of advice I'll try to offer you. Leave it alone. Go back to Tampa. You won't be doing yourself or anyone else any favors by pushing this thing."

She gave him a hard look. "Doesn't it bother you that it's been six years and you've never found even one lead to who killed her?"

"No. I know who killed her. One of these days I'll break his alibi and we'll have him."

"After all this time?" She was flabbergasted.

"I'm a patient man."

"Why didn't you tell Griffin the baby wasn't his?" She threw the words at him like darts.

Dangler showed no reaction. "I was sure he knew. That's why he killed her."

"Well, he didn't," she spat at him, climbing into her car. "Maybe it's time for you to start looking somewhere else."

Her tires squealed as she pulled away from the curb. Her head was pounding again and her rage was so fierce she could almost touch it. Hot tears spilled down her cheeks, blurring her vision, until she pulled off onto a side street and gave vent to all the stored-up anguish. She cried until her eyes ached and her chest hurt, beating the steering wheel with clenched fists. A long time passed before she was calm enough to start the car again.

She was soaking in the bathtub, every bit of strength gone, when she heard Griff calling her name. "Up here," she called.

He took one look at her and kneeled beside the tub. "Not the best of days, was it?" He smoothed stray curls away from her forehead.

"You could certainly say that. I have stuff to tell you but not now. I'm too exhausted to think."

He cared for her as he would a sick child, with a tenderness she would never have thought him capable of. He let the water out of the tub, lifted her out and dried her with a gentle touch, then found one of his own large tee shirts and slipped it over her head. She stood, unresisting, while he ministered to her.

When he was through, he carried her to her bed, slid her under the covers and lay down beside her. Cradling her in his arms, he crooned soft words to her until she dozed off.

* * * * *

The room was dark when Cassie woke up. She was aware that Griffin's body was still spooned against hers, his arm lightly thrown over her body. She moved slightly and he was instantly alert.

"Better?" he asked softly, brushing her hair back from her face.

"Much." She laced her fingers through his, so grateful for the feeling of his warm skin, his hands so tender and magical.

"Lousy day, right?"

"Worst than most." She turned over and sat up. "What a bunch of sanctimonious hypocrites. If I'd had a gun I think I'd have shot everybody there."

"Such bloodthirsty words from such innocent lips," he grinned.

"These people are amazing," she told him. "I feel like I'm living someone else's nightmare."

He insisted that she eat something, even if it was just soup. He watched her finish it while he ate the sandwich he'd made for himself. "Just eat as much as you can," he said. "If you don't put something in your system you'll get sick."

She obediently spooned the soup into her mouth and munched on a cracker. When the bowl was empty, she sat back and recapped the day for him. She told him about the funeral service, about Neil and Cyrus and even Donald. And about Chief Dangler and what he'd said.

Griffin's eyes darkened as he listened, especially to the part about the chief. His jaw clenched but he sat in silence until she finished.

"Someone killed her and it wasn't you." This had become her mantra. "And no one in this town is going to look any further to find out who it was. It's going to be up to us."

"We're hardly detectives," Griffin pointed out.

"We couldn't do a worse job than the police have already done—which is nothing," she replied. "Griffin, if we don't find answers to this, it will dog us forever and we'll never have any peace."

He picked her up and sat down again, cradling her in his lap. His lips touched her hair, her forehead, her eyelids, her cheeks. She could feel his heart thudding against her and spread her palm over his chest, letting the beat travel into her body.

"I'm tainted, Cassie," he reminded her once more. "You should keep that in mind."

"You know what?" She sat up suddenly, nearly knocking both of them over. "That's getting old real fast. Do you think I didn't know who or what you were that first night I let you take me up to your bedroom? Do you think I don't know who you are now? I'm an adult, Griffin. I make my own choices. This is one of them. How many times do I need to tell you that?"

In answer he kissed her, gently at first, then hard, his tongue probing and insistent. His hand roamed over her body, touching her everywhere, branding her as his. Finally he lifted his head and looked at her. "All right, then. We go on from here. But it won't be an easy ride, sugar."

"If I wanted easy I never would have walked up onto your porch that night."

They knew one of the first things they had to do was make some sense out of the signals Cassie was getting from everyone. She thought again of all the offers to help her go through the house. Which of them had an ulterior motive? Was it more than one? Was the little clutch bag what they were looking for, or was there something else out there that was even more damning? Because the baby hadn't been Griffin's, there was a man out there with a dreadful secret to hide. A good enough excuse for killing.

They carefully looked over the list of items the chief had given Cassie but nothing in the catalogue of Diane's belongings gave them any kind of hint.

"What did you do with the rest of her things after... Afterwards?" she asked.

"Boxed them up and gave them to your folks. I missed a few of her things, which I brought to you the other night. That's it."

She tilted her head, forcing him to look at her. "So they're probably still in this house somewhere."

"I guess. Your mother looked like she wasn't ever going to let go of them."

"We have to find them. There may be something there." She stood and carried their plates to the sink. "I can't think anymore today. Tomorrow while you're working I'll be going through this house room by room. I need to make lists anyway, what I want to keep, what I want to get rid of, stuff like that. It will give me a good chance to really dig through this house again."

"Don't you want to wait until I get home tomorrow night?"

"No. I need to get into this. Besides, it will keep me busy during the day."

"I've got someone coming by tomorrow to paint the trim for you. A guy who does pickup work for me. I hope that's okay."

"Lordy, yes. I had no idea who to call."

"We should leave here after lunch on Thursday to get to the airport in San Antonio on time," he told her. "When I go by my house to check on it tomorrow, I'll pick up some clothes for the weekend. I don't want your friends to think you found me in a homeless shelter."

Cassie burst out laughing. "Claire could care not less what you look like. She'd probably like it if you didn't wear any clothes at all."

"What kind of friends do you have?" He grinned, happy to see her relaxed a little.

"You'll like Claire and she'll like you and she's the only one I really care about."

He gathered her in his arms, his breath quickening. "Don't you think it's time to go to bed?"

"Make me forget," she whispered. "Make it all go away."

In the bedroom he stripped off the tee shirt and was out of his clothes in seconds and lying next to her. His hand automatically sought the familiar shape of her breasts, his tongue probed her ear and his hot breath whispered over her skin.

"Cassie," he crooned. "God, touching you is like touching a flame. You make my blood boil and my skin catch fire."

Cassie felt his lean, muscled body pressed against her side, the mat of hair on his chest teasing at the side of her arm. The rough stubble of his beard abraded her cheeks, suddenly making them erogenous zones. No matter where he touched her, or how, she was so aroused her body begged for satisfaction.

Needing to connect with him, she reached for his cock, already hard and throbbing, the soft tip probing against the flesh of her thigh. When she wrapped her hand lightly around it she heard him groan, felt his body tighten in response.

"Your touch is like a feather. So light but so hot. God, Cassie, I can't get enough of you." He laved her ear again. "Come on, sugar, talk to me. Tell me how I make you feel. It's okay," he crooned. "I want to hear you say it. Tell me from your heart."

Cassie had never dreamed of doing what Griffin asked, of verbalizing. But then, she'd never dreamed she'd be fulfilling all her erotic fantasies with him, either. And somehow saying the things he wanted to hear only cemented the connection between them.

"Say it, Cassie," he urged.

"You make me feel…good," she gasped.

"Hot?"

She nodded, barely able to think.

"Tell me, then." His mouth closed over one breast, his teeth rasping the nipple, biting it, tugging on it. His hand slid down her soft abdomen, trailed through the silken curls and his fingers slipped beneath her labia.

Without any urging, Cassie opened her legs, thrusting her hips at him. "Yes, hot. Empty without you inside me."

"Do you like my fingers inside you, sugar? Talk to me. Tell me what to do."

"Put...put your fingers inside me. Oh, God. Yes! Like that!" She felt him slide two long, lean fingers inside her and then she couldn't stop talking. "Fill me with your fingers, Griff. More. More. That's not enough." She shoved her hips at him. "Give me more. I want you way inside me. Do it. Do it."

She couldn't believe she was saying these things but Griffin stripped away all her inhibitions, all her reserves. And she did want more, that soul-shattering feeling only he could give. "Inside me, Griffin. Feel inside me. I'm already wet for you."

He nudged her legs until her knees were bent and her feet were flat on the mattress. "God, you're dripping." He slipped another finger inside with the other two, stretching her, the muscles now loose and pliable. Curling his fingers, he lightly scraped her vaginal walls with his nails, smiling in satisfaction when she jerked in response. "I could leave my fingers inside you forever," he whispered, "feeling your muscles clamp around them. Your hot, slick moisture is like warm cream. Oh, sugar, you are so sweet you take my breath away."

Cassie was wild, her senses on overload. Every coupling with Griffin seemed more intense than the last. She craved his fingers, his tongue, his thick, hard cock. There wasn't a nerve in her body that wasn't inflamed. The more he touched her, the more she wanted.

"Fuck me with your hand, Griffin." In all her life Cassie had never whispered graphic, erotic words to anyone, but with Griffin she couldn't seem to stop herself. Everything he did and said excited her. "Do it. Hurry." She pressed herself upward against his touch. "Yes. More. Oh, God, I can't stand it anymore. Put your mouth on me. Please."

"All right, darlin'. Let's see if the little nub likes my tongue as much as your mouth does." His lips closed over her clitoris, sucking it into his mouth as if he'd never let it go. When he caught it between his teeth, biting it oh so lightly, her hips thrust at him so violently she almost knocked him away from her.

"Don't stop," she gasped. Her entire body seemed focused on the one little spot, jolts of electricity spiking through her, every nerve screaming at the intense stimulation.

Griffin sucked hard, his tongue relentless as his fingers stretched her vaginal walls. When he lifted his head, his lips were slick with her moisture. He watched her face flushed with desire, her eyes wild and glazed. "You taste like fine wine, sugar. Better than anything that comes in a bottle. I could get drunk on you, Cassie, you know that?"

"Yes, yes. Drink me, Griffin. Use your mouth. Oh, God, please, please." She was desperate in her need, her body begging for release, for satisfaction.

His fingers kept working their magic, moving her closer and closer to her peak and all the while he crooned to her in his low, rich voice. "Sometimes when I'm working I think about how you taste. How you feel, like velvet and satin. I don't know which turns me on more, sugar—making you come wide open, so I can watch those pretty pink muscles clench, feeling you with my hand, or having you clamp tight around my cock while I spurt into you. When I think how it feels to have my cock inside you, my zipper nearly pops open."

She was moving harder against his hand now, moaning soft little sounds, her body arching in her frantic search for fulfillment. "Make me come, Griff. Please. Now. Now. Now."

Her skin was slick with the sheen of perspiration and her breasts swayed with each toss and turn. The walls of her vagina were fluttering against his fingers in a way that drove him crazy. He wanted to be inside her but he wanted to feel her spill herself into his hand even more.

"Come for me, Cassie." His mouth was against her ear again, his tongue dipping and swirling. "Let me feel all that good hot liquid pour into my hand."

His words pushed her over the edge and she climaxed, bucking wildly, grabbing his hair, screaming his name over and over. Her fluid pooled in his palm, a feeling so erotic he nearly came just lying there. His fingers stroked and probed and teased inside her as she came in what seemed an endless orgasm.

When the fierce movements of her body slowed, he removed his hand slowly, brought his fingers to his mouth and with great deliberation licked them.

Through slitted eyes Cassie watched him licking her dew from his skin and the pulsebeat deep in her channel began all over again. She'd barely finished with one orgasm and she could feel another already building.

With her body was still throbbing with aftershocks, Griffin moved over her and sheathed himself with a condom from the nightstand. His fingers opened her labia as if he was peeling back the petals of a flower and he entered her with one hard, swift thrust. She was so damp with her own moisture he slid in easily, seating himself to the hilt.

"Like that better, sugar?" His voice was raspy with desire. "Like my cock inside you? Oh, Cassie, you don't know how good you feel. Or what heaven it is being inside you."

Her tender flesh surrounded him like a velvet glove, the little spasms still gripping her vaginal walls like so many tiny flames against his cock. The hard points of her nipples stabbed into the curly mat of hair on his chest, flooding him with sensation.

As aroused as they both were, he barely stroked her before they both exploded in a fierce orgasm. Bodies slick with sweat crashed against each other. Then he collapsed on top of her, his lungs begging for air, little pulsations still gripping their bodies.

When he could breathe again, he rolled onto his back, taking her with him, holding her against his body. "Jesus, Cassie. I think we might kill ourselves."

"I...do things with you I never thought I'd do with anyone." Her voice was shy, her face turned away from him.

"Good, sugar." He kissed her shoulder. "Because I'd hate to have to go out and *really* kill someone." He bit her shoulder, a tiny love nip. "I love you, Cassie. There should be no boundaries between us."

"Will you keep teaching me?" She could hardly get any words out. Every muscle, every nerve in her body was wrung dry.

"You bet. We've just begun, darlin'."

"Griff?"

"What, honey?"

"I think you made today all better."

He chuckled, turned on his side and molded her against him. The outside world might conspire against them but what they had, no one could destroy. Whatever else happened, he would cherish this woman forever, his life brighter and warmer since she'd come back into it. He was still smiling when they fell asleep.

Chapter Sixteen

ℰℭ

Griffin left before sunup in the morning, planning to go by his house to check it out and pack before he started his first job of the day. He had mixed feelings about taking this trip with Cassie but he wasn't about to let her do it alone. He'd certainly never have a peaceful moment with her driving back from Tampa by herself, on the highway for two days.

He was aware of the chattering tongues in town and the parade of cars past her house, hoping for a titillating glimpse of the two of them together. Cassie would have thrown up the window shades and told them to take a look. Griffin, however, insisted on protecting her from prying eyes as much as possible, the hot and heavy scene in the backyard the other night notwithstanding. He promised himself that would never happen again.

While Griffin was trimming shrubs and shoveling mulch, Cassie was again working her way through the house room by room. She decided to start with one more look in Diane's room, in case they had missed anything. All of her sister's clothes were stacked in a corner, ready for packing in cartons when she got back from Tampa. There were plenty of places to donate them to. They hadn't yielded anything.

She stripped the sheets from the bed, tossing them in the washer and folding away the blanket, leaving the mattress to air out for the time being. Then she scoured every inch of the room, even checking to see if the carpet had been pulled up anywhere but found nothing. If Diane had hidden something in the house, she had hidden it well enough that Cassie was having a difficult time finding it.

Going through her mother's room, where her parents had slept together until her father's fall from reality, was equally as difficult. The stale air of sickness hung in the air, along with something more. Neglect? Failure? Retreat? Cassie found it very depressing.

She followed the same process with the clothes and the bedding. Then she dumped everything from the nightstand drawer into a sack and put it in her room along with her mother's jewelry box.

By the time she'd finished with the upstairs she was hot and dusty and still had no answers. She drank nearly a whole pitcher of iced tea with her lunch, then began with the downstairs.

By four o'clock, she'd accumulated a lot of trash to haul to the curb, another sack of papers to go through but she was empty-handed as well as discouraged. She felt in her bones that Diane's secret was hiding somewhere close at hand but no clue jumped out at her.

She decided to use up some of the food she'd bought and make spaghetti sauce for dinner. A salad, French bread and the bottle of red wine she'd picked up rounded out the menu. Not quite the gourmet meal she had in mind but for once they wouldn't be eating takeout or sandwiches.

Griffin greedily ate everything she put before him, complimenting her with each bite. After dinner they sat out on the patio again, in the fading light, discussing their options. Cassie reported on the fruitlessness of her search.

"We just need to drop everything until we get back," he told her. "Whatever our unwelcome visitor is looking for, if I couldn't find it today, as much as I tore the house apart, he or she won't either."

"You shouldn't leave that jewelry and all those papers lying around, though," Griffin told her. "I wouldn't put it past dear sweet Carol Markham to do a little snooping while we're gone, either."

Cassie chuckled. "We do have nasty suspicious minds, don't we? You'll be happy to know that tomorrow morning I'm going to run by the bank and rent a big enough safety deposit box to dump everything into."

"I asked Phil to check on things every once in a while 'til we get back." Griff saw her open her mouth to object. "I know, I know, Phil's just Phil. But maybe he'll see something that will help us."

Phil was not the person she would have picked to keep an eye on the house. She wouldn't put it past him to do a little light burglary if given the chance but she decided if Griffin trusted him, she should too.

After they finished their wine they made one more sweep of the house, then hit the garage where they discovered some old cartons stacked haphazardly in one corner.

Cassie dumped all the clothes into them for the time being. "I'll do it more neatly when we get back. I just wanted the closets and dressers emptied in case Carol troops people through here this weekend. She's putting the For Sale sign up tomorrow and I'm sure it will attract plenty of snoops. Thank God the trim is painted. And you worked miracles with the yard."

"Don't you have to be a serious buyer to have someone show you a house?" Griffin wrinkled his forehead with curiosity.

"Sure." She mimed dialing the phone. "Hello, Markham Realty? I'm a serious buyer. You have a house listed I want to see."

Griffin shook his head. "Maybe there's a lot to be said for being out of the mainstream. People sound less appealing to me all the time."

Cassie laughed. "Try being a reporter. You get to see a side of people you wish they'd shipped on the *Titanic*."

When they dropped Griffin's truck back at his house the next day, Cassie waited while he double-checked the locks on the doors. "You surprise me every day," she told him, watching him reset his alarm system. "I'd never have thought you were the kind for such fancy gadgetry."

He grinned but with a touch of bitterness. "When you're as popular in town as I am, you need to cover all your bases."

"You mean people might try to break in and damage your things?" She was totally aghast.

Griffin shrugged. "They make me uneasy enough I wouldn't put anything past them. Especially with Diane's murder still unsolved."

"My God, Griffin, what a way to live. With these people treating you so horribly, why haven't you left here long ago?"

He slid into the driver's seat of her rental car, leaned over and kissed her lightly. "Maybe I was waiting for you to come back, sugar."

Cassie could feel the warmth spreading through her that always came with his touch. *Heaven help me,* she thought, *I'm becoming a sex maniac.* She giggled slightly.

"My kisses are funny now?" he asked.

"No. Just a little private joke. I'll tell you tonight if you're really, really nice to me."

* * * * *

The flight was on time, smooth and easy. In Tampa, they retrieved their luggage and went outside to the cab stand.

"You didn't leave your car here?" Griffin asked.

"No." Cassie shook her head. "My friend Claire chauffeured me. She thinks all airport parking lots are treasure chests for thieves."

"She's probably right."

They finally snagged a cab and in less than thirty minutes Cassie was unlocking the door to her apartment. Griffin carried their bags inside, then stopped in the living room, looking around curiously.

"Something wrong?" She moved around the room, opening drapes and letting in the light.

"No, just interested in how you live. How come the place looks so temporary? It's almost like a hotel room."

Cassie looked around, trying to see things through his eyes. She was struck by the fact that he saw what she hadn't— everything looked as if she'd bought it from a discount showroom and plunked it down without thought or scheme. Which was pretty much what she'd done. She'd always promised herself to fix it up the way she wanted to, but somehow the urge had never quite stirred within her.

Griffin came up behind her and hugged her. "You really weren't planning on staying here forever, were you, sugar." It was a statement more than a question.

She shook her head. "I guess not. Claire always told me I should make more of a home out of this place and I see now what she meant." She turned in his arms. "Maybe you were right, Griffin. Maybe I was just waiting to get back to you, to have you in my life again."

They stood holding each other for a moment, then she broke the contact.

"Okay. We'll just open the suitcases on the floor in the bedroom and take out what we need. Shower, fresh clothes, food and drink. In that order."

Cassie didn't want to go to any of her usual places to eat. She knew they'd be bound to run into people she knew and she wasn't yet ready to share Griffin with anyone. Besides, Claire would kill her if she didn't get the first look. They went, instead, to a little pub in a strip center near her apartment where they had thick steaks and aged bourbon.

"So this is Tampa," he said, polishing off the last of his dinner. "This is where you've been hiding from me?"

"Maybe hiding from myself."

"You came here that summer after…"

"Yes. After. I called Claire and told her I needed emotional first aid. She never blinked, just told me to pack my bags and come on down. I'd spent vacations with her before so it wasn't like I was a stranger. Her folks were very welcoming and really gave me some space."

"Just out of curiosity, what did you do all that summer? You had a long time before classes started again."

"Actually I got a job as a summer intern at the newspaper. They had just fired the one they had. I walked in looking to find anything at all and they hired me on the spot. That's how I met Mike Rivard, my editor at the sports publication."

"So you worked there the next summer too?"

She nodded, sipping at her drink. "Semester breaks and vacations I just hung out with Claire and her family."

"Didn't your folks ever want you to come home?" He raised an eyebrow at her. "I can't believe they were happy to let you just opt out of seeing them at all."

Cassie stirred her drink with the tip of her finger, weighing her words. How to explain this to someone and not have it come out wrong? "When Diane was killed, I always had the feeling my folks would have been happier if it were me. It didn't make me anxious to hurry back to the bosom of my family."

"Shit, Cassie. That's an awful way to live."

"You get used to it. And they never stinted on money. Until my dad began drinking after Diane's death and just sort of faded away, finances weren't a problem. They paid all my college expenses and sent me a check every month."

Griffin reached across the table and took both of her hands in his, gently rubbing his fingers over the knuckles, caressing the skin. "Life hasn't been much better for you than it has for me, has it, sugar?"

"Oh, don't get me wrong," she told him. "I didn't spend my time wallowing in self-pity. I went to work full-time at the paper here right after graduation, then went with Mike to this new publication. I'd saved a lot of the money my folks sent me, so I was able to get my own apartment, buy a car, things like that."

He still had so many unanswered questions to ask her but he knew tonight wasn't the time to get into them. He reached across the table and took her hands in his. "What do you say we get out of here. We'll be a long time making up for what we lost and I don't want to waste a minute."

Chapter Seventeen

ള

As soon as they were up in the morning Cassie took care of her apartment situation. Next she called Claire and arranged for them to meet her for lunch.

"I want to stop and get some moving cartons." She stood in front of her open closet. "Tonight we're going to pack up my clothes and the few things I want shipped to Texas. I'll hire a mover and ask Claire to be here for the pickup."

"What about the rest of your stuff. You don't plan to just walk out on it, do you?"

"Nope. I'll talk to Claire about that too. She'll have some ideas."

And she did but not before she had given Griffin a thorough once-over. Cassie knew he had dressed with care, wanting to make a good impression for her. The blue polo shirt was nearly the exact color of his eyes and his black slacks fit his body as if he'd had them custom-made. His deep tan set off his sun-bleached hair that just brushed the collar of his shirt.

"Wow!" Claire let her eyes travel the length of his lean body. "So you're the guy who broke her heart."

Cassie reddened and kicked Claire under the table.

Griffin smiled his sexy smile and said, "I'm also the guy who gave her his to hold—and would never break her heart again." He placed his hand casually over Cassie's and rubbed his thumb over her knuckles.

Claire grinned. "Well, I can certainly see what the fuss is all about. Cassie, my dear, you didn't half do him justice. I'd give my soul to have some guy look at me this way."

174

"Hands off," Cassie laughed. "He's all mine."

Claire smiled at Cassie. "Oh, I can see that. I just have one favor to ask. If there's another one back there like this one, crate him up and ship him to me directly."

Throughout lunch Griffin constantly touched her, rubbing the nape of her neck, brushing his fingers against her cheek. He was advertising ownership, silently sending the message to Claire to spread the word and Cassie had to admit it made her feel good. When they rose to leave, Claire reached out and hugged her hard, blinking back tears.

"Take care, my wonderful friend. Don't let him get away no matter what you have to do. But remember. I'm always here if you need me, though."

"I know you are. And thanks for agreeing to take care of things for me."

Cassie promised to call the next week so they could check in with each other. Then Claire was gone, not looking back.

"She really is a good friend, isn't she," Griffin said.

"The best," Cassie replied. "The very best."

After picking up cartons at the U-Haul place, their last stop before going back to the apartment was to say goodbye to Mike. That was nearly as hard for Cassie as lunch with Claire.

Mike was his usually gruff self, helping her clear out her desk, handing her a final paycheck. "Something happens to her, you'll answer to me," he told Griffin, taking a hard look at him.

Griffin rested a proprietary hand at Cassie's waist, giving Mike the same look back. "I'll be taking good care of her." His voice was firm.

Mike just grunted but gave her an uncharacteristic hug. "Anything at all, you call me." Then he waved them both away.

"You made quite a life for yourself without me," Griffin commented when they were back in the car. He stared out the windshield, trying to shut down the unreasoning jealousy he'd felt all day.

"Did you think I wouldn't? If so, you really don't know me at all."

He shook his head. "No, you did exactly what I was afraid you'd do. You locked me away and moved ahead." He leaned close to her and kissed her ear, teasing it with his tongue.

She nearly ran the car off the road. "God. Don't do that when I'm driving."

"But not quite completely away, right, sugar?" His voice sounded like warm honey.

"No. Not completely." She smiled to herself. "I think you know that by now."

"It's nice to see how everyone respects you, though. You're a complex person, Cassie. People appreciate you. But so do I. Just don't forget that."

Dinner was sandwiches from the deli, eaten while they took a break from packing and cleaning. Cassie was cleaning out the drawers in her bedroom when she heard Griffin say, "Well, well. What have we here?"

She turned to see him holding a narrow black case from her nightstand drawer.

"Give it here." She'd forgotten her vibrator was stashed there. She should have snuck it into her suitcase when Griff wasn't looking.

"Uh-uh." He held it above his head. "Was this your substitute for me, sugar?"

She felt her cheeks redden and dropped her eyes. "Yes. Now come on. Give it back."

"Under one condition." He tilted her face up, forcing her to look at him. "Let me watch you use it. One time, here in this place. Okay?"

She couldn't believe how embarrassed she was, after all the intimate things they'd done together. "I...don't think I can."

"Sure you can. I'll help you. Come on. We can finish this other stuff in the morning. We're almost done anyway." He pulled her against him, his lips brushing her temple, his hand smoothing her hair. "Cassie, I love you. I would never do anything to make you feel uncomfortable. Whatever we do together is good and right. It would please me to see the pleasure on your face when you make yourself feel good, knowing that you're thinking of me when you're doing it." He brushed his lips against her forehead. "But if you don't want to, it's okay."

"No, it's all right," she whispered on a shuddering breath.

He pressed soft kisses to her cheeks and eyelids. "Trust me. Please."

While they showered he let his hands roam lightly over her, murmuring in her ear exactly what he wanted her to do and how he wanted her to do it. They'd picked up a bottle of wine and he'd brought a glass of it into the shower with them, feeding her light sips as he whispered to her. She began to shake just from listening to him.

By the time he'd dried her off and led her to the bed, she was already flushed with the first heat of passion.

"All right, sugar. Like this." He lowered her to her back, then bent her legs so her feet were flat on the sheet. With a gentle touch he spread her legs as wide apart as he could get them. "Lick your fingers, Cassie. Just the tips. Yes, like that."

She ran her tongue over her fingertips, wetting them with her saliva, her eyes never leaving his face.

"Okay. Put your hands between your legs and pull those sweet lips apart. Let me see that beautiful cunt that I love so much. Do it, Cassie." As he talked, he'd shed his clothes and now he was sitting on the bed at her feet, eyes focused on the spot between her legs.

Still self-conscious but wanting to share her private pleasure with Griffin, she slid her hands down through the nest of curls and separated her labia, already tingling with anticipation. She was wide open to him and his eyes feasted on her in greedy appreciation.

"Good, honey. Very good. Oh, yes, I love that sweet place so much. Now show me how you tease that little clit when you're by yourself and thinking of me. Yes, that's it. Pull back that tiny hood and let me see it all."

She closed her eyes and in her mind she was in her bedroom alone, Griffin's face dancing beneath her eyelids, her body craving his. She used her fingertips to expose her swollen nub and without any prompting began moving one finger back and forth over its tip, feeling the heat inside her escalating.

"Now inside, Cassie." His voice was a whisper and his hands were lightly caressing the outside of her thighs. "Put your fingers inside."

Obediently she slid two fingers into her vagina and began stroking herself as she'd done so many times before. Her body began to move with the rhythm, one fingertip still moving in a steady rhythm on her clitoris, now so sensitive she could hardly stand to touch it. In and out her hand moved, while the coil in her body wound tighter and tighter and like windswept clouds, any embarrassment fell away.

"Okay, sugar. Now the big guy." He handed her the vibrator, already turned on. "God, Cassie, you don't know how hot it makes me to know you did this imagining us together." He placed his hands on her knees, his thumbs drawing gentle circles, his eyes hot with need.

She fell into her remembered pattern, stroking the instrument over her clitoris, into her channel, around and around the opening damp with the evidence of her desire. As her nerves caught fire, she slid the vibrator all the way inside her, holding it with one hand while she stroked herself with the other.

"Beautiful," Griffin murmured. "Just beautiful." As he crooned to her he rubbed the backs and insides of her thighs, ran his fingertips along the crease where her thighs joined her body, brushed lightly against the curls now so wet they were plastered against her skin. "I'm going to give you an orgasm that will blow your mind, sugar. Just keep your eyes closed and feel."

She couldn't even think any more, she was so intent on reaching that elusive peak. Her body was one sensual flame, so aroused and so alive she felt as if her skin had been peeled back.

"I love this cream, darlin'." He was holding the little tube he'd found with the vibrator. "It smells like peaches. Just like you. Do you use this on the vibrator when you're fucking yourself? I've got a better use for it." She could hardly process what he was saying, she was so lost in a sensual fog. But then she felt Griffin's hand slide into the cleft between her buttocks, rubbing and massaging the cream into her skin.

He moved his hand back and forth, rubbing the crevice, tickling at the entrance to the one place he hadn't yet plundered. And then, just as she pressed harder with the vibrator and her hand moved faster, she felt him slip one finger inside that hot, dark place. His thumb caressed the tender skin just below her vaginal opening, he pressed a second finger into her anus to join the first and she came, an orgasm so shattering she didn't think her body could stand it. She cried his name over and over, bucking, twisting, pushing—wanting it to last, wanting it to end.

And then it did end and she fell back exhausted, panting for breath, her heart thundering, a fine layer of sweat coating her body.

But Griffin wasn't done. As she lay there trembling with aftershocks, he kissed his way down her body, nipping at her breasts, her navel, the soft hair between her legs. He slid the vibrator out and replaced it with his tongue, drinking the fluid she'd spilled for him, feeling the heat rise in her again.

She reached automatically for his penis, feeling it so engorged she didn't know how he kept from going off.

"God, Cassie," he whispered, "I can't ever get enough of you. You turn me on like no other woman ever has. I worship you, dewdrop."

With gentle hands he turned her over and began trailing kisses down her spine, just as he had the other night. No area was left untouched. His lips slid over the satiny skin of her calves, the backs of her knees, her inner thighs. He inhaled her fragrance, peaches and strawberries mingled with the scent of her sex. Then he was at her hole again, pressing the head of his cock against the tight opening.

"I've wanted to do this since that very first night six years ago." His voice was soft, loving. "I didn't think you trusted me enough then. You trust me now, though, don't you, Cassie?"

"Yes." The word hissed out between her teeth. She was so lost in an erotic fog she couldn't think. She only knew this was Griffin, who could do whatever he wanted with her body and she'd take pleasure in it.

He leaned forward and licked her shoulder. "Good, darlin', because I want you so bad this way I can hardly see straight. I love you, Cassie, more than I ever thought I'd love another human being. I want to have you every way I can, to make you totally mine. Is that okay, sugar? Tell me, Cassie."

As he talked he squeezed more cream from the tube he'd found, lazily rubbed the globes of her buttocks and slid his fingers along the separation. Then, wanting not to frighten her, one knuckle at a time he eased his finger into that place he had yet to fill with his cock, feeling the heat grab the cream from his skin until he was sure she was well-lubricated.

"It's all right, Griff. I love you." Then she jerked, tensing, as his finger intruded further. "Griffin?"

"It's okay. Everything we do is okay, remember? I promise you'll love this. I promise I'll never do anything to hurt you. Any time you want me to stop, just say so." He was fighting to keep his voice even. "Cassie, I wouldn't do this with just anyone. It's too intimate. Trust me, all right?"

Hastily he rolled a condom onto his swollen penis. Scooping the fluid still seeping from her vagina to moisten his cock, he positioned himself behind her, pulled her to her knees, separated her buttocks and pressed steadily inside her. When she cried out at the unexpected entrance, he began kissing her skin again and pressed his hand against her mound to pull her tight against him.

"Just relax. You'll be fine in a minute. Breathe, Cassie."

Slipping the tip of one finger onto her clitoris and gently massaging it, he continued his invasion until the entire length of him was swallowed up by her hot, tight rectum. He began thrusting in and out of her, with long, slow strokes. He gritted his teeth as he felt control slipping away from him, willing himself to hold off so he could make it good for her.

Cassie bit down against the first shock of invasion but in a moment it was replaced by a feeling she could only call lust. Every nerve, every muscle in her body responded to this new assault. Before she even realized it, she was moving in rhythm with him, shoving her hips back against him, driving him deeper, her body wrapped in sharp, fierce pleasure. She felt him filling the hollow of her body, his penis so large she didn't know how he got it in, yet it wasn't enough.

She felt his body against hers, his skin heated and she wanted to wrap herself in him and stay there forever. He whispered in her ear, erotic words, sexy words, love words. Everything receded except herself and Griffin in this time, this place.

And then it began to build, swiftly, the tremors, the spasms, sensation piling on sensation and she heard herself screaming. "Now, Griffin. Now. Now." As she shouted she forced herself hard against him.

When they came in a simultaneous explosion, they shook the bed, Cassie's screams so loud Griffin thought the neighbors would hear. His own body convulsed with such force he thought his heart would stop. When they collapsed, he slid out of her and pulled her tight against him, raining kisses on her forehead, her cheeks, her nose, stroking her arms and her shoulder.

"I love you, Cassie. And you're mine. I will do anything in the world to make you happy. All that matters is that we're together."

"I love you too, Griffin. More than my life." And she did. Never had she expected to have this kind of connection with someone, be so treasured by them, so worshiped.

He left the bed long enough to dispose of the condom. She heard the water running in the bathroom, then he was beside her again. She snuggled her body against him, feeling the slow thud of is heart against her back.

And they slept.

Chapter Eighteen

ॐ

They were ready to leave as the sun was coming up, wanting to cover as much distance as they could.

"I hope the next residents living here enjoy it as much as we did." The corner of Griffin's mouth turned up in a teasing grin as they took a last look around.

"Impossible." Cassie laughed and hugged him. "Just plain impossible."

The memory of the things they'd done the night before made her body glow. Her last vestige of self-consciousness had vanished and she wanted to tell Griffin how eager she was to explore more uncharted sexual waters with him.

As they emerged into the parking lot, a white convertible squealed into the lot and stopped in front of them. Cassie was stunned to see Claire emerge.

"I can't believe you got up this early." Cassie hugged her tightly.

"I wanted one last look at the gorgeous hunk," Claire whispered.

Griffin was leaning against the car, giving them some space. In his soft jeans, tee shirt and aviator shades, with the wind riffling his wheat-colored hair, he could have stepped from the pages of a romance novel.

"Don't let him get away," she told Cassie. "He loves you. It's there in his eyes and the way he touches you. If you ask me, he always did."

"Don't worry. I'm hanging onto him this time." She gave Claire a lingering look. "I'll call you when we get to Stoneham.

Thanks again for taking care of everything. And you'd better start planning a trip out west."

"If there are any more like him back there, I'll be hard on your heels."

One more stop at a drive through for coffee and they said goodbye to Tampa. They followed U.S. 19 north nearly to Jacksonville where they picked up Interstate 10 heading west. Cassie tried to find a comfortable place to put her body but the activities of the night before had left her tender in places she didn't even know she had.

Griffin reached over and squeezed her knee, trying to hide the self-satisfied smile teasing at his mouth. "A little sore today, are we?"

"Get that smug look off your face, buster." Cassie grimaced but said, "I'm fine."

Griffin laughed, a rich, full sound. "Can I tell you that making love with you is a most extraordinary experience?"

Cassie laced her fingers through his fingers still resting on her knee. "For me too, Griffin."

She started to say something more when his cell phone rang. He spoke briefly, then snapped the phone shut, his jaw clenching.

"What? What is it?"

"That was Phil. He's been cruising by your house like I asked, checking things out. Apparently sometime last night our mysterious visitor decided to show up again and got inside."

"What do you mean?" She was shocked. "You mean someone broke into my house?"

"Exactly. It happened sometime between about ten last night when Phil went by the first time and four this morning when he checked it on his way home from a late night out. He decided for some reason to walk around the house, just in case and found the glass in the back door broken."

"Did he go inside? Was anything taken?"

"He went in only a little way. He said it was obvious from what little he could see that someone had been in there searching but he didn't spend much time checking it out."

"What should I do? Should I call Dangler?" She gripped her hands together. "You were afraid something like this might happen."

"Don't call anyone yet." His hands gripped the steering wheel. "First of all, I don't want to put Phil in a spot. Secondly, I don't think they'll be back, at least for the moment. They don't know when we're supposed to return. Plus people are around more on the weekends and the intruder won't want to take any more chances than he or she has already taken."

"I need to call Carol. What if she's showing the house while we're gone?"

Cassie swallowed against the nausea rising in her throat. Someone had actually broken into her house. She felt violated, defenseless. Griffin reached over and took her hands in one of his. The warmth from his body seeped into hers and chased the away the cold creeping over her.

"Don't sweat it. It might even be good if she were the one who found the break-in."

"But…"

"I know it will be hard but you've got to put it out of your mind 'til we get back. Besides, this is good, in a way. It means we were right. Someone's definitely looking for something. We just have to figure out what it is."

Before either of them could say anything else, Cassie's cell rang.

"This is Carol," the breathless voice said. "Something awful has happened. Where are you?"

"We're passing Mobile, Alabama. Why?"

"I went by to check on your house. I actually have a showing already, believe it or not. And it's a disaster."

Griffin glanced at her quickly and she mouthed *Carol.* "What do you mean by a disaster? The showing or the house? What's wrong?"

"Cassie, someone's broken into your house. It's just awful." Carol's voice was a mixture of horror and excitement.

Cassie could almost hear her drooling at the thought of the gossip she'd have to pass around. "I-I don't know what to say. Did they do much damage?"

"Luckily no. I called Barry Dangler and he said he'd send someone by to take a look but I couldn't wait. I did make arrangements to get the back door fixed, though, since someone broke the glass in order to get in." She paused. "But I don't think I can show it again until you come back and figure out what's going on. My client won't want to buy a house that's a target for robbery."

"I think someone just saw an empty house and tried their luck." Cassie rubbed her forehead. "I'll call Barry and see what's going on. Can you hold onto your client a little bit?"

There was a long pause. "Did you say 'we'?" Carol said at last.

Cassie wanted to laugh out loud. Her house was burglarized, she had a jittery buyer and Carol was looking for dirt. "Yes, I did. Griffin Hunter is with me."

"I see." More silence. "It's really none of my business but…"

"I don't mean to be rude but you're right, Carol," she interrupted. "It really *is* none of your business. Anyway, we should be back very late tomorrow night. I'll call you early Monday."

"Carol giving you advice?" Griffin grinned when she hung up.

"What do you think? Let me tell you something. She may be holier-than-thou but she and every other woman in that town would give their household treasure to trade places with me."

"You don't know what you're talking about." His voice had an edge of anger. "All those *nice* ladies would run me out of town in a hot flash if they could."

"All those *nice* ladies would rip their clothes off for you if you gave them half a chance. It's all about forbidden fruit, Griffin. When the town bad boy is wickedly sexy, it makes the forbidden fruit that much more tempting. You were every female's guilty pleasure. They might point fingers at me now but every one of them wishes they were in my shoes—or bed."

Griffin threw back his head and laughed and the sound broke the tension the calls had generated. "Well, damn, Cassie. If I'd known that I'd have figured out how to take advantage of all that free flesh long before this."

She thumped him on the thigh again.

"You'd better quit that or we'll have an accident. That was just a joke, sugar, although I must say, it was good for my ego." He reached his arm over and slid his hand between her thighs. "They're nothing, Cassie. This is where my heart is." He gave her a slight squeeze that made her squeal and he pulled his hand back. "And don't go thinking it's just sex again, because you have to know it isn't. Sure we're great in bed. But that's because of how we feel about each other. You're the only good thing that's ever come into my life. Like I keep telling you, this is real."

She slid over as close to him as the seat belt would allow. "It is real," she told him. "I can't tell you how free I feel when we make love but that's only because I do know it's more than sex."

"For me too, darlin'. I do things with you that with anyone else would just be physical exercise. But every time we make love, I feel as if our souls are mating."

Cassie felt a tightness in her throat. Griffin was not a man given to poetic declarations, so his words had all the more meaning for her. She touched the locket around her neck where the tiny heart was enclosed. "I'll always keep your heart safe, Griffin. Always."

* * * * *

They pushed themselves hard for two days and pulled into Cassie's driveway late Sunday night.

"I'm not even sure I want to deal with this now." She was tired, depressed, dreading what they'd find and angry at the violation of her privacy.

"Tell you what." Griffin came around the car. "Let me go take a quick look and I'll tell you if we need to do something tonight. My guess is no."

"Uh-uh. I need to go in, just to see for myself what the damage is. Then we can make a decision."

He made her give him her keys, though, insisting he should go in the front door ahead of her. What she found wasn't as bad as she'd imagined. Things were moved around slightly. Some drawers in the old-fashioned desk were still pulled out a little and the kitchen cupboards hung open. She could tell where furniture had been moved.

Griffin went through the upstairs and came back to report it appeared to be the same as the downstairs. "No real damage," he told her. "But you can certainly tell someone's been through here."

"I checked the back door. I guess Carol had them replace the whole door with one that doesn't have glass panes."

"Probably a good idea. I say leave it for tonight and in the morning you can call Dangler and get him out here. You at least need to make a report and Carol's alerted him."

She sighed heavily. "You're right. At this moment I want a shower and bed more than you can imagine."

"Come on, then." Griffin hustled her back out to the car, locking the door behind him.

"Where are we going?"

"My house." He backed out of the driveway. "I can pull your car into the garage and I have an alarm system."

"Griff, I don't think…"

He knew what was on her mind. He reached over and gently touched her cheek. "I know what's on your mind and I understand. But our only other option is going to a motel and you know everyone in town would be parked outside our room come morning."

"I hate this." She pounded a fist on her knee.

Griffin pulled over to the curb and put the car in park. "Listen, Cassie. Diane and I slept in that room but it was a long, long time ago, if that's what's on your mind. I've lived in it by myself for most of my life. It's my personality, not hers in there." He grinned. "I even bought a new bed and sheets."

"Oh, Griffin." She leaned over and put her head on his shoulder. She was too worn out even to cry. "All right. I guess if you can do it, I can. Maybe it's just one more thing to get past."

It seemed only minutes before they were at Griffin's house. He opened the garage door with the remote control he'd taken with him and pulled her car inside. After disarming the alarm panel, he led her into the house, carrying only the overnight bag they'd used the night before at the motel.

Cassie stopped in the living room and stared. Whatever she'd expected, it wasn't what she found.

The house was spotless. The kitchen they came through gleamed as if it had just been polished and the living room, although threadbare, was neat as a pin. When she followed Griffin upstairs to his room, she got another shock. The room was definitely furnished for a man. A king sized bed was covered in a navy and tan quilt. Bookshelves lined two walls. And everything, not just the bed, looked fairly new.

Griffin chuckled, watching her. "Were you imagining one step up from the homeless shelter?"

"I didn't know what to expect," she said truthfully. "I'm amazed."

"Bad boys don't have to live like slobs, you know." Pain flashed briefly across his face. "After my father died I was determined never to let the house go the way he did."

In the bathroom he handed her towels and soap and gave her privacy to shower. He knew instinctively she'd need time to adjust to being in his house, the place where he'd lived with Diane, even for such a short time. He used the bathroom off what had been his parents' bedroom.

He could have moved into the bigger room any time since his father died but he'd shied away from it. What he really wanted was to get rid of the house altogether but that would take some planning and finagling. This was one of the things he and Cassie could handle together.

She was waiting for him when he got back to his room, standing by the window with her hands clasped behind her back.

"It's okay to get in the bed, sugar," he told her. "No one's ever slept in it but me. Come on. Let me show you." He led her over to the bed, turned back the covers and gently nudged her into it.

She lay back, her eyes never leaving his face. Then he was lying next to her, cradling her in his arms, soothing her with his hands and his voice. She was strung tighter than telephone wire. He rubbed her back, her shoulders, her neck, his hands warm against her. He put his lips next to her ear.

"Shall we chase some ghosts, Cassie?" His voice was quiet and low and then his mouth came down on hers.

Tired as they were, it was what they both needed. A door needed to slam shut for them and now was the time to do it.

It wasn't the frantic lovemaking of that first night, or the sensual exploratory kind they'd indulged in since then. It was more a blending of soul and mind and heart—a recognition that while the past might always be with them, they wouldn't let it hurt them.

Griffin's mouth and hands were everywhere, kissing and licking, teasing first her nipples, then her throbbing clit. He penetrated her channel first with his fingers and then with his mouth, building the pleasure in his body.

Panting heavily, she suddenly pushed hard and shoved him onto his back. Rising to her knees, she took his shaft into her mouth, probing the slit in the head with her tongue and stroking his balls with teasing fingers. When she squeezed them his whole body tightened next to her and he pulled her head away.

"Inside you," he whispered. "I want to be inside you when I come."

Barely taking the time to sheath himself, he pushed her knees back against her chest to open her wide to him and slid inside. She gripped him with the muscles of her cunt, milking him, knowing they were both close. So very close.

The climax this time was like the gentle rolling of a heavy tide, the spasms like white caps beating against a shore. Griffin dropped the condom into the wastebasket beside the bed, then pulled Cassie tightly against him. She could feel the rhythmic beat of his heart, feel his breath against her skin.

"I love you," she whispered.

"I love you more."

And strangely, in this place where it should have been the worst, Cassie no longer felt Diane hovering over her, mocking her.

In the morning, however, the real world intruded again and not very pleasantly.

Chapter Nineteen

ဢ

Cassie stood in her living room listening to Barry Dangler and getting angrier by the minute.

"This was a real break-in, Barry," she spat at him. "Don't try to make out it's nothing."

"Well, why in the hell would anyone want to break in here?" he demanded. "What could they even want?"

"That's what I'm trying to find out and that's what I'm asking you to check into." She was furious. "Why is it you just want to sweep it under the carpet, the way you did with Diane's death?"

"Whoa, there." Now *he* was angry. "Back off there, Cassie. Nobody's sweeping anything under the rug. And I'm still convinced that somehow, some way, Griffin Hunter engineered what happened with your sister."

"Well, he didn't break into my house. He was with me in Florida when it happened."

"There's always his friend, Phil. We noticed him cruising by here a few times."

Cassie wanted to stamp her foot or throw something. She was beyond frustrated. "We asked Phil to keep an eye on the house, Chief, because we were afraid something like this would happen. And Phil wouldn't have to break in like that. He's a locksmith. He could have done it without any trace. Besides, what would be his motive?"

Dangler glanced casually around the room. "Lots of valuable stuff here, you know. Mighty tempting."

"Oh, please. Now you're reaching. First you tell me there's no reason for a robbery, now you tell me I've got stuff anyone would want to steal. You can't have it both ways, Chief. What's going on here, anyway? Why are you giving me such a bad time?"

Dangler gave her a hard look. "You run with the wrong people, Cassie, most anything can happen."

Just like that it was clear to her. As long as Griffin Hunter was sleeping in her bed and was a part of her life, she'd be tarred with the same brush the town used on him. This was exactly what he'd warned her about but she hadn't realized just how serious bad it could be.

With a supreme effort she controlled the anger raging in her. "Fine." She turned away from him. "Just write up some kind of report so I'll have it for the insurance company. I won't bother you again. If I have a problem, I'll take care of it myself. Just remember, I still have a sister whose murder hasn't ever been solved. I won't stop poking my nose around until I get some answers."

"You might not like what you find," the chief said in a flat voice.

Cassie gritted her teeth. She was tired of hearing this from everyone. "At least I'll be the one to find it, since you and everyone else seems to think we're not worth bothering about."

"Cassie, I didn't mean..."

"Yes, you did. You can show yourself out."

She spent the morning putting the house back in order, dusting and vacuuming as she went along. She needed to keep it in shape for any prospective buyers.

At noon she called Carol, thanked her for everything she'd done and told her the place was ready to show again.

"I know I shouldn't be saying this, Cassie," Carol began.

Cassie interrupted her. "That's enough. Do you want the listing or not, Carol? I certainly don't mind calling somebody else."

"Who on earth would you call?" Carol sounded so astonished Cassie nearly laughed.

"Strange as this may seem to you, there are other real estate agents in Texas."

"But we're the experts in this area." Carol still couldn't quite get herself under control. "We're the best you can get."

"Then I suggest you do your job and leave my personal business out of this. Let me know when your client wants a showing again." She hung up the phone a little more vehemently than necessary but it gave her some measure of satisfaction.

Cassie spent the rest of the morning unpacking her car and putting things away. The cartons coming on the moving van she would store in Griffin's garage on a temporary basis.

She called the bank, relieved to learn all the papers for the annuities had been processed and the appropriate checks transmitted electronically. In the end she had chosen to take only one in a lump sum, opening a money market account with it. The other she would continue to receive payments from until the balance had been reduced to zero. She realized she still hadn't told Griffin about the windfall and made a mental note to do so.

That done, she decided to go through all the clothes in the garage. Family Services always needed clothing so after checking everything thoroughly she would ship it all over to them.

But before she could get started, Neil called.

"I just wanted to make sure you were all right," he told her.

"I'm fine, Neil. Why wouldn't I be? Is there something I should not be fine about?"

"Not at all, not at all." Cassie could almost see him thinking of how to rephrase his words. "I heard about the break-in and I just felt a responsibility to check on you."

She bit down on her temper, but failed to keep the sarcasm from her voice. "I didn't realize the break-in was in the paper so soon. News sure gets around this town in a hurry."

"Stoneham is a small town," he reminded her. "We all look out for each other."

"If that's true, how come Barry Dangler is trying to blow off what happened? If Griffin hadn't been with me, I'm sure he'd have him in jail for it. And if everyone is so very concerned, how come Diane's murder is still unsolved?"

There was a long silence at the other end of the line. Cassie could almost hear Neil turning sentences over in his mind.

"Cassie, you need to leave Diane alone. She's dead and that's unfortunate but your sister lived a life that could only end in some kind of violence. You need to get on with yours. Away from Stoneham. Away from Griffin Hunter. Maybe coming back here wasn't such a good idea for you after all."

"Is that a threat?" she asked quietly. "Or do you know something you'd rather I didn't find out?"

"That's totally unfair," he protested. "I'm just saying let sleeping dogs lie. If you hadn't gotten yourself mixed up with Griffin you wouldn't be on this kick."

"You are so wrong. Diane was my sister, no matter what you think of her. And she's not just dead, she was murdered. I'm entitled to some answers."

"Fine. But don't blame me if you don't like the ones you get."

They terminated the conversation without either of them saying goodbye.

Cassie's rage, which had been slowly receding, threatened to erupt again. She decided the best thing would be to attack the project out in the garage.

* * * * *

Despite the heat of the day, the garage wasn't too unbearable. Cassie found an old fan in the corner, which she plugged in and opened the back door to get some circulation. Sitting cross-legged on the floor, she pulled the first box toward her and began lifting things out. Her mother's things.

The familiar scent of the rose sachets her mother had used for as long as she could remember still clung faintly to the garments. On impulse, she held a blouse to her cheek, the material soft against her skin. Tears welled up for all the hugs she'd never received and for the last six years when she might as well have had no mother.

One by one she lifted out each garment, examined it for usability and folded it neatly, stacking everything in piles around her. In an hour she had gone through several cartons, rejecting only a few items. When she was nearly finished, she was startled to see it contained her father's clothes. The box must have been in the garage all this time.

Out of habit she checked each of the pockets, not really expecting to find anything. But in the back pocket of one pair of slacks, her fingers encountered a slip of paper. She withdrew it carefully and unfolded it. Something was written on it, faded now with age and she had to walk to the open door to get better light. Her heart thumped when she read what was written.

You'd better rein in that bitch daughter of yours or you and she are both dead. Ten o'clock tonight.

Cassie's hand began to shake. Did this mean her father knew what was going on with Diane? And what would that have been? How did her father figure into it? Who had he been meeting? The questions came so fast she got dizzy.

Pulling herself together she picked up the portable phone she'd brought into the garage and dialed the chief's office. Knowing she'd get precious little from him, she still had to try.

"What is it now, Cassie?" He sounded tired — of her, more than anything. "Haven't you stirred things up enough already?"

She forced herself to swallow a quick retort. "I was going through some things in the house and it just occurred to me I never actually saw a report of my father's suicide. Do you have one?"

"Shit, Cassie, now you're seeing problems where none exist. Maybe if you'd come home for the funeral you'd have found out then."

"I didn't call for a lecture, just to ask a simple question. Can you answer it for me?"

"I guess so." His sigh carried through the connection. "Otherwise you'll be down here driving me crazy again. Yes, there's a report. Cut and dried. Nothing funny."

"All I ever knew was he became depressed after Diane's death and six months later someone found him in his car, in the park. He'd shot himself with that old gun he kept around."

"That's correct. That's all there was to it. I suppose you want a copy of that report too?"

"Yes, if you don't mind. I'd like to come by and pick it up now."

"I do mind but I don't guess there's any getting around it. But you need to give me a day or two, just like with Diane. All those old files are in storage."

Cassie blew out her breath in exasperation. "All right. Wednesday afternoon, then. But don't put me off."

"I'll have it for you." She could tell he was irritated. "But I'm getting real pissed off at all the cans of worms you want to keep opening. Go back to Florida, Cassie. You don't belong here."

"You won't get rid of me that easily. For your information—and everyone else you'll share it with—I quit my job and gave up my apartment. I'm back to stay."

She waited for him to say something. To show some reaction. There was such a long silence, she didn't know if he was still there.

"Chief?" she prompted.

"I think that's a big mistake," he said finally. "You're making yourself pretty unpopular around here, you know."

"I didn't know I had to win a popularity contest to stay in this town." She was getting madder by the minute.

"Go away, Cassie. Anywhere. And take that damned Griffin Hunter with you. Good riddance to you both."

She pressed the disconnect button as viciously as she could. She was glad she and Griff had already decided to move when this was all over. Stoneham was making her sicker by the day.

Her hand was still on the telephone when it rang again.

"Hello, Cassie. Just checking on you since you got back."

Cassie exhaled heavily. "Hello, Harley. I'm fine, thank you. And apparently still sticking my nose in where it isn't wanted."

"Cassie, honey." His voice had his best bedside manner tone to it. "We're just looking after your welfare, you know. You're stirring up a lot of things best left untouched. If you plan to stay in this town, you don't want to be raising everyone's hackles. Especially over nothing."

"You call my sister's murder nothing? Harley, I thought you were a friend to my family."

His sigh traveled through the connection. "I am, sweetheart. I'm still trying to be one."

"Duly noted. And who says we're staying in Stoneham, anyway?"

"I don't understand."

"And you don't have to. Thanks for the call. Goodbye, Harley."

The one box she had yet to open was the one containing all the papers from her father's desk. After finding the slip of paper, she couldn't bring herself to face any more discoveries at the moment. She'd need Griffin beside her to do that.

By seven she had finally showered, changed into fresh shorts and shirt and was lying on the couch letting aspirin work on her headache when Griffin came home. He carried two white paper sacks.

"I figured you'd be too busy today to cook," he told her, dropping a kiss on her forehead. "And it's too hot for anything heavy. I got fruit and veggie platters from the deli along with some chicken wings. Okay?"

"That's wonderful," she said. "You're wonderful. Come here and let me show you how wonderful."

"Wait 'til I shower," he said. "I'm sweaty and dirty. I'll just be a minute."

When they'd finished eating and were sitting at the kitchen table, drinking their iced tea, she pulled the slip of paper out of her pocket.

"I found this today." She watched his face for a reaction.

"What the hell is this about?" He was as puzzled as she was. He turned the paper over, looking at both sides to see if he'd missed something.

"I guess that's what I'm asking you. Does this mean anything to you?"

"No." He smoothed it out with his fingers. "But let's see if we can figure it out."

Cassie nibbled on her thumbnail. "I know this is a terrible thing to ask you but could Diane have known who the real father of her baby was and been blackmailing him?"

"Anything is possible where Diane was concerned." His words were tinged with bitterness. "I think there's a lot none of us knew about her."

"And how does my father fit into all of this? Who could he have been meeting? I'm more confused than ever." She closed her eyes for a moment, then snapped them open. "I almost forgot. I called the chief today to ask about a report on my father's suicide and he wasn't any too happy with my request."

"I'm sure he wasn't." Griffin laughed shortly. "You're giving him the biggest headache he's had in a long time."

"Something's not right here, Griffin." She swallowed the last of her iced tea, then rolled the glass against her forehead. "There's just too many unanswered questions floating around. Like, did my father really commit suicide?"

"Don't get carried away, Cassie, seeing bogeymen where there aren't any."

"I'm not," she insisted. "I know my father was very depressed after…what happened…but I never could see him killing himself. It just didn't make sense, no matter what my mother said. I told the chief I'd pick up the report on Wednesday. He didn't seem too happy but he couldn't very well refuse me."

"We have a lot to check out," Griffin agreed, "and we need to do it carefully and quietly. You can't charge around anymore with a big sign on your forehead. If someone out there really killed your father as well as Diane, he won't hesitate to get rid of you, either."

Cassie shivered as a sudden chill raced over her. "You know, everyone seems to want you and me to leave town. Do you have that feeling?"

Griffin laughed out loud. "Hell, they've been wanting me to leave for years. That's nothing new."

"I want to talk to you about something," she said slowly, "and I don't know if this is the right time or not."

"You look like I might bite you. Why don't we go sit outside?" He stood up and took her hand. "It's always easier to talk in the dark."

When they were sitting in the lounge chairs, hands linked in the space between them, she asked, "Were you serious when you asked me to marry you?"

His fingers tensed on hers. "I thought I made it pretty clear that I want the whole ball of wax. You, a home, kids. I thought you understood that."

"I needed you to say that again," she told him. "Because that means we're partners in everything, right?"

In a moment he was beside her on the edge of her chair, his hands on her shoulders, his mouth hard on hers. "But I remind you I have precious little to offer you," he told her, when he raised his head. "I have plans but haven't quite figured out how to make them all happen yet. And as long as you're with me, you'll be an outcast here. But I love you and I want to marry you." He moved back to his own chair. "So, what's this all about?"

She drew a deep breath and let it out. "If we sell both houses and you sell your business, we'll have a nice little bundle of cash. I told you my mother had two good-sized annuities my father left her. I kept one of them as-is because it gives me some income but I cashed out the other one. The money's already in the bank. I want us to buy that land you showed me and the nursery. You know how much is there. We've got enough cash that by the time we combine everything we'll be free and clear of debt."

She sat very still, waiting for him to say something. For a long moment she thought he was going to get up and leave. Had she offered too much too soon? Hurt his pride in some way?

"I can't take your money," he told her at last. "I'd feel bought and paid for."

"That is just so ridiculous," she exploded. "Why did you take me out there if you didn't think it was something we could both share? Answer that for me."

When he didn't say anything, just sat quietly in the dark, she sat up, spitting fire. "You aren't *taking* anything. This is for both of us. Let me be part of this, please. Knowing we're doing together this will make everything else we have to do that much easier. Please, Griffin."

She clenched her teeth so hard waiting for him to speak again she thought her jaw would break. "We're either together or we're not. Here's your chance to show me you meant what you said. We can do this. Together."

"All right." He rubbed his forehead. "I do want us to have a life together. I'm just not used to this. You know that." He looked at her intently. "But your name goes on everything too. Whatever we do is for both of us."

"If we're getting married, I guess so." She moved over to his chair and hugged him, leaning close to him. Suddenly she felt more lighthearted than she had since they'd gotten back into town. "It will make leaving this town a reality."

"But I have something I want to do first," he told her.

"What?" She scrunched her eyebrows, puzzled.

"You'll see. Tomorrow." And that was all he'd tell her.

Chapter Twenty

ഇ

The moving van arrived at Griffin's house the next day and the men stacked all of Cassie's cartons in the garage. Not much to show for six years, she thought, then shook herself. Her life wasn't in the past but in the future with Griffin.

Carol called to tell her she had two showings she'd like to schedule. When would be good for her? Two possibles. Cassie crossed her fingers. They settled on Wednesday afternoon while Cassie would be out.

"I'd be ecstatic if we got rid of this place that soon," she told Griffin that night. "Some people have fond memories of the house they grew up in. Not me. Good riddance, I say. So. How was your day?"

He picked up one of her hands and rubbed his thumb over her knuckles in a gesture rapidly becoming both familiar and comforting.

"I took you at your word," he told her. "I called the owner of the nursery and asked if we could come by and talk to him. I also called the agent listing that property."

"And?" she prompted.

"We can go by and see both of them Saturday." He looked hard at her. "You sure we're not rushing this too fast? I feel like we're on a roller coaster."

"It's time to move fast, Griffin. We spent the last six years standing still. And as soon as my house sells, you need to list yours." She laughed. "That'll certainly give the town something to talk about."

"Like they don't have enough already."

"Maybe if they talk enough," she pointed out, "we'll find out something no one wants to tell us."

"Don't hold your breath," he snorted, then reached into the pocket of his jeans. "But I have a requirement."

"Oh? Does this have to do with the business you wouldn't tell me about?"

"Everything to do with it. Close your eyes."

"Why?"

"Cassie, just for once don't ask questions and do as I say."

She closed her eyes and in a moment felt him taking her hand and doing something with her fingers.

"Okay, open."

Her eyes nearly popped out of head at the sight of the solitaire diamond Griffin had slipped onto her finger. "My God, this must have cost the earth."

"I told you I had some money put away. I want to advertise what we're doing to all of Stoneham. It's very important to me that everyone know I love you and we're making a life together."

Cassie laughed. "This is better than an ad in the paper. But you shouldn't have…"

His mouth closed over hers. "Yes. I should. I should have done it six years ago." He searched her eyes. "Do you like it? If not…"

"Are you kidding? I love it." She held her hand out so the moonlight could catch the sparkle.

"Maybe we should go upstairs and make this official." His grin was wicked.

She was already ahead of him, stripping off her clothes as she moved through the house.

"Impatient, are we?" he asked, as he caught up with her.

"You bet."

By the time they reached the bedroom they were both naked. Tonight they were too eager to take their time. Cassie reached for Griffin's cock as he lay down next to her, stroking and pulling, the tip of her nail seeking the familiar slit in the velvety head. Thick moisture was already seeping from it. She loved the feel of the soft skin over the hard rod it covered and the heaviness of his balls as she reached down further to cradle the sac in her hand.

"I'll go off in a second if you keep doing that, sugar." His voice was husky, strained with the effort at control.

"Good. That's what I want."

"But not until I'm inside you." He lifted her legs over his shoulders and, as he had done the other night, spread the petal-soft lips of her labia as wide as he could. Liquid was already coating the flesh of her vagina. Griffin could hardly tear his eyes away from it. "God, you are so pink and perfect. I could look at you forever. But I have to be inside you. Right now."

His hands trembled as he rolled on the condom. Then one hard thrust and he filled her completely, the tip of his cock touching her womb. "Look at me, Cassie," he commanded.

She opened her eyes but they were glazed with desire.

He could see the pulse beat at her throat accelerating. Pulling her tight against him, he reached down and fully exposed her clitoris, then pinched it between thumb and forefinger. Eyes fastened on her, his cock moving in and out, in and out, he rubbed the hot little bud faster and faster.

Cassie began to writhe, unintelligible cries escaping her throat, her hands gripping the sheet. When he felt her orgasm begin to roll through her, he let himself go, jetting every bit of his semen into the condom, tilting her to reach all the way to her womb.

"Will we live to make it to the wedding?" she asked in a weak voice.

"I don't know, dewdrop." He was still reaching for air to fill his lungs. Sex with Cassie destroyed him in the most pleasurable way possible. "But what a way to go."

* * * * *

Wednesday Cassie picked up the report on her father's death from a reluctant and very irritated Barry Dangler.

"Cassie," he admonished, "I'll tell you one more time. There's nothing here you can do except stir up more trouble. This is a quiet town, just like when you grew up here. You make a mess, people won't forgive you."

"As if I'd care," she retorted. "All I've gotten from anyone in this town since I got back is grief of one kind or another. Well, everyone can go to Hell. Someone's covering up something and I'm going to find out what it is. If you won't do your job, I guess I'll do it for you."

Dangler threw up his hands. "Have it your own way. Just don't forget I warned you."

She stomped out of his office, seething.

At home she found a note Carol had left for her on the kitchen counter.

"I may have some good news. Both women want to see the house again, with their husbands. Saturday's convenient for them if it's okay with you. Call me."

Good. Maybe someone would make an offer. She called Carol and told her Saturday would be fine.

"I'm keeping my fingers crossed," she told Griffin when they met at his house. "We can go take care of business that morning."

He kissed her forehead. "Let's hope," he told her.

After dinner she took the box with all the papers from her father's desk, the folder with the police reports and her laptop and set everything up on the kitchen table.

"What's that?" Griffin asked, looking at the sheet of paper she was studying.

"The report on my dad. And I want you to read the one on Diane. Can you do it?"

His mouth tightened but he nodded.

The report on her father was just a single page. James Fitzgerald had been found in his car at Stoneham Municipal Park about eleven o'clock at night, reeking of scotch, with a revolver still in his hand and a bullet hole in his head. Everyone knew he had been very depressed over Diane's murder.

The only blood stains found were his and there was gunshot residue on his hands. There was also a bullet hole in the window on the driver's side but the police on the scene had surmised that on his first try her father had lost his nerve and jerked the gun away. Case closed.

"You know, there's another explanation for this." She leaned back and pushed her hair away from her face. "Someone else could have shot him, then fired a bullet through the window to get the residue on his skin."

Griffin scratched his head. "Wouldn't they have opened the window first?"

"Maybe." Cassie shrugged. "Or maybe they were just sloppy."

"But I ask again. Six years later, where do you start?"

She looked at the report, brows drawn together. "I don't know. I have to think about that. But my reporter's nose tells me there's something underlying here."

"Reporter's nose, huh?" he chuckled. "If it's half as nice as the rest of your body, I'll follow it anywhere."

She threw a pencil at him, grinning. "Did you get anything from Diane's report?"

He scowled. "Not really." Then he snapped his fingers. "Remember I told you she had this kind of purse she always kept with her? The one that wasn't with her things that Dangler has? And nobody found in the park, or anywhere else?"

Cassie nodded, waiting.

"Just now I remembered how she looked when she left. She grabbed her keys off the hall table but Cassie? *She didn't have that purse with her.*"

"Are you sure? You're not mistaken? Think again. Griffin. It's important."

"I'm sure. Positive." He described again everything she'd been wearing, the keys in her hand but *no purse.*

"What about her driver's license? Money? Anything like that?"

He shook his head. "I don't know, I'll have to think again. But she didn't have that purse with her. That's for sure." He sat up suddenly. "You know what that means, don't you?"

"It's still in your house," she almost whispered. "Hidden somewhere. We've been going about this all wrong."

"What do you mean?"

"I mean, what we're looking for is probably not in my parents' house." She stood up, dumping everything into the box on the table. "Come on. Let's go see what we can find."

* * * * *

They stood in the foyer of his house, just looking around.

"We need to do this methodically," he said. "Go through one room at a time. And cover every inch of it. We can't do every room tonight, so let's take the logical ones first."

They started with the living room, barely used and a likely place to stash something, then the dining room and finally the little room Griffin used as an office. Nothing.

"She wouldn't put it in my office, anyway," he said. "Too much chance I'd find it." He pulled Cassie against him, gently rubbing her back. "Let's go to bed, sugar. We're both too tired to do any more good tonight."

"I guess." But she couldn't wipe the look of dejection from her face.

He moved her slightly away from him, looking down at her. "Why don't you spend the day here tomorrow while I'm working, instead of going back to the other house? You've done all you can there, anyway. And tomorrow night we'll go through that box of papers."

She nodded, knowing he was right. At the moment she just wanted to lie down and close her eyes and forget about everything. She was tired of the town, tired of looking for a needle in a haystack, tired of everyone's attitude. Only her anger kept her going.

"Okay. Just point me to a bed and I'll try to keep my eyes open 'til we get there."

But her mind was already focused on the next day.

Chapter Twenty-One

Griffin was out of the house when Cassie awoke the next morning but he'd left a note on the pillow next to her.

Back in a minute with breakfast. Extra toothbrush in bathroom. Love, G.

She smiled, stretched and went to shower. She liked having someone watch over her. By the time she was dressed again, although in yesterday's clothes, Griffin was back with two bags from McDonald's.

"McMuffins and coffee. Hope that's okay."

"An excellent choice. Thank you." She kissed his cheek. "You spoil me."

They munched breakfast in an easy silence, each preoccupied with their own thoughts.

"Okay," Griffin said when they finished, throwing away their trash, "I'm off. All my fans are eagerly waiting for me. I have a longer break than usual in the middle of the day, so I'll be here at lunch. There's not much food in the house at the moment, so I'll pick up something and you can give me an update."

As the morning wore on and she had little success, she was afraid she wouldn't have much to tell him. The downstairs yielded nothing but as she started up the stairs, she noticed a tiny closet wedged under the stairway. The door was locked but she'd faced that problem before.

In the kitchen junk drawer she found a small screwdriver. In less than five minutes she had jimmied the lock and dragged the door open. Inside she found an odd collection of old and dusty suitcases of every size and shape. She guessed after Griffin's mother died, no one did any traveling. Pulling them all out into the hall, she sat down to open them one by one.

The third one yielded a treasure, a small packet of papers held together with a rubber band. Cassie pulled them out to look at them and discovered they were notes written on scraps of paper. Her heart nearly stopped as she read each one.

Meet me tonight, same place. I only have an hour.

I can take a long lunch today. You know where.

You were fantastic the other night. I can't wait any longer to be with you again.

The notes were printed, not written, obviously an attempt to disguise the handwriting but an expert could make a match if he had something to use as a comparison. Cassie's hands shook as she read first one then another.

Some of them were explicit, suggestive, even erotic at times. Whoever wrote the notes was meeting regularly with Diane. Put these together with the note she'd found in her father's slacks and a picture began to emerge.

Cassie didn't know why Diane risked keeping the notes, except that even at twenty-four she still had a teenager's perspective and having a secret lover would have been romantic to her. The danger in keeping the notes and hiding them would have appealed to her.

She set the bundle aside and resumed her search.

By the time noon rolled around, she'd added two expensive-looking bracelets and two notes Diane had written to herself. She was reading those when she heard Griffin come in.

He shook his head when she pointed to the space under the stairs. "You know, I'd forgotten all about that little cubbyhole. We sure never had any use for suitcases after my mother died. What did you find?"

"After lunch." Cassie got up and walked into the kitchen.

"Is it that good or that bad?" he asked apprehensively.

"After lunch," she repeated firmly. "Go wash up."

She deliberately kept the conversation light during lunch. They talked again about the possible buyers for her house and what she would do if one of them made an offer. Griffin told her he'd called both the nursery and the agent for the land and made appointments for Saturday.

After they were finished eating Cassie retrieved her morning's treasures and put everything on the table. "Look at these and I think you'll see a picture emerging."

"Quite a haul," he commented when he was finished.

"Do you recognize the bracelets?" Cassie asked.

Griffin shook his head. "No. Not at all."

"She never wore them?"

"Not around me. They look pretty expensive. I could never have bought anything like that for her. Not then." He picked up the papers and looked at them again.

"I'm not showing these to Dangler," she told him.

"No?"

She shook her head. "First of all, he's still determined to prove it was really you. And secondly, I think if he gets this stuff in his hands it will disappear. He's much more interested in protecting the reputations of the upright citizens of Stoneham than yours or mine or Diane's." She swept everything into a pile.

"That's no lie."

"No," she continued, "I think we're going to have to do this ourselves. Also, these two sheets of paper lead me to believe Diane kept a diary. She probably couldn't get to it when she wrote these notes, for whatever reason. I'll just bet she's got some names in there nobody wants made public."

"That has to be what someone's looking for." He'd been keeping himself under tight control but how long could he do that?

"I'm going back to my house later." She began clearing everything away. "I want to take one more look around, so come there after work, okay?"

"Okay. Watch yourself, though." He kissed her and was gone.

She refused to go through the room Griffin's parents had shared without him there, so she forced herself to go into his room. Closet first, she thought. But nothing remained of Diane, not the smallest trace. Griffin's clothes hung much more neatly than she would have expected, everything arranged with almost military precision.

She dragged a chair in from the guest room, stood on it and searched around the closet shelf. Nothing. She even tested the ceiling to see if there were any panels that might lift. Nothing there, either. As little as the contents of the closet revealed, Diane might never have been in the room.

She figured the rest of the furniture would be a waste. Griffin had told her he bought everything new after Diane's death. If there was been anything to find, it would have turned up then. Curiosity got the better of her, though and she couldn't resist peeking in his drawers.

Again, everything was stored precisely and neatly. Nothing unusual. Underwear, socks, tee shirts. She lifted one of his tee shirts out and held it to her face, wishing it held his male scent. As she did so, the pile shifted and she saw a wallet hidden under the pile. It wasn't the one he carried now and it piqued her curiosity.

It was obviously old, the leather worn and faded. When she opened it, there was only one thing in it and it made her catch her breath. She was looking at a picture of herself that had to be ten years old. She was standing with two of her friends in front of the high school in her cheerleading uniform. Someone must have said something funny because her head was thrown back and she was laughing.

She hadn't even known the picture was taken, or who had snapped it. Or how Griffin had gotten hold of it. He would have been twenty at the time, not given to hanging out with high school students, virgins or not, so he must have had a reason for wanting this. It amazed her that he'd kept it all this time.

She replaced it in the drawer and put the tee shirts neatly back in their stack. Suddenly she was tired and a dull headache throbbed behind her eyes. It was time for her to get out of this house until Griffin could help her with the rest of it.

* * * * *

The rest of the afternoon was not only fruitless but depressing as she returned to her home knowing she wouldn't find anything new. When Griffin showed up after work, he bullied her into her car and made her follow him home. Over pizza they dragged up every detail of everything they knew but still found no clue as to the whereabouts of the diary.

"It has to be somewhere we haven't thought of." Cassie gathered their trash and dumped it in the wastebasket. "And I'm certain that whoever killed Diane killed my father. It just fits too well."

"We'll finish going through this house tomorrow night but we also need to think of other places she might have chosen to stash it. We're missing something but I don't know what."

"Whatever it is, we want to find it before our mysterious stranger steps up his activities."

* * * * *

Cassie was barely dressed the next morning when Neil McLeod called her cell phone to give her what she called his Griffin Hunter speech.

"I see you've already moved into Hunter's house," he abruptly began.

"Leave it alone, Neil." She closed her eyes and tried to imagine herself stabbing him with his letter opener.

"In good conscience I feel I have to make one more attempt to talk sense into you," he told her. "You don't know what a big mistake you're making here."

"Actually, Neil," she told him, taking great pleasure in her words, "I think for the first time in my life I'm *not* making a mistake. I know exactly what I'm doing and I'm enjoying it."

"I'm worried about your inheritance, is all. I feel a proprietary interest in it and you."

"My inheritance?" She was dumbfounded. "What are you talking about?"

"I understand Griffin is planning to buy a business and some property over in Marble Hill. Is it your money he's using, Cassie? Has he already got his hooks into you?"

Cassie was so furious she was nearly speechless. She swallowed twice to control herself. "First of all, I don't know how you found out about Marble Hill but it's none of your business. Neither is my money. It's mine and I can do what I want with it."

"So that's the way he plays it." Neil was nasty. "Well, it's no less than I expected from him."

"Neil, I'm getting really tired of singing this song. Stay out of my business. Our business. If I had wanted your advice I would have asked for it."

"Your mother always took my advice."

"Well, my mother isn't here anymore," she pointed out, "and I'm a little better prepared to make my own decisions."

"You know the chief still thinks Griffin's the one who killed Diane." His tone was harsh and filled with irritation.

"Is that so? Well, I may be digging up a few surprises on that score."

There was dead silence on the other end of the line. "Don't let Griffin Hunter sell you a bill of goods." His anger vibrated across the connection.

"For your information, Griffin and I are planning to be married. So save your breath from now on."

"Walk away from this, Cassie." He hung up without even a goodbye.

The coffee was ready and Cassie had just filled a mug when her cell rang again.

"I wanted to touch base with you and make sure you were doing all right." Donald Brandon's oily voice slid over the phone wires. "I know this has been a sad and trying time for you."

"No offense, Donald but it would be a lot less trying if all of you would just leave me alone."

"Why, Cassie, no offense taken but I'm sorry you feel that way. We all only want to make this time of grief easier for you and help you settle things here."

And get out of town, she thought.

"I'm fine, Donald. I'm handling things well."

Silence hung between them for a moment. "I see Griffin Hunter is still hanging around, sucking up to you. I hope you're on your guard with him."

"For God's sake, Donald," she snapped. "That's insulting. As a matter fact, Griffin and I are engaged."

Cassie chuckled to herself as she pictured Donald at an uncharacteristic loss for words.

"I would feel derelict in my duty," Donald told her, his voice pinched, "if I didn't remind you that the chief still believes Griffin is Diane's killer."

"You know," she said, "the chief would do a lot better to stop pointing the finger at Griffin and try to identify the real killer."

"Go away, Cassie. Leave Stoneham and we'll leave you alone." He hung up much more firmly than Neil had.

She made short shrift of Cyrus McLeod's call, the next one on the tag team. His professed paternal concern sounded like so much garbage to her and she told him so.

"You're burning a lot of bridges," he pointed out. "The sooner you finish up here and leave, the better for everyone."

"Well, chew on this. When I came here I planned to get out as quickly as I could. But now I find there's still so many questions about Diane's death—and my father's—there's no way I'm leaving until I have all the answers and I know the truth. Maybe if everyone hadn't been so quick to hustle me out of town and cover everything over, I'd be long gone. You can pass that along to all your very good friends."

"Your father?" A different tone entered his voice as he picked up on that reference. "Your father committed suicide. Don't go making problems where there aren't any."

This time is was Cassie who hung up first.

She was out in the backyard, lying on one of the lounges and trying to blot everyone out of her mind, when Harley Graham walked up behind her.

"You didn't answer the bell so I thought I'd check out here."

She jumped at the sound of his voice. "Oh, my God. You scared me half to death, Harley."

"Sorry, honey. I didn't mean to startle you. Okay if I sit down?"

"As long as you're not here to lecture me about Griffin Hunter or tell me I need to get out of town."

Harley chuckled. "That bad, is it?"

"Worse," she groaned. "I'm just so sick of everyone telling me what they think is good for me."

"I guess that's what some people consider the charm of this town. What they like to call closeness."

Cassie snorted. "Too damned close for me. Excuse my language."

"No problem. I'd bet by this time you've got plenty to swear about." His eyes dropped to her hand. "Nice ring, by the way. I guess that means you and Griffin are serious."

She nodded. "And serious about getting out of here too."

"Okay, let's hear it all." Harley leaned back in the other lounge chair and listened while she described the day's phone calls. He was the least judgmental person she'd ever known and easy to talk to. Just being in his presence cheered her up.

"Cassie, not much has changed here since you left. Griffin Hunter isn't ever going to live down his reputation, Barry Dangler isn't going to stop trying to hang Diane's death on him and the upright folks around here aren't going to stop giving anyone who'll listen a piece of their mind. You just do what you need to do and forget about them."

"Hah! Forget about them. That would be a neat trick." She sat up and looked over at him. "Harley, I need to tell you about some things I've found out, strange things and some stuff that's happened and ask you some questions. Is that okay?"

"Fire away, kiddo. I'm all ears."

Slowly, trying to remember all the details, she told him what she and Griffin had found out about Diane, about the things that weren't in the police report and the surprises that were, such as the baby's parentage. She told him about the notes she'd found and the jewelry. And finally she told him about the report on her father's so-called suicide and the note she'd found in his clothes.

"So what do you think?" she asked, when she finally wound down.

Harley shook his head. "That's some story, Cassie. Have you talked to Barry Dangler about it?"

"That idiot?" she spat out. "All he wants to do is find one piece of proof to lock Griffin up and throw away the key. He's not interested in anything else."

"Still singing the same song, it seems."

Cassie leaned toward him, an earnest expression on her face. "But this is evidence of something. Harley, I didn't mention this to anyone else but Diane was seeing someone, a person who needed to keep his identity secret. Probably the baby's father. And the jewelry? She was trying to get money out of him. That's what the warning note to my father was all about."

"I signed your father's death certificate," he told her.

"And did you examine him yourself?"

"I guess I probably took what Barry said and I didn't bother looking for anything else." He stroked his chin thoughtfully. "I had no reason to. Everything seemed so cut and dried. And I had been treating him for clinical depression, you know."

"No, I didn't. But I do know that my father was not a person who would take his own life. Diane's death may have upset him but he would never have just left my mother alone like that."

"You may be chasing at shadows, you know," he pointed out. "Diane had a vivid imagination and loved to conjure things up. Did you ever think she might have written those notes herself?"

"No." Cassie shook her head vehemently. "She wouldn't go that far. Someone killed her, Harley and it wasn't Griffin."

"Forgive me but I can't see any decent person getting involved with her. If there is someone lurking in the shadows, it would more likely be one of that wild bunch she ran with."

"But they wouldn't have any money," Cassie protested. "Someone was giving her expensive gifts. Keep in mind, none of the men Diane ran with would have much that she could blackmail them about. Also, it had to be someone who'd kill my father to keep his secret. Griffin had no reason to do that. Neither did anyone else in that crowd."

"You never can tell what someone will kill to protect. Be careful," he warned her. "If you're right, that means there's a dangerous person out there who thinks he's safe. He won't like having things disturbed after all these years."

"Don't worry. Griffin's taking very good care of me. You aren't going to give me grief about that like everyone else has, are you?"

He sat up and grinned at her.

"Not a chance. I figure you're old enough to know what you're doing and if you don't, it's your problem. That doesn't mean I don't care but I'm not your self-appointed keeper."

Cassie leaned over and hugged him. "Thank you for that. At least I have one person I can count on."

"Just call me if you need me," he told her and headed off to his car.

Chapter Twenty-Two

Deciding she needed to cook again and give Griffin some real food, Cassie made a quick trip to the grocery store, picking up three bottles of wine along with everything else. When Griffin got home he found her in the kitchen, basting a roast and halfway through one of the bottles.

He raised an eyebrow. "Having a tough day, are we?"

"You don't know the half of it," she told him.

He sniffed the air. "Dinner sure smells good. I didn't know you were such a good cook."

"It's pretty basic but I decided I'm letting you eat way too much takeout."

He came up behind her, wrapping his arms around her and resting his chin on the top of her head. She leaned back against him, thankful for the feel of him.

"I'm dirty and sweaty and I need a shower but I couldn't wait to do this." He turned her around and kissed her so tenderly that she nearly cried. Ignoring his disheveled condition, she reached up and put her arms around him tightly, pressing her body against him.

"I love you, Cassie," he murmured. "I don't think I'll ever get tired of telling you that."

Then he was gone, up the stairs and soon she heard the shower running. Cassie hummed happily as she finished dinner.

He came into the kitchen as she was serving the food, scrubbed clean and smelling deliciously of spicy aftershave. He stooped and kissed her again.

"So, did the news get out today?" He lifted her hand with the ring on it.

"Enough so they won't have to print a paper this week."

"Good. I only wish I'd been able to tell everyone myself."

After they were finished cleaning up, they took some of the wine out to the yard and sat in the lounge chairs. Cassie gave him chapter and verse on the telephone calls and on Harley's visit. Whatever campaign was going on, it seemed to be stepping up in intensity.

"I'm curious as to why everyone is trying so hard to get me to drop what I'm doing and get out of town," she said. "I'd hate to think there's some big conspiracy going on but it sure seems like someone's pulling some strings."

"No one knows about the notes we found, or the jewelry," Griffin reminded her. "They think you're just looking for someone to pin everything on because of what's going on with you and me. Remember, it would make everyone sleep better at night if I just confessed and Dangler could close the file."

"The notes aren't quite the secret they were," she apologized. "I told Harley about them when he was here but he's the only one." She chewed her thumbnail. "I'm trying to attack this as if I were after a story but it's a lot different when it's personal. And when I mentioned there might be something suspicious about my father's death, you would have thought I cursed the pastor."

"If they discount the suicide decision," Griffin told her, "that means they have to look at Diane's death again because they might be connected and that's not going to happen. Your questions are making people nervous so they want you to go away."

"We'll just have to keep searching for the diary," she sighed.

"I agree. That could be the key to everything."

The sun disappeared completely while they sat outside. Now bright stars twinkled in a clear sky overhead and for a change there was a faint night breeze stirring the sultry air.

Griffin stood up and reached for Cassie. "I think we need to discuss this with fewer clothes on." He grinned. "And we've given the neighbors enough to think about for the year. Let's go upstairs and see what comes up."

He leered at her and wiggled his eyebrows. Cassie burst out laughing, then followed him into the house.

* * * * *

They left Griffin's house early Saturday morning.

"I don't think we have to worry about another break-in at your place," he told her. "Too much commotion over the last one. If someone still wants to get in, they'll figure something else out."

"What a comforting thought." Cassie bit her cheek. "Maybe I should just buy a gun."

"You'd probably shoot yourself instead. No, I think what we need to do instead is try to see if anyone follows us around. Whoever it is may have decided it would just be easier to let us find what they're looking for and go from there."

"And what, kill us too?" She was incredulous. "You don't think we'd be two deaths too many? Suicide wouldn't work this time."

Griffin's eyes darkened and his jaw tightened. "No but they could easily make it look like I'd killed you, just like Diane, then killed myself in a sudden fit of remorse."

"My God!" Her jaw dropped. "But that's unbelievable."

"Whoever we're looking for has managed to kill twice and get away with it. By this time they have great confidence in their ability to get away with anything."

Cassie shivered and reached across the seat for Griffin's hand. She remembered when the only thing that bothered her was her dark, erotic dreams about him.

They still hadn't gone through the carton of papers from her father's desk. They'd carted them to Griffin's the night before. Now he suggested bringing them along and looking at them over a picnic lunch.

But first things first. They spent most of the morning at the nursery, talking to the owner. Cassie was impressed with Griffin's knowledge and business sense and she could tell the owner was too.

Finally Griffin shook hands with the man. "Thanks for all the information. I think my fiancée and I need to discuss this but we'll do it quickly. I'll give you a call Monday or Tuesday, okay?"

The owner nodded, although he seemed reluctant to let them get away.

"What do you think?" Cassie asked when they were back in the truck.

"I think tomorrow we should sit down and do a financial projection. Then Monday we can call him with a formal offer."

"How soon would we have to close?"

"Probably ninety days, which gives us time to wind up everything else."

At Marble Hill they found a deli where they could buy cold cuts, salads and drinks for lunch, then drove out to the property Griffin had taken her to. They had an hour before the agent was to meet them, so they let down the tailgate on the truck, spread out their food and, over lunch took their first good look at the papers from the desk.

Most of them were run-of-the-mill but underneath the jumble they found a tiny envelope with a key in it.

"Griffin, this is a key to a safety deposit box." Cassie could hardly contain her excitement. "I recognize it."

"Yeah, me too. You think it's just been lying in here all this time?"

Cassie nodded. "It could have belonged to my father but I have an itchy feeling Diane stuck it in here. She probably wanted a safe place for it, figuring no one would open this envelope. She was right."

"Your mother wouldn't have found it?"

She shook her head. "No I'm guessing that after Dad died, all my mother did was shove papers in the drawer and forget them. She really left everything for Neil to deal with."

Griffin narrowed his eyes thoughtfully. "Why do you suppose he never asked her what she kept at home, or where she kept personal papers? I'd have thought he'd want to get his hands on them."

Cassie shook her head. "I don't think he gave it a thought. He was too sure my father had given him everything important. Unless he's the one looking for the diary, why would it even occur to him?"

"Monday, you need to call that idiot at the bank and see if either of your folks had a safety deposit box that he conveniently forgot to mention to you." He bit into a sandwich as if it was Howard Cook's head.

Cassie giggled, then turned sober. "But Neil or Howard would have told me when we went over all the paperwork, wouldn't they?"

"Not necessarily. If one of them is our killer, they'd probably just as soon not have you find out. If it's not at Dimwit Howard's bank, you could try Bank of America where you have your account. Or maybe we need to start checking the banks in San Antonio."

Cassie blew out her breath and grimaced. "That's certainly a job and a half." She snapped her fingers. "But if we need to do it, I think I know someone who can help us. She's very good at sneaking into computer records."

"You can't go hacking into the banks' records, sugar. I think they put you in jail for that."

"Only if they find out," she reminded him.

"I didn't know I was marrying a potential felon," Griffin joked. He leaned over and kissed her lightly.

Cassie ran her tongue over his lips. He tasted of ham and potato salad and the special essence that was Griff. Kissing him was one of the most pleasurable experiences of her life.

They had just finished bagging their trash when the real estate agent drove up. He handed Griffin a folder with all the information on the land, then suggested they walk at least part of the property. When they reached the crest of the hill, Cassie drew in her breath. The land sloped away to a creek below and everywhere she looked the land was guarded by old oak trees and sycamore. Wildflowers grew in abundant profusion, coloring the land with their brilliant reds and blues and yellows.

She reached for Griffin's hand and squeezed it, hard. His answering pressure told her he knew what she wanted and he did too.

In another hour they were done, signing a contract to purchase and giving the agent a deposit check. They could hardly contain themselves on the ride home.

"Our very own piece of property," Cassie crowed. "We need to start thinking about plans and getting an architect."

"In a hurry, are we, darlin?" Griffin smiled.

"You bet. I feel like we're in a different world out here."

"We are. And a lot closer to Austin than San Antonio, so even our city trips would be different."

"Oh, Griffin." She hugged his arm. "I can hardly believe our good luck."

Their luck continued to hold, because as they neared Stoneham, Cassie's cell phone rang.

"Carol Markham," she told Griffin as she glanced at the Caller ID.

"Cassie, you won't believe this," the woman gushed. "I just have to pat myself on the back."

Cassie rolled her eyes. "What is it, Carol?"

"We actually have a buyer. And almost the full price you want. Am I good or what!"

"Yes, Carol. You're terrific." Cassie forced enthusiasm into her voice. And in truth, she was happy. She would be more than glad to get rid of the house altogether.

"I've got a signed agreement to purchase and a good faith check. If you're okay with this, I'd like to drop by tonight so I can get your signature and we can proceed to closing."

"That's fine. I'm staying at Griffin's, so why don't you come by there?"

Cassie knew she should have been used to the long silences she always received any time she paired herself with Griffin.

"I see. Well. All right, if that's what you want. Is seven okay?"

Cassie stifled a laugh. "Yes, that'll be fine." She snapped her phone shut and let the laugh bubble out. "We won't have to worry if someone hasn't heard the news anymore. Oh, lordy, Griff, I'd give a month's pay to have seen her face."

"Tonight should be interesting, sugar. Very interesting." He squeezed her hand. "Now if we can just find that safety deposit box, we'll be in clover."

*   *   *   *   *

The air was thick with tension when Carol walked into Griffin's house that night. Cassie refused to let him hide in another room, reminding him that after all, it was his house. Carol pointedly ignored him while they all sat at the kitchen table but it was hard for her not to notice the engagement ring, which Cassie took every opportunity to flash.

"Yes," Cassie said, noticing Carol's avid glances, "Griffin and I are getting married. Just as soon as we can."

Carol's eyes slid from one to the other. "I see. Isn't that interesting?"

Later Cassie told Griffin she wished she'd had a camera to take a picture of the woman's face at that moment. The careful mask disintegrated and her eyes bulged. Her mouth looked like a gaping fish. With a visible effort she pulled herself together and gathered up her materials.

At last everything was signed, Carol handed a copy of the agreement to Cassie and put everything else back into her folder.

"The buyers are a very nice couple. Older. Retired. They want to close and take possession in three weeks, if possible. Is that going to be a problem for you?"

Cassie shook her head. "My biggest problem is going to be getting rid of the furniture. Otherwise, I'm okay."

"I'm guessing you'll have a place to stay." It was a statement, not a question and tinged with more than a little sarcasm.

"Yes, that's not a problem." Cassie stood up and moved closer to Griffin.

"I guess you know what you're doing but if you ask me, you're making a huge mistake."

"Then I guess it's a good thing I didn't ask you." Cassie's voice was sweeter than sugar. "Thanks for coming by. Just let me know when the closing is."

Carol literally ran from the house.

Griffin and Cassie looked at each other and burst out laughing.

"Well," Griffin said, "You're right. We won't have to worry about telling anyone our news."

"Good." Cassie hugged him. "I'd put it on the front page of the paper if they'd take my ad."

"If you think people bothered you before, just wait until tomorrow."

"By the time church is over, it will be better than an ad," she agreed.

She was right. They had barely finished a late breakfast before they heard a car in the driveway followed by the ring of the doorbell. Cassie opened the door to the McLeod triad— Neil, Cyrus and Leslie.

"Wow," she said. "The big guns, huh? To what do I owe the pleasure?"

"Hello, Cassie." Leslie stepped forward, the picture of poise and elegance. "We thought we'd stop by after church. May we come in for just a minute?"

"I think you should ask Griffin. This is his house, after all."

Three pairs of icy eyes swept coldly over Griffin who stood behind Cassie.

"By all means," he drawled. "Welcome to my home."

They trooped with military precision into the living room, arranging themselves on the furniture.

"We're a little busy," Cassie told them, "so I hope this won't take too long. I'm right in assuming this isn't just a friendly Welcome Wagon visit?"

It appeared Leslie was taking the lead today. "Cassie, you know how fond we all are of you and how fond we were of your parents," she began.

"No, Leslie. Tell me. I don't seem to remember being invited to any of your parties. Diane either. And when did your parents ever socialize with mine?"

"I think you're being deliberately obtuse," she said. "You have to know that everyone only has your best interests at heart. We're concerned about what's happening to you. We may not have been close friends but that doesn't mean Neil and I aren't deeply worried about what you're doing."

"After yesterday's phone calls and Carol's visit, I wondered how long it would take for you all to show up. If you're here to ask me if I'm really going to marry Griffin Hunter, the answer is yes." She flashed her ring at them. "It's official."

"Now listen, Cassie," Cyrus began.

Cassie went on as smoothly as if no one had spoken. "If you want to know if I'm going to quit poking into Diane's death, or my father's so-called suicide, the answer is no. You can save yourselves any more visits and phone calls. My answers won't change. Does that about cover it?"

Cyrus scowled. "Funny. I don't remember you as being this headstrong."

"I think determined is more like it," she told him. "I'd sure like to know why everyone is so hell-bent on sweeping Diane's murder under the rug. Don't you want to find the real killer?" She looked at each face carefully. "Isn't anyone worried it could happen again?"

Neil's mouth was set in an angry line. "No, I don't think it will happen again. Unless it happens to you."

Cassie felt white heat consume her, a rage so great she wasn't sure she could control it. "Do you want to explain that to me?"

"You may be blind, Cassie but I think we all know who's the culprit here. It's just a matter of proving it. But if you want to put yourself in harm's way, I guess that's your choice."

She clenched her fists so tightly her nails dug into her palms. Behind her she felt the tension radiating from Griffin's body like a solid mass. "You come into a man's home and insult him that way? Who the hell do you think you are? And why, after all these years, are any of you interested in the Fitzgerald family?"

Cyrus moved a step forward, restraining Neil with a hand on his arm. "Cassie, you were always the good girl in your family. The one with bright promise. You've made a good life for yourself. Why are you throwing it away and putting yourself in jeopardy?"

"Everyone's just concerned for you, Cassie," Neil added.

Cassie snorted. "Yeah, right. If you're that concerned, you can help me get at the real truth here."

"Don't you see, Cassie?" All eyes turned back to Leslie. "All you're doing is bringing up unpleasant memories that everyone would just as soon forget. Poor Diane's murder was the only violent crime in Stoneham for fifty years."

"And my father's. Let's not forget about him."

"Your father's death was ruled a suicide and that's what it was." Cyrus was using his stern legal voice. "Everyone knew how depressed he was. If you'd been here, you would have known that too."

"We'd all be a lot better," Neil said to Griffin, "if you'd get your hooks out of this girl. And if you'd own up to Diane's death and stop filling Cassie's head with crazy ideas."

"Well," he drawled, "I think that's up to Cassie."

She went to stand next to him, purposely putting her arms around him and moving as close to him as she could. The trio stood up.

"You're making a big mistake, Cassie." This from Cyrus. Apparently they each had specific lines in this little drama. "You don't know this man as well as you think you do."

"Maybe so but I'm having a lot of fun getting to know him better." She smiled up at Griffin.

The McLeods filed toward the door.

Leslie turned at before they left. "I really thought we could give you some good advice. When you get hurt, don't come crying to any of us. Your house has already been broken into. Who knows what could happen next."

"Is that a threat?" Griffin's voice was deceptively calm.

"Of course not." Leslie looked at him as if she was smelling something bad. "We just don't want any harm to come to Cassie. I'd say you're the only threat she has to worry about."

"By the way, Neil," Cassie called out. "Did you forget to tell me about the safety deposit box my folks had at the bank?"

They all stopped dead.

Neil turned slowly to face her. "I have no idea what you're talking about."

"You know, a box in the bank for important papers. I believe they had one. Weren't you going to tell me about it?"

"You must be mistaken," he said, his body rigid. "I gave you everything of theirs I had. You should stop making crazy accusations."

"Well, you can pass the word that I'm going to keep stirring the pot until I get the answers I want. The sooner I get them, the faster I'll be out of everyone's hair."

Cassie watched them get into Neil's car and back out of the driveway. She was holding onto her temper by a slender thread.

Griffin sensed it and came to stand behind her, his hands resting on her shoulders. "Let it go, sugar. They have their own agenda and nothing you say will change it."

"Don't you think it's very interesting that every time I get a little closer or a little more aggressive, someone jumps all over me about it? My telephone calls the other day must have stirred up more of a hornet's nest than I thought."

"You might have gotten a little more than you bargained for," he warned. "I don't trust any of these people. Someone out there is dangerous. I've about decided that whoever Diane's mysterious lover was, a lot of people know about it and aren't anxious for it to come out. And I'm not so sure he was the only one she was involved with."

"Oh?" Cassie raised an eyebrow at him.

His voice took on a bitter tone. "Money meant everything to Diane. It was a huge shock to her when she discovered the money I threw around was all I had. There wasn't some big pot of gold hidden away. I wouldn't be surprised if she was pushing more than one person. I'd sure like to find proof of that."

"Me too." Cassie pressed herself against his chest. "Do you really think someone will try to hurt me?"

"I hope not but we're getting into some murky waters here. Malicious mischief may be more their style at the moment. You should call Carol Markham and get her to put out a Sold sign today. You don't want any more damage to your house. They might leave the house alone if they know it's sold."

"On the other hand, if someone's in a real panic, they might want to break in to search it one more time."

"I still think the sign's a good idea but we'll keep an eye on it. Asking Dangler to watch it is like spitting in the wind."

"Okay." She reluctantly let go of him and moved toward the kitchen. "I'll call Carol right now."

They spent the rest of the afternoon going over the information on the nursery and preparing a counteroffer. Griffin had really done his homework. He had a thick file of information from other nurseries he'd talked to so they had some idea of where to start.

"I'll call the guy in the morning." He stacked everything together. "I think what we're offering is a fair price and close to what he's asking."

Cassie poured herself a glass of iced tea and sat at the kitchen table with her ever-present pad of paper, trying to make a list of anyone Diane might have been involved with. Finally she threw the pen down, shoved the pad away from her and looked at Griffin. "This is impossible."

"No, just difficult. But I have a feeling we're getting close, so don't give up now."

Chapter Twenty-Three

෨

And then it was Monday. Cassie drove to the Bank of America office and met with the manager. She presented her letter from Neil and the death certificate, explained what she was looking for and the manager, Janet Colburn, scrolled through her computer.

"I don't see a box here for either your mother or father," she said. "Are you sure they'd have come here? I don't believe this is where they did their banking."

"For this I think they'd have wanted some anonymity," Cassie explained. "Can you see if there's a box under Diane Fitzgerald or Diane Hunter?"

Again Janet searched her database and again she came up empty.

"Thanks, anyway." Cassie tried to hide her disappointment.

"Hold on a second," Janet said. "Let me go into the main database and see if there's one at another branch."

Cassie sat crossing her fingers while Janet's computer did its thing.

"All right, Miss Fitzgerald." Janet looked up at her. "I have a box listed for a Diane Hunter at a branch in San Antonio. Is that where she's living now?"

Cassie was shocked. "My sister died six years ago! I don't understand. Who would even be paying for it now? Doesn't it have to be paid for each year?"

"Yes but according to my records, when Mrs. Hunter rented the box she paid for ten years in advance."

Planning, Cassie thought. Covering her bases.

Cassie left the bank in a daze. She sat in her car with the air conditioner on and called Griffin on his cell phone.

"Hunter," he answered.

"It's me. You'll never believe what I found out. Can you talk?"

"Hold on a sec." She heard a door slam and assumed he had climbed into his truck. "That's better. I can crank up the A/C for a minute and have some privacy. What's up, sugar?"

He listened as she gave him all the details of her meeting with the bank manager, not saying a word until she was finished.

"But that's too weird," he said finally. "Why did she pick that location? And pay for so many years in advance?"

"I'd say she wanted it to be as far away from Stoneham as possible where it would be lost in the records of a big bank but close enough for her to access it when she wanted to. As to paying for it, I think she wanted to hedge her bets. Life was pretty unstable for Diane."

"Tell me about it. So what can we do next? You said they wouldn't give you access to the box, right?"

"Yes but you could get into it. You were her husband. I think all you'd need is a copy of the marriage license and her death certificate."

"All right." He thought a minute. "We'll do it tomorrow afternoon. Can you call and find out how late they're open?"

"Sure but what about your jobs tomorrow? You can't keep blowing people off."

"I'll just start early. Anyway, don't worry about me. These people may hate my guts but right now I'm the only game in town. Besides, I'm hoping we won't have to worry about this much longer."

"I just don't want you to have any more hassles than you've already got."

He laughed. "Honey, that's my middle name. I'll see you later at home."

At least the rest of the day brought them good news. The owner of the land accepted their offer and wanted to close as soon as possible. The nursery owner was happy with Griffin's price and asked when he could come over to sign papers and bring a deposit check. And Carol called with a firm closing date for the house.

"This is all good luck," Cassie said, hugging Griffin. "Everything's going to work out the way we want it to. I just know it. And I feel so sure we'll find what we're looking for in that deposit box."

"I told the guy in Marble Falls we'd be able to drive over tomorrow evening," Griffin told her. "Does that work out for us?"

"Sure. The bank's open until five. If we leave here at four, we can get there before closing and hopefully get to open the box with no trouble. That way we can be in Marble Hills before eight."

"All right. Can you call the real estate agent and set up a date to close on the land? Maybe we can sign the final papers for the nursery then too."

"No problem. All I'm doing tomorrow is getting rid of those boxes of clothes."

"Okay. I'll be home early enough to shower and change."

Cassie was surprised at how easily she accomplished her tasks the next day. If only every day was as simple, she thought. Family Services was happy to get the clothes and anything else she wanted to give them. A used furniture dealer in Kerrville said he'd come by Thursday to see what she had and if it suited him, he'd take everything off her hands.

Confirming a closing date on the land was the last thing she did before heading off to shower and change and wait for Griffin. She was sitting in the kitchen reading the police and autopsy reports on both Diane and her father one more time when Griffin came in the back door.

"I thought you'd have those memorized by now." He kissed the top of her head. "You know, sometimes I have to pinch myself to be sure everything is real. How could someone whose life has been so messed up have caught the brass ring?"

"It was always there waiting for us. We just had to reach for it."

He chuckled. "Before long we'll even be like normal people, owning a business, building a new house, starting a new life together." He kissed the top of her head. "I wake up sometimes in the middle of the night in a sweat, wondering if I dreamed it all. Then I touch you and I know it's all real."

"It's definitely real." She rested her head against his chest for a moment. "I just keep thinking we're missing something," she told him. "My reporter's nose is twitching."

"It'll come to you." He set her gently away from his sweaty body. "Give me ten and I'll be ready."

They were silent driving into the city, both tensely expectant at what they might find, worried about the process of opening the box. But that too, followed the rest of the day and everything went smoothly. Griffin's documents were examined and copied along with his personal ID. He pulled out the key and in short order they were in a small room with the box sitting on the table between them.

Cassie and Griffin stared at each other, neither of them making a move.

"You open it," Cassie said. "You were her husband."

"Yeah, right," Griffin snorted but he reached for the box and flipped open the lid. They both stared.

In one side of the box were neat stacks of hundred dollar bills, each stack with a rubber band around it. Next to the money was a soft velvet pouch. Griffin opened it slowly and a bracelet studded with precious gems fell out into his hands. He looked at Cassie, bewildered.

"Blackmail," she said softly. "It has to be."

And finally, tucked in the other corner of the box, a small red leather book that couldn't be anything else but a diary.

"You take it," Griffin said. "I don't know if I can stand to open it."

Cassie took it with trembling hands. Holding her breath, she thumbed the lock and opened the book. Nearly every page was filled with writing that she recognized as Diane's. Would they find the answers to their questions at last? She pushed the book toward Griffin.

"You should read this," she told him.

He shook his head. "No. I don't think I can. In fact, I don't think I can sit here another minute. Dump all that in your purse and let's get out of here. I feel like I'm choking."

Once they were on the way to Marble Hills, they relaxed slightly.

"I can't read that book, Cassie." Griffin gritted his teeth. "I know it probably has clues in it but I'm asking you to be the one to do it. When Diane told me about the baby, I was willing to make an effort to shape up. That bitch had no intention of being straight with me. She must have been on the prowl before the ink was dry on the marriage license." There was more anger than pain in his voice.

Cassie didn't ever remember hearing him sound like this. "Don't let her keep reaching for you from the grave, Griffin. We'll get the answers and be done with it. We have a life together now. Don't let her ruin that too."

She saw the muscles in his jaw working as he tried to calm himself. Finally he reached over and took one of her hands.

"I love you, Cassie. That's the one good thing that's come out of this."

Cassie let out the breath she didn't even know she'd been holding. "Then everything else is a piece of cake." She squeezed his hand, brought it to her lips and kissed his fingers.

"Let's go buy a business. When we get home I'll look through the diary. Right now let's just concentrate on us."

* * * * *

The whole time they were at the nursery, signing papers, writing checks, making arrangements, the diary was like a hot coal in her purse. Cassie could almost feel its heat. Not to mention the money, shoved into an envelope the bank manager had provided. What in God's name would she do with it?

She was thankful when at last they were back in the truck and headed for Stoneham.

Griffin reached over and squeezed her hand. "Even with all the distractions, we did good, honey."

"Did we?"

"You bet. We got him down to an acceptable price and we've got ninety days before we have to close and take possession."

"Can we do that? I mean, I'll be done with my house in another week but you still have yours to get rid of, not to mention your business. And where will we live while we're building our new house?"

"Don't sweat it. I'm putting an ad in the paper tomorrow for the landscaping service and I guess I'll go ahead and get Carol to list my house. Maybe we'll get lucky there too."

"But where will we live?" she repeated.

"We'll rent. The guy in the nursery said there are several small houses in town that are available. Tomorrow you can call the agent handling the land and get him to e-mail you some listings to look at."

"I can't say I'll be sorry to see the last of Stoneham," she said with resentment. "Good riddance."

"Are you hungry?" he asked, when they were finally home. "We haven't eaten at all."

"Yes but I want to look at this diary. I can't wait any longer."

"Then I'll grill some steaks and toss a salad while you read, okay? You can tell me what I need to know."

She took the book into the living, kicked off her shoes and curled up on the couch, the diary in her hands. She looked at it for a long time, knowing that the minute she opened it there'd be no turning back. Finally, she opened the catch and turned to the first page.

The first several pages yielded nothing, just musings about Griffin, about parties, words about nothing in particular. She sat up when she came to a page that said simply, *No one can know. It has to be our secret but I don't care. The secrecy is part of the fun. And I know I can get him to buy me presents. He just wants me to keep my mouth shut.*

The page was dated three months before Griffin and Diane's wedding. So this was where it began. No name yet but it was the first indication of the dangerous game Diane was about to play.

The next entry was dated a week later.

He certainly knows more than the guys I've been hanging out with. I guess sex is really what you know after all. Too bad I can't teach some of this stuff to Griffin or any of the other guys but they'd wonder how I suddenly learned everything. Oh, well. I guess once a week will hold me. For now.

A week later she wrote, *I told him I love the bracelet. He gave me cash too, lots of it, to buy stuff to wear for him. Also I think he knows if he gives me money I'll keep my mouth shut. He doesn't have to worry. I don't want to upset his apple cart or mine.*

The next few pages were more of the same, then a new entry.

If it's good with one, it's great with two. Little did I know there were so many frustrated men in this tiny town. Their wives must sleep in an icebox. Although my cookie has worse problems than that.

But he's a nice addition to my collection. He doesn't mind paying, either.

Cassie felt get sick to her stomach. She felt like a lead weight had dropped into her body and taken up residence. She knew her sister had been wild but this was beyond even her imaginings.

"Find anything yet?" Griffin carried in a tray with two drinks and a plate of sandwiches, which he set on the coffee table.

Cassie looked at him, trying to find the words to describe what she was reading.

Griffin's face got a closed look on it when he saw her expression. "That bad, huh?"

"Griffin, I…"

"Never mind. That's why I wanted you to read it. Here. Eat something."

"I can't." She shook her head. "I don't think I can swallow anything."

"Cassie, you are not responsible for what she did. You have to eat or you really will be sick. Come on."

He placed the salad on the table, then the two plates with their steaks. "Eat," he ordered. "You know. Chew and swallow. And put that stuff away until you clean your plate."

In spite of herself she had to smile and the food did look delicious.

"A real meal." She gave him a weak grin. "How can I let it go to waste?"

She pushed everything aside and picked up her fork. Griff had gone to all this trouble. The least she could do was show her appreciation by eating. When she'd stuffed the last bite into her mouth, she pulled the diary over and scanned through a few more pages. She stopped on one page where the words leaped out at her.

This is getting harder than I thought. I can't ditch the crowd too many nights a week or they'll start asking questions but now I have three wonderful admirers who can't wait to give me presents and money. Well, a smart person like me will just have to figure it out.

She looked up at Griffin, hating the things she would have to tell him. "She was seeing three men on the side, three apparently married men, who gave her gifts and money. Diane wasn't much better than a prostitute."

"Ask me if I'm surprised," he said viciously.

Cassie hated the look of pain on his face. He hadn't loved Diane but he had tried to do the right thing for her. She had repaid him with her self-destructive behavior. Idly Cassie kept turning the pages, hoping for a clue to a name. She stopped when she came to a page that had the words "The baby" at the top, underlined.

I will not have an abortion. I've heard too many scary stories. No, I'll find someone to marry me, have it, then go back to the way things were. But they're all going to pay for this mistake, you can bet on it. Or I'll set this town on its ear.

There was a lot more of the same, including the notes on her marriage to Griffin. Cassie hurried over them, not wanting to read the mean things her sister had written. Then, a week before her death, an entry was written with anger.

None of them wants to take responsibility. Fine. Then I'll make them all pay. I told them each to meet me next week at our usual time and place or they'll see their names on the front page of the paper. If I have to have this kid, I want money to hightail it away from here when it's done. Griffin says he always wanted a family. Well, now he can have one.

Underneath the entry was a string of letters, that at first glance made no sense at all to Cassie. She needed to figure out what they meant but for a moment she had to close the book. She felt as if she'd been wading through slime and would never be clean.

Griffin was looking at her, questions burning in his eyes. "Well?" His face was set in grim lines.

"All right." She sat up and took a swallow of her drink. "Here's the bare outline. Diane was blackmailing three men. Any one of them could have killed her. She never identified which one actually fathered the baby but she was heading for a showdown with all three of them." She opened the book again to the last entry. "Maybe if I could figure out what all these letters mean, we'd know who she was meeting."

She held the book so he could see the page but he sat like a statue, not saying a word. She got up and sat in his lap, curling her arms around him and laying her head in his shoulder.

"Think of this as an abstract puzzle," she told him. "The only thing that's real is us. We've put a down payment on our dreams, Griffin. Let's not lose sight of that."

"You're right." He held her tightly against him and she felt him take a deep breath. "But the sooner we find the answers to this, the sooner we can close the book on Diane and this town completely."

"Meanwhile, let's get some sleep. We can tackle this tomorrow."

But as tired and emotionally spent as they were, tonight the need to lose themselves in each other was stronger than ever. They made such gentle love that night that Cassie thought her heart would burst from the sensations she felt. She had not believed that Griffin could be such a needy lover in a quiet way — his emotions greater than his physical needs.

He sucked her breasts, pulling at her nipples with his mouth until they throbbed from his touch. His teeth nipped at the underside of her breasts then his tongue soothed them, while his warm hands massaged their fullness. Then he did it again. And again, until she thought she would come just from his attention to her breasts.

He licked every inch of her soft abdomen, teasing her navel with the tip of his tongue until every nerve was inflamed. He tugged at her pubic curls with his teeth and then opened her legs wide and slid his tongue from her clitoris down the length of her slit to the very soft, very tender, very sensitive flesh just below her vaginal opening.

He gripped her knees and pressed them back into her chest, opening her wide for whatever he chose to do. It was his favorite position to keep her in, except when he had her on her hands and knees. Slipping his fingers inside her, he sucked her entire clitoris into his mouth, softly but completely. He worked it with his tongue and lips as he fucked her with his hand, rubbing her juices into the walls of her vagina over and over again.

When his fingers were soaked with her liquid, he slid one, then two into the opening between the cheeks of her buttocks, his mouth still fastened on the swollen bud of her sex, his arm holding her in place while she bucked under his touch. He stroked in and out of her hot rectum, touching every sensitive place inside, driving her higher and higher. But he never allowed her to peak. Every time he felt her nearing the crest he backed off, soothed her, then started again.

Tonight there was no talking, only touching and feeling.

When she was ready to scream with frustration, he rolled over onto his back, took her hand and placed it on his thick erection.

Giving him the same attention he gave her, Cassie licked the length of his cock until it was wet with her saliva, probing the tip of the soft head with her tongue until he begged her to stop. She stroked her hand up and down his shaft while her other hand caressed the heavy sac between his legs.

And all the while he kept one hand between her legs, teasing her clitoris, playing with her distended labia, sliding his fingers into her and stretching her walls to make her ready for him. When she felt his balls begin to tighten, she moved over and straddled him. Grabbing the foil packet he'd tossed in the bed, she ripped it open and rolled the condom onto him. Then, taking his penis in her hand, she positioned it at her vaginal entrance, then slid down so he was completely inside her.

Tonight she set the rhythm, moving in the slow cadence he had set, not wanting to rush, feeling him stroke every inch of her sex he could reach. Her fingers found his flat, hard nipples and rasped them with her nails until he cried out. And then, so suddenly it was on them almost before they realized it, a shuddering orgasm rolled over them. Wave after wave of sexual ecstasy crashed through their bodies, until they were completely exhausted.

Cassie leaned forward and rested her head on Griffin's chest. She felt his heartbeat thud in time with hers. As much as he'd teased her tonight, plundered her, sent flames of heated passion through her body, there was none of the usual frenzy or intensity. With every touch tonight he was telling her what an important part of his life she was.

She wanted to weep with the love she felt for him. Kissing his warm lips, her palm on his cheek, she slept with his penis still cradled in the slick walls of her vagina.

* * * * *

Carol Markham called in the morning to tell Cassie she had a client with rental properties who would take all her furniture if she made him a good price.

"Get whatever you can. I just want to be rid of it."

"You know I'll bargain well for you."

Cassie could almost see Carol setting her shoulders back. "Of course. Thank you." It would save hassling with the man from Kerrville and leave one less thing for her to attend to.

When she was finished, Griffin took the phone and explained he wanted to list his place, also.

Carol barely concealed the surprise in her voice. "Could I come by with a listing agreement after I meet the furniture buyers at Cassie's?"

"That'll be fine." After he hung up he told Cassie, "I think the gossip line will be heating up again in a very short time." He grinned. "Think how much excitement we've brought into their lives."

She giggled. "Think how bored they'll be when we move away from here."

After she called the real estate agent in Marble Hills about a rental for them, Griffin placed an ad in the local paper as well as San Antonio and Austin papers to sell his business and then they sat and looked at each other.

"We're really doing it," he said.

"Yes, we are." Cassie smiled. "Tonight we need to take a good look at what we want from your house and start packing. I know we've got some time but maybe we'll get lucky and your house will sell as quickly as mine did."

Carol came by late in the afternoon, trying to balance her distaste for Griffin with her greed for a commission. She kept up a running chatter about nothing in particular while she took inventory of the rooms and the yard. The tension in the air was like thick, wet cotton. Her eyes kept straying to the ring on Cassie's finger. The expression on Carol's face said plainly she wanted to ask a million questions but couldn't figure out a way to do it gracefully.

Griffin conducted his business with her, then he and Cassie sat back and waited for her to leave.

"Well, I'll get this listing in the computer first thing in the morning," she told them, fussing with the signed contracts. "I'll call as soon as I get a nibble."

"Thank you." He opened the door and ushered her out onto the porch.

"'Bye, then."

"Goodbye." Griffin smiled as he watched Carol hustle to her car, then turned to Cassie. "She had her cell phone out of her purse before she even cranked the ignition. Can't wait to spread the word, I'd say."

"Let's order a pizza and go to sleep," Cassie said. "You've got a lot of work to make up tomorrow. And you've got to start telling your clients what you're doing. And my morning project is going to be trying to solve the puzzle of the diary."

Good luck to that, she thought.

She cuddled closer to Griffin and willed herself to sleep. She had a lot of checking to do in the morning.

Chapter Twenty-Four

ೞ

In the morning Cassie stopped by the police station to turn over the money and jewelry from the safety deposit box to Dangler as evidence of Diane's blackmail. The only request she made was after the case was settled it be used for some community purpose. The chief nodded, his eyes troubled. When he took the envelope from her, he touched it as if it burned his fingers. And in a way, maybe it did.

"Maybe this will give you the urge to open this case again," Cassie taunted. "That money didn't come from Griff and you know it."

"We'll see," was all Dangler said but he looked decidedly uncomfortable.

Cassie picked up a few things at the grocery store, then went home, made herself a sandwich and opened the diary. She tried every type of code she could think of but nothing seemed to work. By the time Griffin came home, her head was throbbing and she felt physically ill.

"Bad day, sugar?"

"Frustrating. I'm not getting anywhere." She threw down her pencil. "Go take your shower. I bought some thick steaks today which you can grill while I throw a salad together."

He planted a quick kiss on her lips. "Sounds good to me. Give me ten."

Cassie splashed cold water on her face at the kitchen sink, then took out two bottles of beer from the refrigerator.

She opened them and began to drink from one as she looked at the diary again. Suddenly something clicked in her brain, she tore off a clean sheet of paper from the pad and began constructing an alpha code. By the time Griffin came back downstairs she was both excited and dismayed.

He saw the glint in her eyes. "Got something?"

"Yes." She took another swallow of beer. "I think I know who the three men were that Diane was sleeping with and blackmailing. And it isn't pretty." She pulled the pad over. "I don't know why I didn't remember this before. Diane and I made this up as kids to write notes to each other our parents couldn't read."

"How does it work?"

"Too easily. We split the alphabet, then substituted letters. See? A=N, B=O and so on. I used that to decipher the three lines at the end of the diary." She bit her bottom lip. "Look what I came up with."

They both stared at the names wordlessly. In the end, the answer to the riddle had been simple, staring them in the face if they had looked beneath the surface of the town.

"This isn't really proof," Cassie said. "There's nothing in here to really identify them except what I've figured out. We need to set some kind of trap for them."

Griffin shook his head vehemently. "I am not letting you put yourself in any kind of danger. It isn't worth it."

"But we have to do something," she protested. "I refuse to let these people get away with this. And no way will I let this town continue to lay two murders at your doorstep."

"Cassie, they've already got blood on their hands. A little more won't make a difference. I say we go to Dangler."

"You don't think he knows this already and has been covering up for them?"

"I think when we show him the diary he'll cave."

She chewed her lip again, frowning. Then she sighed. "Fine. I guess that's the smartest thing to do. But we can't wait to do it."

"Just until the morning, okay? No one's going to do anything tonight."

Cassie nodded her head.

Later, lying in bed, Griffin sleeping beside her, she thought again of the men involved. She couldn't imagine any of them being part of something this sordid. But then, she thought, did you ever really know anyone, or know what they would do under certain circumstances?

She finally fell asleep but she dreamed of a faceless man pushing her over a cliff, his hollow laugh echoing in her head.

* * * * *

"You knew about this all the time, didn't you?" Cassie stood in front of Barry Dangler's desk, her tone accusing, her face tight with anger.

Beside her, Griffin's body was rigid with tension.

"Cassie, I..."

"You're the police chief, for God's sake," Griffin exploded. "And you would have been very happy to see me rot in jail for a crime someone else committed. What kind of man are you, anyway?"

Dangler's face was stamped with defeat, his shoulders slumped, his body posture one of resignation. "Try to understand," he pleaded. "These men are my friends. My backers. They put me in this office."

"So that gives you the right to cover up a murder?" Cassie's eyes glinted with fire.

Dangler held out his hand, palms up. "An apology is useless now. What do you want me to do?"

"I want to set a trap for them and I want you to catch them."

He shook his head. "Too dangerous. Besides, it's police business."

"Oh, right." She slammed her purse down on her desk. "I don't think that excuse will fly. There hasn't been much police business conducted on this case until now. Why ruin a good thing, right?"

Dangler's eyes were filled with shame. "I deserve whatever you say, Cassie. I guess none of us thought you'd ever come back here. Or if you did, that you'd even care about what happened."

"I've wasted six years of my life because of this mess and what Diane and all of you did. I'd like to see it finished. Over and done with. Either you do this with us, or I'll go to the media with my speculations. You'd be amazed at the damage innuendo can do."

He threw up his hands. "All right. What choice do I have? Tell me your plan."

* * * * *

I have the diary and I know everything. I want something out of this or the police will have it. I will contact you with further details. Be ready.

That was the message that rolled out of three fax machines that afternoon. They'd decided that was the best method of contacting all the men. While Griffin followed his usual routine, Cassie drove into San Antonio and used fax machines at three different office supply stores on the east side of town. That way no one could pinpoint a single source for the messages.

Shortly all three men were connected on a conference call.

"I knew that bitch was trouble. A diary. Of all the childish things for that female to do. What the hell do we do now?"

"Why couldn't Dangler have just shoved Griffin Hunter through the system and been done with it?"

"You know the answer to that. So what the hell do we do now?"

252

"Call Dangler?"

"Let's wait and see if we hear anything further."

* * * * *

From the moment she sent the last fax, Cassie was tense and anxious. She was convinced this was a good plan but there was real danger involved with it. She glanced at her watch. Right about now they should all be sweating over their faxes. It would be interesting to know if they were all involved, or just one or two of them. And did they each know about the others?

Diane, you played too close to the fire and now other people are getting burned. How could you do this?

She looked at her watch again. A long time until Griffin came home. She needed to find something to occupy herself during the day or she'd go crazy.

* * * * *

"Cassie?" Griffin dropped his keys in the dish on the hall table. "You here, dewdrop?"

Cassie ran from the kitchen and launched herself into his arms. She locked her hands behind his head as if she'd never let go and pulled his face down to hers.

"It's nice to be missed." Griffin grinned, when they finally broke the kiss. "Unfortunately, I don't think this has to do with my masculine charms. Right?"

She leaned her head against his chest, her arms still wrapped firmly around him.

"Honey?" He tilted her face up to him. She was trembling and he could feel her heart beating heavily against his chest. "What is it? Did something happen? Damn. I knew this was a bad idea to begin with."

"No, nothing happened." She stood on tiptoe to kiss him again. "Just my nerves, is all."

"Did you see anyone today? Did someone do something?"

"No. Nothing like that. I stayed inside all day. I was afraid I'd run into one of them and give myself away."

"All right. Come on. Let's go in the kitchen and get something cold to drink. Do we still have any beer left?" She nodded. "Good. I think you could use something to settle your nerves."

Griff had built a deck running along the back of his house and put huge pots of colorful flowers at the corners. They hadn't exactly taken time for relaxation since Cassie had moved in with him, but now he insisted she come outside and sit there with him.

"You need a break," he cajoled, holding up the beer he'd plucked from the fridge.

"You're right. As usual."

He put down the bottles and took her hand in his, linking their fingers together and planting gentle kisses on her forehead. "I've done a lot of thinking about this today, Cassie, and I'm not really crazy about putting you in any kind of danger. I don't think I could handle it if anything happened to you."

"Chief Dangler said if they agree to the meet, he'll be there with plenty of backup. And you'll be there. I'll be fine."

* * * * *

Tonight. In the park where Diane died. One hundred thousand dollars and the diary is yours. Otherwise I go to the police.

The second fax had been sent and the conference call was on again.

"I think whoever it is, they're bluffing."

"Are you willing to take that chance?"

"Hell, we don't even know for sure there's a diary. This whole thing could be a hoax."

"Then exactly how did they know who we are? I don't know about either of you but a hundred thousand is a small price to pay to keep my life intact."

"Nobody's arguing that. Just that we've got to be sure. We've all got the same thing to lose, you know."

"I don't think all of us need to show up. One of us can carry the money and get the diary."

"No. We're all in this together. Besides, if there's a problem, we need to take care of it together."

"Are we back to the idea of elimination again? We can't just keep doing away with people, you know."

"We're not killers."

"God, don't even use that word."

"Well, we're not. Diane was an accident."

"And her father?"

"Collateral damage that made me sick for months. I couldn't do it again and I don't think either of you could, either."

"We're paying for our stupidity."

"All right. Let's decide exactly how we're going to do this. We only have a few hours and we all need to get to the bank."

"You know Howard Cook will be asking questions."

"I'll handle Howard. Let's just get on with this."

* * * * *

"I'm going out in the back so we can test this thing and see if it works." Barry Dangler made sure his earpiece was solidly set, while his officer who handled most of their technical stuff packed up the wireless microphone kit. "Count to twenty, then say something."

Cassie finished buttoning her blouse, her hands trembling only slightly. This had to work.

Griffin slid one arm around her waist, his touch reassuring. "You'll be well covered," he reminded her. "I don't think any of these guys will do anything. I think they've had their taste of killing but we still need to be careful. Desperation does funny things to people."

The most interesting part of the preparation had been the noticeable decrease in hostility on Dangler's part toward Griffin. The chief wasn't cutting him any slack but something in his attitude had obviously changed. A new Griffin had emerged when the chief wasn't looking, one they could see he was having trouble reconciling with the bad boy image the man had always carried.

"Go ahead and try it now, Miss Fitzgerald," the young deputy said.

"All right." She cleared her throat. "Can you hear me, Chief?"

"Loud and clear, Cassie." He came back into the house. "Okay, then. I'd say we're ready to go."

"I still think I should be right there with you," Griffin said, his voice plainly stating his unwillingness to leave her by herself.

"We've already discussed this, Griffin. It will only work if they see just me. Besides, you'll be just a few feet away behind the restrooms with everyone else."

She could see he still didn't like it but he was through arguing. Ignoring the presence of everyone in the room, he pulled Cassie close to him and kissed her thoroughly. "That's for luck," he whispered. "You get the rest of it later." He hugged her tightly, then let her go. "All right, Chief. Let's go."

Cassie watched them all leave and get into the two unmarked police cars in the driveway. They would arrive at the park far enough in advance not to be observed. She checked her watch. One more hour. She could do this. She could confront them and it would all be over. When she and

Griffin left town, they'd have no unfinished business. Nothing they needed to look back on and regret they hadn't handled.

* * * * *

Keeping out of the halos thrown by the park lights, the three men trudged silently into the park's interior, grateful that at this time of night the park seemed deserted.

"I don't see anyone. What if this is all a hoax?"

"It's not a hoax. Get serious. Whoever it is, they'll be here. No one is going to walk away from this much money."

"That's right, no one is. I'm over here, gentlemen." Cassie stepped out from behind a giant oak next to the public restrooms.

"Cassie?" Harley Graham's jaw dropped.

"Yes, Harley, it's me. Surprised?"

"I have to say, I am. I think all of us are. You're the last person we'd expect to try this kind of thing."

"What kind of thing is that?" she taunted. "Making the people who murdered my sister and my father pay for it?"

"Blackmail," Cyrus McLeod said sharply. "It doesn't seem quite your style."

"We were all good to you, Cassie," Neil told her. "Why are you doing this?"

"Oh, yes. You were all very good to me. You killed most of my family and shortstopped every effort I made to get the facts. Thanks to you, Griffin Hunter's been walking around town all this time with people speculating behind his back. Is that fair?"

"I hardly think Griffin's reputation is anything for you to defend." Neil's jaw worked, a sign of his growing anger. "This is more his type of thing, anyway. He had to put you up to it. We all told you to stay away from him. He's bad news."

"Actually, Griffin tried to talk me out of this. We're leaving town as soon as his house sells and he wanted to just walk away. I couldn't do that. His name needs to be cleared and my father and Diane deserve justice."

"If you wanted justice you'd give this book to the chief. All you want is the money. That makes you no better than the rest of us."

"We actually haven't admitted anything," Cyrus pointed out in his lawyer voice.

"But you did do it, didn't you."

"Diane was an accident," Harley blurted out.

"Shut up, you old fool," Cyrus hissed.

"An accident? Then why didn't you come forward at the time?"

"We had our own reputations to think about." Harley shook off Cyrus' restraining hand.

"Then none of you should have started fooling around with my sister. And what about my father? What was the problem with him?"

"Your father stuck his nose in where it didn't belong," Cyrus said.

"So you admit you killed him? I want to hear you say it."

"We're sorry about that." Harley mopped his sweating brow. "Diane too. But neither of them would listen to reason."

Cassie moved one step closer. "But I will. Three hundred thousand of them. Do you have the money?"

"It's right here." Neil held up the briefcase. "Where's the diary?"

Cassie held up the package in her left hand. "I'll put it down right here. You toss the briefcase over. I'll check inside and if the money's there, I'll just walk away."

"You don't think we're going to stand here and let you have both the money and the diary, do you?" Neil's tone was vicious. "Toss the diary over here."

"Uh-uh. I don't trust any of you. Look here. I'm putting it down. Toss the briefcase."

"You think we're going to stand still for this, you little bitch?" Neil's self-control had snapped. In three long strides he was at Cassie's side. Before she could back away, he had an iron grip on her arm and was trying to wrench away the diary.

"Let go of me." She tried to pull away but he was too strong for her.

"Give it to me, or you'll get what your tramp sister got."

The sound of a gunshot stunned everyone. Barry Dangler and two of his deputies stepped out from behind the restrooms. Griffin was with them, instantly moving to Cassie's side.

"The next one won't be in the air," Dangler said. "Step away from the girl. And don't even think about running," he added, as Harley tried to back away. "I have deputies at your cars and two more here with me."

As he spoke, the two men he indicated stepped up, guns drawn and forced the men to kneeling positions. The only sound that broke the night was the clink of handcuffs.

"You'll regret this, Barry," Cyrus threatened.

"I already have too much to regret," Dangler said, his tone sad. "I'd like to get a little of my self-respect back."

"You still have to prove this." Neil was in a rage. "I want to see what that diary says."

"Whatever it says doesn't matter." He held up a small tape recorder, pushed a button and the entire conversation began to play back. "I've covered for you all long enough and I have to say, I'm ashamed of myself. But I have a chance to correct things and I'm doing it."

"Are you all right?" Griffin asked Cassie in a soft voice, wrapping his arms around her. "I swear my heart stopped beating when I heard that shot. Tell me you're okay."

"I am now." She was shaking and he could feel her heart thudding against his chest. "I just want to get away from them. Take me home, please."

Griffin held her tightly against his body and looked inquiringly at Dangler, who was watching them.

The chief nodded. "Go on. I've got a busy night ahead of me. I'll catch up with you tomorrow." After the three men had been led away, he walked over to Griffin and Cassie. He held the briefcase and the diary. "Cassie, I'll need to take your statement but it can wait until tomorrow." He paused. "I just want to say I'm sorry. About a lot of things." Then he was gone.

Griffin placed a soft kiss on her lips. "Okay, sugar. Let's blow this pop stand."

Chapter Twenty-Five

ॐ

They lay naked on the bed, Griffin's hands touching Cassie with learned familiarity. That afternoon they had driven into San Antonio, paid for their marriage license at the courthouse and emerged as Mr. and Mrs. Griffin Hunter.

Barry Dangler, in his effort to make amends, had arranged for a judge who was a friend of his to perform the ceremony quickly. Griffin had taken Cassie shopping for wedding rings first, then stopped at a florist to buy a rose.

"One perfect rose, dewdrop. Just like before. That's you. My perfect flower." He had tucked it in her hair, then bought her a bridal bouquet of roses and mums and baby's breath. All in white. "For fidelity," he told her. "Just in case there's any question on your part."

He grinned when he said it but Cassie knew the message he was giving her. The past was really finished and done with. There was no one else for either of them now or ever again. When he kissed her at the end of the ceremony and told her she'd always hold his heart for safekeeping, even the judge got a little teary-eyed.

In two days they'd leave for a week in Hawaii but tonight they were spending the first night as man and wife in their rented home in Marble Hills. As soon as they returned, construction on their new home would begin, one with plenty of bedrooms for the family they planned to have.

On the way home from the city they had teased each other with words and touches so that by the time they reached the bedroom they were both at fever pitch. She moved her body restlessly against him, urging him, small whimpers escaping from her mouth.

"Easy, sugar," he crooned, as Cassie shifted under his languid stroking. "We've got all the time in the world." His thumbs brushed against her nipples, which were already in tight peaks and stroked down the soft slope of her breasts. Wherever he touched with his hands, he followed with his mouth.

She wanted to reach out and pull him tightly to her but he took her wrists in a firm grip, pinning her hands over her head. His tongue drew feathery circles at her navel as his other hand drifted lower yet, gently parting her thighs and stroking the dampness between them.

"More," she moaned and jerked as his fingers found her clitoris and massaged it gently.

"More what?" He watched her with heavy-lidded eyes. She had become a lot more comfortable with their erotic conversations as they made love, not shy anymore about saying things to him.

"Rub my clit more. Rub my slit more." She shifted restlessly, trying to urge him into action with her body. They were so attuned to each other now, so comfortable in what they did, that talking to him this way had become second nature for her. The words excited her as much as they did Griffin.

"And what else, sugar?"

"Fuck me with your fingers. Slide them into me. You know." As if for emphasis, she arched her body against him, pushing against his hand.

"Into you where, darlin'?"

"Into my vagina." She was panting heavily now. "Way…in. Further. Further. Touch me way inside."

Sliding one long finger into her hot sheath, he felt her wet heat enveloping him.

"And what else? What else do you want me to do?"

"Suck me." She could hardly get the words out. She was panting with need, her body writing under his touch. "Suck me, lick me, stick your tongue in me. Do it, Griffin. Now."

When he replaced his hand with his mouth he felt shivers race over her entire body. His erection was hard and throbbing, testing his self-control but he was determined to draw out her pleasure.

Separating her folds to plunge his tongue inside more deeply, he felt her convulse violently, twisting, clenching at him as shudders overtook her. Her liquid poured like a waterfall into his mouth. He continued to touch and stroke as the storm subsided, only the aftershocks still producing light quivers.

"Good, sugar?" he whispered.

"Yes but I want it all. I want to feel you inside me. Fill me, Griffin."

"You want my cock inside you, sugar?"

"Yes. Yes. Now. Oh, God, now."

Releasing her hands and bracing himself on his forearms, he entered her in one smooth stroke. This was the first time they'd fucked without the thin barrier of latex between them and the sensation consumed him with heat. Skin to skin. He could hardly stand it.

Cassie let out a low moan as she felt him filling her. At once he could feel her becoming newly aroused. He kept his tempo even, watching her face for signs that she was reaching her peak again. When her body surged against him, he plunged hard, once, twice, then a final hard thrust as he poured into her. Her legs wrapped around him and her hands clutched at his straining muscles.

Finally they were quiet again, lying with their arms around each other, the lazily turning ceiling fan cooling their sweat-soaked bodies.

"I love you." She reached up and brushed her hand lightly against his cheek.

"I love you too, Cassie." He cradled her head against him. "God, I thought this day would never get here."

"I know what you mean."

Time had dragged in the month since the McLeods and Harley had been arrested. Cassie gave a detailed statement to Barry Dangler and they'd been shocked when he actually reached out his hand to Griffin. He didn't say anything—that was as much of an apology as he was giving to the town's bad boy—but they shook hands firmly, banishing the past.

The story had made every newspaper in Texas and some on the national scene. After all, three upstanding citizens arrested on double homicide charges was fodder for gossip everywhere. And especially in Stoneham. Cassie and Griffin had to let the answering machine pick up calls and stopped answering the door. Everyone, it seemed, wanted a firsthand account.

"They don't deserve anything at all," Cassie spat, "not after the way everyone in this town has treated you."

"We can forget about them now," he'd said soothingly. "We'll be gone soon enough."

Griffin's business sold more quickly than they expected. A man who read the lurid story in the *Dallas Morning News* saw the item about Griffin selling out. He and his wife wanted to leave "the big bad city" as he called it and regroup in a small town. The notoriety had served at least one useful purpose.

Carol had paraded a steady stream of potential buyers through his house, most of them just satisfying their avid curiosity. But then the couple who'd bought the landscaping business asked if they might get a better price if they made it a package deal.

Preliminary contracts were signed, the Marble Hills agent found a rental house for them and they concluded the transaction on the purchase of the nursery. The movers had arrived and carted away their belongings to the rental house, although much of what they had would go into storage until the new house was ready.

Now Cassie looked at her wedding ring catching the light filtering in from outside. She wore it and her engagement ring even when she was naked, insisting they were her talismans.

"Any regrets?" Griffin asked.

"Not a one." She wrinkled her forehead at him. "You?"

"Are you kidding? I feel like the kid who woke up and found out there really is a Santa Claus." He kissed her, letting his lips linger over hers. "Tomorrow's a fresh start, sugar."

"I know. I never thought we'd get to this point."

"Are you still okay about coming back to testify?" He worried constantly about how she'd handle it.

"As long as you're with me, nothing bothers me." She snuggled tighter against him. "And I'm glad that everyone will finally know the truth about my sister and my father."

"Dangler's been more than polite and accommodating to us."

"He should be, damn him." She sat up abruptly. "None of this might have happened if he hadn't had it in for you from the beginning."

"Let it go, Cassie." He pulled her down again. "Tomorrow is the first day of the rest of our lives."

"Yes, it is, isn't it."

"And I know just how to start it." He turned her toward him, his mouth coming down on hers. Cassie moaned under him, little bursts of pleasure that told him how heated her blood was becoming. Their bodies were so finely tuned with each other, their give and take so natural.

When they again lay gasping, side by side, Griffin pulled her against him the way he liked to, stroking her satiny skin, dropping little kisses here and there.

"I think it's against the law to be this happy," Cassie smiled. Running a fingertip along the arm wrapped around her. "But we deserve it."

"I don't know how I got so lucky," Griffin murmured, "but I'll spend the rest of my life treasuring you."

"Mmm. Yes. I can't wait."

Cassie looked into Griffin's hot, blue eyes and saw everything there—love, desire, caring and a future. The past six years had been hard on both of them. Seeing each other again could have been a painful end rather than a new beginning. Whenever he looked at Cassie, he saw complete love and acceptance in her eyes, a love she surrounded him with eagerly and happily.

Griffin wasn't a praying sort of man but he gave thanks daily that circumstances had brought Cassie back into his life and given them a second chance. For the first time in his life he knew peace. Real peace, after years of anguish and uncertainty.

The long, tormented journey was over. He and Cassie has each other and the lies and deceit has been washed away. Cassie was where she belonged and Griffin Hunter was finally content.

Also by Desiree Holt

ɛɔ

eBooks:

1-800-DOM-help: Delight Me

Cougar Challenge: Hot to Trot

Cupid's Shaft

Dancing With Danger

Diamond Lady

Double Entry

Driven by Hunger

Ellora's Cavemen: Flavors of Ecstasy I (*anthology*)

Emerald Green

Escape the Night

Hot Moon Rising

Hot, Wicked and Wild

I Dare You

Journey to the Pearl

Just Say Yes

Kidnapping the Groom (*with Allie Standifer*)

Letting Go

Line of Sight

Mistletoe Magic 2: Touch of Magic

Mistletoe Magic 4: Elven Magic (*with Regina Carlysle & Cindy Spencer Pape*)

Night Seekers 1: Lust Unleashed

Night Seekers 2: Lust by Moonlight

Night Heat
Once Burned
Once Upon a Wedding
Riding Out the Storm
Rodeo Heat
Seductive Illusion (*with Allie Standifer*)
Sequins, Saddles and Spurs 1: Trouble in Cowboy Boots
Switched
Teaching Molly
Texas Passions 1: Eagle's Run
Turn Up the Heat 1: Scorched (*with Allie Standifer*)
Turn Up the Heat 2: Scalded (*with Allie Standifer*)
Turn Up the Heat 3: Singed (*with Allie Standifer*)
Turn Up the Heat 4: Steamed (*with Allie Standifer*)
Until the Dawn (*with Cerise DeLand*)
Wedding Belles 3: Something Borrowed
Wedding Belles 4: Something Blue (*with Allie Standifer & Cerise DeLand*)
Where Danger Hides

Print Books:
Age and Experience (*anthology*)
Candy Caresses (*anthology*)
Cougar Challenge: Tease the Cougar
Demanding Diamonds (*anthology*)
Ellora's Cavemen: Flavors of Ecstasy I (*anthology*)
Erotic Emerald (*anthology*)
Mistletoe Magic (*anthology*)
Naughty Nuptials (*anthology*)
Rodeo Heat
Where Danger Hides

About the Author

ຂໍ

I always wonder what readers really want to know when I write one of these things. Getting to this point in my career has been an interesting journey. I've managed rock and roll bands and organized concerts. Been the only female on the sports staff of a university newspaper. Immersed myself in Nashville peddling a country singer. Lived in five different states. Married two very interesting but totally different men.

I think I must have lived in Texas in another life, because the minute I set foot on Texas soil I knew I was home. Living in Texas Hill Country gives me inspiration for more stories than I'll probably ever be able to tell, what with all the sexy cowboys who surround me and the gorgeous scenery that provides a great setting.

Each day is a new adventure for me, as my characters come to life on the pages of my current work in progress. I'm absolutely compulsive about it when I'm writing and thank all the gods and goddesses that I have such a terrific husband who encourages my writing and puts up with my obsession. As a multi-published author, I love to hear from my readers. Their input keeps my mind fresh and always hunting for new ideas.

Desiree welcomes comments from readers. You can find her website and email address on her author bio page at www.ellorascave.com.

Tell Us What You Think

We appreciate hearing reader opinions about our books. You can email us at Comments@EllorasCave.com.

Why an electronic book?

We live in the Information Age—an exciting time in the history of human civilization, in which technology rules supreme and continues to progress in leaps and bounds every minute of every day. For a multitude of reasons, more and more avid literary fans are opting to purchase e-books instead of paper books. The question from those not yet initiated into the world of electronic reading is simply: *Why?*

1. *Price.* An electronic title at Ellora's Cave Publishing and Cerridwen Press runs anywhere from 40% to 75% less than the cover price of the exact same title in paperback format. Why? Basic mathematics and cost. It is less expensive to publish an e-book (no paper and printing, no warehousing and shipping) than it is to publish a paperback, so the savings are passed along to the consumer.

2. *Space.* Running out of room in your house for your books? That is one worry you will never have with electronic books. For a low one-time cost, you can purchase a handheld device specifically designed for e-reading. Many e-readers have large, convenient screens for viewing. Better yet, hundreds of titles can be stored within your new library—on a single microchip. There are a variety of e-readers from different manufacturers. You can also read e-books on your PC or laptop computer. (Please note that Ellora's Cave does not endorse any specific brands.

You can check our websites at www.ellorascave.com or www.cerridwenpress.com for information we make available to new consumers.)

3. *Mobility.* Because your new e-library consists of only a microchip within a small, easily transportable e-reader, your entire cache of books can be taken with you wherever you go.

4. *Personal Viewing Preferences.* Are the words you are currently reading too small? Too large? Too… ANNOYING? Paperback books cannot be modified according to personal preferences, but e-books can.

5. *Instant Gratification.* Is it the middle of the night and all the bookstores near you are closed? Are you tired of waiting days, sometimes weeks, for bookstores to ship the novels you bought? Ellora's Cave Publishing sells instantaneous downloads twenty-four hours a day, seven days a week, every day of the year. Our webstore is never closed. Our e-book delivery system is 100% automated, meaning your order is filled as soon as you pay for it.

Those are a few of the top reasons why electronic books are replacing paperbacks for many avid readers.

As always, Ellora's Cave and Cerridwen Press welcome your questions and comments. We invite you to email us at Comments@ellorascave.com or write to us directly at Ellora's Cave Publishing Inc., 1056 Home Avenue, Akron, OH 44310-3502.

Make each day more *EXCITING* With our

Ellora's
Cavemen
Calendar

✝ www.EllorasCave.com ✝

ELLORA'S CAVE

Romanticon

Annual convention
for women who
refuse to behave

Discover for yourself why readers can't get enough
of the multiple award-winning publisher
Ellora's Cave.

Whether you prefer e-books or paperbacks,
be sure to visit EC on the web at
www.ellorascave.com
for an erotic reading experience that will leave you
breathless.

CPSIA information can be obtained at www.ICGtesting.com
Printed in the USA
BVOW071202200312

285610BV00001B/39/P